DEDICATION

Everyone deserves a hero. For all the girls, big and small, who don't neatly fit into society's boxes—Shattergirl is yours.

Sign up for our newsletter to hear
about new and upcoming releases.

www.ylva-publishing.com

OTHER BOOKS BY LEE WINTER

The Red Files

Requiem for Immortals

COMING BOOKS IN THE SUPERHEROINE COLLECTION IN 2017

The Power of Mercy
by Fiona Zedde

The Shadow Hand
by Sacchie Green

More books coming in 2018

SHATTERED

LEE WINTER

Ylva

THE
SUPERHEROINE
COLLECTION

ACKNOWLEDGMENTS

My thanks go to Charlotte, Lisa, Kim, and Sam for your unique insights that made my book so much better.

To Astrid at Ylva, I really appreciate how much you believe in Shattergirl. Thanks for letting her shine so brightly.

And thanks, finally, to the love of my life, for sharing our home with the isle of Socotra, random, made-up swear words, and a six-foot superhero for so many months. I'm sure Nyah appreciates it, even if she's not one to show it.

CHAPTER 1

LENA MARTIN STOOD STILL UNDER the falling snow and listened. She held her breath, willing herself to hear beyond the yowling wind ripping through towering pine trees. Actually, *not* breathing was a mercy in Oymyakon, Siberia. With the temperature at −70ºF, a thousand needles stabbing her throat probably felt more pleasant than inhaling would right now.

She resisted the urge to stamp her feet for warmth, knowing that any noise would alert the nearby marauder. Beast Lord. Three hundred pounds of muscle and sinew wrapped up in an unstable guardian. Supposedly one of Earth's beloved superheroes, Beast Lord seemed to have lost his mind in the middle of this godforsaken place.

She couldn't entirely blame him. Oymyakon wasn't exactly a balm for the soul, frequently topping the coldest-place-on-Earth lists.

Lena had come across Beast Lord half a dozen times in the several months she'd been out here, catching glimpses of his furred arms and shaggy head. She had been adept at each encounter in not earning his wrath, which could result in a howl so loud it would perforate eardrums, shatter windows, and flatten trees with its percussive power.

Once or twice he'd swiveled his head her way, their eyes locking. Beast Lord's deeply lined, craggy face was disturbing when his burning, wild, red eyes fixed on hers. His tanned face was sunken; his clothes torn and dirty. He'd sure gone to hell in a hand basket since she'd last seen him on the news feeds. Maybe the Paleo diet wasn't agreeing with him.

She had never been as close as she had been today. Lena could smell his body odor, earthy and primal, and could easily make out deep, long, clawed footprints in the snow. She frowned as she examined them. They stopped in the middle of nowhere, as though Beast Lord had leaped off to one side suddenly.

Lena spun around, her heart leaping as she tried to pick his shape from the trees. Where the hell was he?

Her answer came as the blurred, hairy giant hurled himself toward her without warning, in three enormous bounds. Stretched across his powerful shoulders was a sleeveless, worn, black leather jacket. His ripped jeans were dark with grime, beneath which emerged thick-soled, bare feet, fast and large, and dark with hair.

Lena flung herself to the side, only just avoiding his bulk squashing her. The "whumpf" as his body impacted next to hers caused the snow to shudder, and Lena bounced off the ground, landing on her knees.

Beast Lord's clawed hand flashed out sideways, slashing blindly. Lena lifted her arm to block him. She stared at the rush of blood with a strange, stunned detachment. A second later the pain registered and seared through her.

He backhanded her, tossing her onto her back. Beast Lord flung his arm across her chest, pinning her in place with such force it crushed the air out of her lungs. Lena lay helpless and dazed, acute pain engulfing her.

"You're persistent for a common, I'll give you that," Beast Lord growled.

She wheezed by way of answer, feeling like a wrecking ball had landed on her chest.

Beast Lord lifted his head and howled, a primal, eerie, aching cry that shattered the stillness. It created a wind blast—trees bent, groaned, and uprooted themselves, and snow flurries slammed into Lena's body. She shivered uncontrollably beneath her three layers of thermals and thickly padded coat.

Lena waited the roar out, studying her target. She had long wondered if wolf sensibilities applied to Beast Lord. Now she was close enough to test it out, she'd try that tack. Her eyes watered as the howl persisted, and snow and plant debris shuddered and vibrated, the wind whipping it all up in her face.

He stopped, waited for the echo to die down, then turned to look at her. His arm at last shifted off her chest, and he stared intently. Surprise lit his features when he tilted his head for a better look at her ears. Probably expected to see blood running from them.

Asshole.

If she wasn't using a special set of earplugs, she'd be deaf by now, her eardrums pulped from the acoustic blast this close to its source. The high-tech ear pieces filtered sound and turned into white noise everything except for humanoid voices.

His body reared up suddenly and then dropped forward to crouch over her, a meaty, hairy fist planted on either side of her head, his massive thighs pinning her narrow hips.

"Tell me why I shouldn't end you now," he demanded. "I'm tired of you following me. How long am I to be your prey? Do you never give up?"

"No," she said as air began to flow back into her lungs. It still hurt like hell. "I don't give up. And no, you won't end me. Because guardians aren't killers. You're heroes, remember? You protect humans like me. The commons. You're forces for good."

"It would be so easy," he said, eyes flashing in realization at the truth of his statement. "So easy to just make you go away and give me some peace. I thought you'd give up. But you never quit."

He peered at her and seemed to be weighing his options. Lena felt no fear, just a strange calmness as he decided her fate. She inhaled deeply, regretting it as the frigid air clawed at her lungs. The pain woke her up. To hell she'd go out like this.

"You think I don't know how it feels for you?" she asked softly. "I know you miss them. Your people. The guardians. They're like your pack, aren't they? They miss you. They want you back."

"*Tagshart*," he swore in his native tongue. "I'm an embarrassment."

"No," Lena said earnestly, staring into his eyes. She lifted her bloodied arm up and touched his shaggy beard with her gloved hand. "You made a few mistakes. You didn't mean to. The locals got scared about some strange beast running around shattering their windows and frightening their animals. But it's just a mistake and it can be made to go away. That's what I do. Fix the mistakes. No one outside of the Facility would ever know. Besides, don't you know what the most important thing is?"

He leaned forward, listening intently.

"Without you, they're incomplete. A pack without one of its members is like a body missing a limb."

He inhaled harshly. "Don't you know what they'll do to me?" he rumbled. "I can't go back. I need to be free. I need to be out here. Not trapped in some city, playing fetch for the commons."

"I know," she said. "I know. It's like a call for you, isn't it? Being out here?" She began combing his shaggy hair softly, soothingly, with her fingers. "You need to be free," she repeated back to him. "You need to roam. It's in your blood."

"Yes." His head dropped forward in agreement. "Yes. I have to. I can't be what my people want. Or what your people want."

"Hey, it's okay," Lena said. "Your leader understands. He's not angry with you. He knows why you're out here."

"Tal's not mad?" His head tilted up, hope lighting his eyes.

"Of course not. He misses you. He wants you to come home, so he sent me to ask. You're needed back there." She ran her fingers behind his head and patted the back of his neck like one might a domesticated dog, and watched his body language shift to even more docile.

"I didn't mean to run." Beast Lord's voice cracked and his strange blood-red eyes implored her to believe him. "I just *had* to get out of there. The city. The demands. You don't know what it's like. How could you? You're a common."

"We can never know what you go through," Lena agreed, injecting every ounce of sympathy into her voice. "Being a hero has its burdens, I know that. But you can't carry them alone. Don't forget, your people are waiting for you. They can help. They understand. It's time to stop running. Come home with me. You'll wonder what you were so afraid of. It'll be okay."

She gave his shoulder a thump of solidarity.

His body sagged.

She had him. She knew she had him. Lena just needed to…

A vibration and soft ding came from her FacTrack. She frowned. Her employers wouldn't contact her mid-assignment unless it was an emergency.

Beast Lord sat back on his haunches warily as Lena gingerly shifted her jacket sleeve off her wrist to study the screen. She narrowed her eyes.

An urgent recall order?

She tapped out "1d?" asking for a day's delay before returning home. Even with half a day's grace she knew she could bring Beast Lord in, docile as a puppy, now she'd gotten through his defenses and connected.

The screen lit up instantly: "NOW."

Damn it.

She tugged her sleeve back down and looked at the guardian, who hadn't taken his eyes off her. Lena didn't like his expression as he fought to work out what was going on through the haze that had been weakening his faculties of late. He'd have figured out she was a tracker weeks ago, but until this moment her subtle manipulations had gone unnoticed.

Beast Lord's face darkened as he joined the rest of the dots. Yes, of course, she'd been hired to return him to his people, with force if necessary. There was no kinship between them. No bonding whatsoever.

This was business.

The dawning expression of awareness, doubt, hate, and mistrust told her the exact moment he realized he'd been played—and well. "New orders?" he hissed.

"You might say that," Lena said quietly. "But that doesn't change anything. We…"

His eyes became mere slits.

Lena knew that look. *Ah crap*. An ego-dented Beast Lord was an especially dangerous creature.

"Piece of *tagshart*," he suddenly howled at her, and his enormous arm lifted high to deliver a vicious blow.

She kicked her legs out and away from his thighs, which had been bracketing her knees, and rolled quickly to her side, unsheathing her hip Dazr under her coat as she moved. He leapt to his feet, towering over her.

Lena had to waste precious time pulling off her glove, which was too thick to manipulate the weapon. She hadn't been expecting a direct confrontation today or she might have risked frostbite and worn her thinner pair.

The split-second delay was all it took to give him the advantage.

"Lying *shreekopf!*" Beast Lord thundered. His fistful of rapier claws sliced toward her.

Lena forced herself to stay calm and, with practiced skill, tapped off the safety and flicked up the Dazr's setting to maximum with her thumb.

"You have no soul!" he thundered.

She squeezed the trigger.

"You know you're a broken piece of…"

A blue electrical field shot out from the gun, and Lena cartwheeled to one side to avoid the now paralyzed guardian crashing back to the ground.

She slowly got to her feet, pissed beyond belief. Why had she been recalled now? What a waste. She thumped the snow off her knees with her hands, peering at Beast Lord's prostrate form in distaste. A voluntary return was always so much easier. They knew that. She'd been so damned close.

Beast Lord was staring at her mutinously, but his vocal cords were as locked up as the rest of his body trapped under the shimmering electrical netting.

Lena gave him a slow, unimpressed smile. She shifted the safety back on her Dazr and rammed it into her holster. "I *am* aware by the way. What you said? Broken and soulless. Yep, nailed it. That's me."

She lowered herself to a squat and met his flashing eyes. "You also left out a cynical, cold-hearted, manipulative, scheming bitch with massive trust issues."

Lena tilted her head and added: "You really think anything that your kind could say to me could have any effect? I've heard it all. But as worthless as you think I am, for all your people's alien powers, none of you has ever beaten me. Your attitude's the worst. All guardians ever do is whine. 'Oh poor me, life's so hard, I can't take it.' Hell. You *do* remember that we let you take refuge on Earth? All we asked in return was that you use your skills to help us. As an added bonus, everyone loved you. Not that you're worthy. Shit, it's the biggest con going."

She peered harder into his eyes and offered him a sneer. "Aww…look at you, all bitter and angry because I played you and said what I had to so you'd want to come home. You're *alive*, asshole. Alive to moan about your sorry life thanks to *my* people. So show a little damned respect."

She lifted her arm and flicked her FacTrack to a different menu, selected the emergency evacuation code, and hit the "Retrieve" button. She pointed a focused blue beam at Beast Lord, and waited three seconds for it to lock on to him and give an acknowledging beep.

"All right. I've relayed your coordinates to the guardians at Moscow's Facility. They'll pick you up in an hour or so. I won't wait; I have somewhere else to be—urgently, apparently. You'll be fine. After all, you've got all this nice fresh air to suck in and all this freedom that you love so much. I'd make the most of it if I were you."

At his venomous glare, she gave him a knowing look.

"You'd kill me now if you could, wouldn't you?" Lena taunted. She rubbed her forearm through its shredded sleeve which bore three deep, bloodied, curling, parallel scratches running up it, courtesy of his attack earlier. "Well, just be glad us commons who you hate so much have more restraint than you do."

She shook her head and turned, leaving him in his awkward tangle of limbs.

"Humanity's heroes, my ass," she muttered, as she began the trek back to her base camp. "You're fucking pathetic."

CHAPTER 2

LENA HOPPED FROM FOOT TO foot, wrenching on her black jeans. Her ass briefly landed on the lime-green armchair that had come with her semi-furnished apartment along with the crappy, glass coffee table that should have met its end dozens of times. God knows she kept almost running right through it when she was late. Like today. First day back at work after her recall from Siberia. She'd landed back home late last night.

Thick black socks, shiny black boots. Check. She dumped the boots beside her with a thud and shook out the socks. She slipped one on and, thanks to the jet lag, almost landed face first on the coffee table. Instead, she managed a last-minute dive onto her lumpy sofa that was drowning under the bright pink cushions her neighbor had bequeathed upon her as a housewarming present.

Lucky her. Until then she hadn't known pink came that loud.

Bra. White T-shirt. Done and done. Lena raked her fingers through her blonde hair, which fell in a messy sweep that never quite stayed out of her eyes. She was overdue a haircut, but it was a low priority. Black padded bomber jacket. Lena slid it on, zipped it up, and almost felt human.

Finally, the pièce de résistance. Black leather cuff. She'd made it herself at shop class back in high school. Turned out halfway decent, much to the teacher's surprise.

Armor on. Good to go. She tightened the wrist buckle on her cuff, pleased to see it covered the claw marks left by Beast Lord, as she headed to the bathroom.

She studied herself in the cracked mirror. Lena had never gotten around to asking the landlord to fix it when she'd moved in. She was rarely here enough to care. Yup, ready. She gave a savage nod. Both visions of herself nodded back.

Okay, if she sprinted the six blocks to the subway, she could just make the 7:40 a.m. express and be in before it was obvious to everyone that she was late. Her fitness, unlike the condition of her one-room apartment, was outstanding, so it was totally doable.

BANG! BANG-BANG-BANG!

Her apartment door almost rattled off its frame.

Lena sighed. No one but her neighbor—she of the lurid pink cushions—ever bothered her. And since the elderly woman knew not to bug her in the morning unless it was an emergency, Lena knew her day was about to turn to crap.

She forced on her civilized smile and opened the door.

Mrs. Josephine Finkel stood before Lena, a frantic expression on her face. "Blood!" she gasped. "*Everywhere!*"

Lena's eyebrow lifted and she nodded once, as though being called to random bloodied emergencies was common. Which, come to think of it, for her it pretty much was. Not that Mrs. Finkel knew that.

"Lead on," was all she said, locking up behind her.

On her hands and knees on a small balcony, hemmed in by potted plants in various states of age and morbidity, Lena scrubbed a widening pool of blood and feathers. It was a rather vicious-looking double pigeon homicide. She side-eyed Bernstein, the plump, smug-looking cat responsible.

It shut its moody green eyes and yawned.

This was not quite Bernstein's worst crime scene, but it was up there.

Lena plucked an errant feather out of her hair and considered the feline's owner. Mrs. Finkel was a sprightly woman for her age. Seventy-one years young, she'd tell anyone who'd listen. Which lately mostly extended to telling the ruthless Bernstein, her goldfish Woodward, and Lena.

The chatty widow had worked all over the US on some of the biggest newspapers—as Lena knew all too well from having her ear bent whenever Lena surfaced to collect her mail, still shaking off the dust from far-flung places.

Pinkish water spattered as Lena dunked her scrubbing brush in the bucket. She wrinkled her nose in disgust, trying to keep it off her clothes.

Damn it, she should be at work by now, finding out what the big emergency was that had yanked her out of Siberia so suddenly. But it was a bit hard to argue a work emergency with Mrs. Finkel given the old woman had no clue what she did for a living, let alone why it was occasionally vital to the human race. For all her neighbor's natural curiosity, as befitting her former profession, she had never once asked Lena what she did. Nor had she ever enquired too closely about the array of injuries—from black eyes to strange scars and crippled knees—that Lena often brought home from various assignments.

No, she held her own counsel. Lena liked that about her. She also liked her sharp mind, which made her tales from the news desk not entirely terrible to bear for the tenth or eleventh time.

Lena hefted the bucket and trudged inside to flush it down the drain. One more rinse across the balcony, and she'd be out of here. Easy.

Lena perched on the edge of a blue, embroidered, oversized sofa, gaze sweeping a mounted stuffed pheasant to her right, a faded world map on the wall behind her, a typewriter by the windowed desk, and a now relieved Mrs. Finkel in front of her.

Lena was stuck with a cup of tar that her neighbor liked to pretend was coffee. In all their years living across from each other, the other woman had never mastered the art of making liquid caffeine that tasted ingestible.

"Thank you, again, dear," she was saying, stroking her fat black cat.

Bernstein swished his tail in Lena's direction and blinked at her. She narrowed her eyes. Smug little shit.

Grimly swallowing more tar, Lena said: "No problem." She wondered whether two sips was sufficient before she could put the cup down and bolt. She wasn't sure which was worse—the coffee or having to be sociable.

Mrs. Finkel laughed. "So uptight, dear. We need to find you a way to relax."

"So you keep telling me."

"I'm never wrong. You know, my granddaughter's about your age. And no, no, don't give me that look again—she's not like most other young women. Diane's a war correspondent. Oh, the stories she can tell. She's very engaging. She's stateside at the moment, and climbing the walls for things to do and new people to meet. She'd drag even you out of your shell."

"I like my shell," Lena said honestly.

Mrs. Finkel laughed. "Well, if you ever change your mind, here's her card. She's always telling me how boring people her age are. You aren't boring, though, are you, Lena?" Her grey eyebrows lifted with a hint of mischief, as they always did when she subtly probed Lena's working life.

It was a game they played. The shrewd widow always inched the door open a sliver, in case Lena was feeling chatty for once. But Lena never could say a word. No one even knew guardians had meltdowns or went rogue, let alone needed trackers, such as Lena, to find them. That didn't fit the heroic narrative at all.

"Oh, I'm very boring," Lena said, pocketing the business card out of politeness. She'd stick it on the fridge and promptly ignore it. "You know me."

"I wish I did," Mrs. Finkel said wistfully. "It's not for want of trying. Whatever it is you do that has you disappearing at all hours, for months on end, it can't be all that your life is, can it? You need friends, dear. A hobby, perhaps?"

She pinned hopeful eyes on Lena, who smiled, placing the unfinished drink on the wooden coffee table and rose.

"I have to go. I'll have to run for the train."

"All right, then. Sorry to have detained you. Thanks for all your help with the mess. Don't forget, call Diane. Make friends. Live a little!"

When Lena made no comment, Mrs. Finkel gave her a long-suffering sigh, her eyes twinkling. "I don't know why I bother."

Lena gave her a wave over her shoulder and opened the door. "Me either. I'm a lost cause."

"No such thing," Mrs. Finkel protested as she shut the door behind her.

Lena caught sight of the clock on the ostentatious spire at the top of her company's American headquarters. She was *really* late. She quickened her pace as she rounded the side of the black glass-and-steel edifice that had been her workplace for half a decade.

The Facility. What a nice, clean, impersonal name for what they did in there. If only people knew. She hurried to the front of the building, taking the stone stairs two at time.

Lena detested being late for one reason—she liked to know what was going on. And all the decent gossip happened before eight on Mondays outside Dutton's office. Not post-ten.

As she entered the Facility's granite foyer, her senses were immediately assailed by the booming, competing giant screens on opposing walls, broadcasting the daily superhero news feeds. Which guardian had saved who and what and how overnight in a light-and-sound spectacle.

Lena rolled her eyes at the excuse to parade an array of straining muscles and cleavages for the commons to get weak-kneed over. Surrounding her in ten-foot-tall, high-definition vision were scenes of adoring fans, their perfect superstars, and the tearful rescued, all on an endless loop.

They were certainly beautiful. But to Lena, the guardians would always be little more than "the talent." It was all kabuki theater these news reels; everything for show. Censorship was rife. No imperfections in their glossy PR image ever allowed. God forbid.

Even so, it was a little hypnotic. She sometimes watched to find out who was ascendant in the Facility's world order. Knowledge was more than just power. Knowledge meant control.

And Lena Martin preferred control in all things.

Her eye caught sight of new Talon Man footage. The orange-suited, lantern-jawed leader of the Guardians' Confederation smiled his toothy, gleaming smile and announced how every guardian lived to serve. His voice resonated across the foyer.

Lena snorted. Sure they did. Three parallel scars on her arm said otherwise.

She flashed her ID at the security guard who was part volcanic rock, part god-only-knows-what. He grunted in reply—which was the most that particular guardian ever said to anyone. She'd never bothered to ask his name, and he'd never volunteered it.

At the elevators, she laid her palm on a chrome wall pad. The doors opened and a computer voice sounded. "ID accepted, Lena Martin, 1342-22A. Tracker First Class. Access granted for sub-levels ten to seventeen. Enter."

She stepped inside and felt the floor drop. It seemed slower than usual.

"Come on," Lena muttered, acutely aware of the time. She stared at the dropping numbers in irritation.

A sharp blue light flashed suddenly around the cabin. A random security check, assessing her credentials at the molecular level. It was an unsubtle reminder that the guardians trusted her, and the other human subcontractors who did their menial work, about as much as she did them.

The elevator stopped at sub-level eleven. Two more trackers got on. She nodded out of professional courtesy, but she had a healthy dislike for both Wills and Rossi.

"Got a big day?" Wills was asking his colleague.

"There's a runner and a splat on the eastern division board," Rossi said. "I'll take the splat. Easier since it's Becky's birthday tonight. My kid's gonna be ten."

A splat. She swallowed in revulsion. When superhero powers failed, they really did. Or sometimes they overestimated their own abilities at stopping an out-of-control train or pulling out of a dive and so on. Why Rossi thought cleaning up deceased talent was "easier," she'd never know. She might not think much of guardians but it was still revolting seeing them in that state. She was glad she no longer did that beat. Having T-stats as high as hers had its perks. She got some say in assignment choice.

"Hey, that's great. Say hi from me," Wills said. "I've got a break on the south side. Shouldn't take too long. They already got him cornered in a warehouse. Keeps calling for his mommy."

Both men laughed.

What asses. Guardian meltdowns—breaks—were happening a lot more often these days for some reason, not that her bosses acknowledged it. In such cases, to be even slightly effective, the Facility needed to send in a tracker who could project empathy. They would pat a guardian's hand and tell them it was going to be okay. That they'd get help. That they'd come to the Facility and be looked after real nice.

What a joke. The Facility didn't have a clue what "help" meant. Their secrets ran a lot deeper than being in denial about the fallibility of its super members.

Rossi turned to her. "What you got, Silver?"

Lena shook herself out of her reverie on hearing her nickname. "Not sure yet. Haven't checked in."

Rossi whistled, glancing at his timeslide. It was some flashy piece of pure platinum in vogue with all the commons right now. Completely redundant, of course, since he also wore his FacTrack which showed the time, as well as being a databank, multimedia player, GPS navigation, and satellite communications system.

"Shit, you're gonna get toasted being this late."

"Whatever," Lena said. "Not like I'm that easy to replace."

And it was true. Rossi and Wills exchanged pointed glances. But she wasn't talking herself up. No one could do what she did. There was daylight between her and the rest of the office. She was the top tracker internationally this year. Same as last year and the year before, when she'd finally beaten Hastings in the London Facility office, which was the international HQ for guardians.

"You just hauled in Beast Lord, didn't you?" Rossi whistled. "Tricky catch."

She shrugged nonchalantly, but her bones were still aching from the cold. She wondered if she'd ever feel warm again.

"We any closer to a result on the pool?" Rossi asked curiously.

Lena gave him a thin smile. Beast Lord was a hotly debated topic. At certain times every decade, he became half wild. No one had ever told the trackers why. Hell, maybe their alien bosses didn't know themselves. So the trackers had a betting pool of theories, ranging from brain-chemistry changes to mating season.

"Nothing new," she replied.

Rossi shook his head. "Figures. He doesn't seem the chatty type." He turned back to Wills. "Here's what I don't get. Those guardians hiding in the middle of nowhere, like Beast Lord, why even bother us with it? Ain't causing commons any problems, right? Just give us the clear-and-present-danger jobs. Not like the masses would be any wiser. They're clueless. They wouldn't know, we wouldn't tell, everyone wins. Right?"

"Are you kidding me?" Lena interrupted, incredulous.

"What?" Rossi's head snapped around, facing her. "I just mean this is such a waste of resources. Come on, Silver, you can't have been too happy freezing your tits off in Siberia over a crazy dipshit like Beast Lord. Look, it's basic math—sometimes the talent runs. So what? Let them, I say, as long as they stay low and off the news feeds. We've got enough crap on our plate with all the extra breaks and splats these days."

Lena glared at him. "You know why. Hell, your kid knows why," she said in exasperation. "People have a right to know that all the talent in the super zoo is being monitored at all times. It keeps the twitchy masses from losing their paranoid minds about having aliens loose among us."

"I know *that*." Rossi gave her a long-suffering look. He folded his arms. "I meant the public doesn't have to *know* they're missing. Why don't we use our trackers better? Stick to the guardians who are actually a threat, not the ones who've gone to ground?"

Lena threw her hands up. "You're a damned tracker, Rossi. You know better than anyone else how much raw power guardians have at their fingertips. Now how much damage could a runner do if they went psycho *while* they were off the grid? What if we couldn't even find them in time, let alone stop them using their powers on us?"

"One is hardly—"

"What if it's not just one?" She glared.

"Come on, Silver, they're harmless." He eyed her uncertainly.

"Yeah? Tell that to the residents of Oymyakon after all their windows have been shattered every time Beast Lord decides to howl at the moon or whatever shit he gets up to. Tracking guardians protects humanity from potentially lethal weapons." She gave the now-subdued man a withering look. "I can't believe I have to explain any of this to a freaking tracker."

The elevator came to a stop with a shudder and a ding. Lena strode out, ignoring the pair, who changed the topic to debating how bad Rossi's splat would be.

Gross.

"Silver!" came a bark from the end office as she took her first step into the Trackers' Control Room. She looked up to see the thin, pinched features of her boss, Bruce Dutton. He was in his mid-forties, and had a nervous tic which made him blink too often. The man reminded her of a highly strung, bespectacled, bureaucratic stork. He was smart, though, and fair, so she tolerated him.

"What time do you call this?"

Lena rolled her eyes. She didn't make a habit of being late, so what was his damned problem? She didn't answer, instead raising her chin and sauntering over. "Need me?"

"Check the attitude." He sighed, pointing at the visitor's chair. "Sit."

She plopped into the seat opposite and folded her arms.

"Welcome back from Siberia. Hope you dodged frostbite?"

Lena drummed her fingers on her forearm, waiting for him to get to the point.

"Fine," he muttered at her non-response. "Upstairs has stepped up the urgency on rounding up all the overdues and getting them back under thumb. Time is a critical issue. We're not stopping for niceties anymore. Just tag them and bag them."

Well, that explained her emergency recall. Lena took no small pride in the fact that when a guardian had been on the run for more than a month, their file stamped "Overdue", it was Lena they called in to get fast results. Due to her survivalist skills, Lena's specialty was the off-the-grid runners—the sneaky, clever ones hiding out in godforsaken places, their communications timeslides torn off as they eluded capture. She wondered how long she'd be packing her bags for this time.

"How late are we talking?"

"This one hasn't checked in for at least eighteen months."

Lena bit back a shocked gasp. *Eighteen months?* Not only was that an unbelievable length of time for an overdue to be gone, but how had she missed hearing about it?

"We've sent four trackers over that time, each with solid leads," Dutton said. "Good trackers too. They all came back saying there was nothing. No trace at all."

He tapped a few keys on his keyboard, and a holographic projection appeared between them. Lena studied the back of the floating image, waiting for it to rotate to the front. "Who is it this time?"

"Surprised you don't recognize her. She was high profile ten years ago. Like, top-tier famous."

Lena leaned forward as the hovering shape turned to face her. A lean, muscled, tall torso encased in a black, figure-hugging costume slowly pirouetted. Dark, smooth skin. A closely cut shadow of hair which emphasized sharp, high cheek bones. Generous, wide lips and deep brown eyes that drilled right into you. Eyes that said she wasn't taking any crap.

Lena started, swallowing her gasp. She was part of history, this one. An actual founder. And she was more elusive than all the other aliens on Earth put together.

Shattergirl had been the forgotten guardian until about ten years ago, when she was outed by paparazzi, catapulting her into the stratosphere as the first lesbian superhero the world had ever seen. Shattergirl had not hidden her displeasure at that. She had an attitude as fierce as her skills, which were twofold—she could fly, and she could fling objects about with her mind, to shattering effect.

"Seriously? Shattergirl's an overdue?" Lena could hardly believe it. Founders never ran. Some of the second-generation guardians did, sure. And their kids' kids were even worse, needing a white-knuckled tight rein. Teenage rebellion crossed all barriers and genetics, it seemed. Most of her day job involved third-generation guardian brats.

But the founders, the original group of aliens to make their home on Earth, were supposed to be the standard bearers of their people. They didn't break or splat or anything else. They were the reason the whole world had fallen in love with their kind. So a founder *running*? Hell. This was unprecedented.

"Yeah." Dutton ran his hand over his thinning hair. "Hence the panic from upstairs. Surprised you, of all people, hadn't heard about it."

"Have you forgotten I was in Outer Buttfuck, Siberia, for the past four months?" Lena lifted her eyebrow. "Only got in last night. When did I get the chance to see any internal briefings on this?"

"Wasn't on the in-house briefings. But I know how good your under-the-table intel is. Thought for sure you'd heard something. For the record, this one is marked as a full news blackout, inside and outside the building. You know the drill."

She did. Their vaunted super bosses routinely censored their people's failings from newscasts if it was within their ability. Occasionally minor stuff slipped out on the indie media channels, such as a costume malfunction, but the guardians' PR machine was pretty effective at controlling the big stuff. It helped enormously that Lena, along with the other commons at the

Facility, had all signed non-disclosure agreements. So, to the world at large, no guardian had screwed up in any major way. Ever.

"So, let me understand this," Lena said, "a founder, an actual icon no less, has been on the run for *eighteen months* and no one's seen her anywhere? How is that even possible? Who'd you send before me?"

"Sachs, Ferretti, Cragen, and Miller."

She stared. They were all elite trackers.

"I suspect," Dutton continued with a sigh, "that Shattergirl somehow knows when they get near. Her spy network must be as good as yours. Every time she finds out we're coming, she relocates before we get close. Hence, the reports that all say 'no trace of her found.'"

Lena considered that scenario, knitting her brows together. Overdues tended to be loners, not part of any network. All her instincts told her Dutton was dead wrong. Shattergirl barely seemed to tolerate her own people, let alone Earth's commons. The idea she was networking expertly to evade capture seemed ludicrous. It had to be something else.

She tapped her lip. From what she knew, Shattergirl did not suffer fools at all, was scary smart, and, unlike her eternally beaming brethren, refused to fake a damn thing. Lena smiled. Having a real challenge and a halfway decent guardian to track would make a change for once. She straightened.

"Why the screaming hurry that you had to recall me from Beast Lord mid-capture? I had to send him home in restraints, but I was *this* close to a voluntary return. You know that's always better for rehab long term."

"I know that, but we've just received a credible tip-off." He tapped his computer keyboard. "Shattergirl's been reported on Socotra. It's the first fresh lead in six months."

"Socotra? Where the hell is that?"

"Did you pay *any* attention at school, Silver?"

"Enough to know it was a waste of my time," Lena said, shooting him a shit-eating grin.

Dutton sighed and pointedly pressed a key. "Okay, I've uploaded it all for you. We need this overdue back by August twenty-first. I know it's less than a week, but at least we've narrowed it down to one tiny island for you. That deadline is fixed, by the way. Talon Man has his thing planned."

His thing. Right. That was one word for the over-the-top extravaganza marking the first centenary of the guardians' arrival on Earth. No expense had been spared. You couldn't even buy tickets for it anymore, no matter how much you offered the scalpers. Obviously it wouldn't do to have only forty-nine of the fifty founders present to celebrate landfall.

"Now I understand," Lena said, checking her FacTrack had uploaded Dutton's data packet. The file blinked at her. She gave him a knowing look. "I get why you so badly need my silver tongue."

"Thought you might," Dutton said. "We need this. Questions from the highest level will be asked if there's a spare seat on that podium come the end of next week."

"Yeah, god help us if the guardians look unable to control one of their own," Lena muttered. "Fine, leave it with me. Fortunately, I have skills the precious guardians don't."

Dutton's shoulders relaxed for the first time since she'd sat down, and he offered a rare smile. "I knew you were the tracker for this." He adjusted his glasses. "Oh, and Socotra?"

"Yeah?"

"It's also called the Island of Bliss."

Lena grinned, pleasantly surprised. "Anything above freezing is bliss to me right now."

"I'll bet." He looked at her seriously. "Pack your Dazr."

CHAPTER 3

LENA UNBUCKLED HER SEATBELT ONCE they hit cruising altitude, little yellow light be damned. She ignored Air Yemenia's shopping channel playing on multiple screens overhead. No, she did not want a "half tola of genuine Arabic oud perfume." She scrolled through her FacTrack and called up the archival vids menu.

The early black-and-white data reels she'd loaded up on the founders before leaving home were interesting. Of course, she'd seen the footage before over the years, but a refresher couldn't hurt. She pressed "Play" on the video of first contact with the founders.

Fifty super-fit humanoid survivors had suddenly appeared on the lawns of England's Houses of Parliament—the epicenter of Earth's power at the turn of the last century—as their spaceship broke up in the upper atmosphere. It was all avidly captured by movie news crews for the cinema houses.

There they sat, strange-looking creatures, barely humanoid a few of them, these oddly dressed refugees from another world. They ignored the growing, fearful crowds of hatted men in long coats and women in narrow, ankle-length hobble skirts and high blouses. They didn't blink at the parade of rickety, black vintage vehicles and horse-drawn carriages, nor even seem to notice when a row of converted double-decker buses creaked to a halt.

From them disgorged a snaking line of soldiers, quickly surrounding the arrivals. In the silent, crackling, monochrome vision, Lena watched an officer with a wide, white mustache and matching bristling sideburns shout a command. The soldiers' weapons snapped to shoulder height.

She held her breath as the gathering mob hungrily watched the aliens' reactions to this provocation. The beings didn't so much as twitch, but their gazes shifted to one among them. Then a shimmer of electrical, flickering energy sprung up around them.

The officer's mouth opened and bellowed a single word. The caption read: "FIRE!"

Smoke, recoiling weapons, contorted faces in the crowd...chaos filled the footage, everywhere except at the very center of the scene. The aliens hadn't even flinched.

Bullets had hit the shimmering protective dome, melting into it.

The commander ordered the men to repeat their attack, yielding the same result. The soldiers lowered their weapons helplessly.

The founders continued to sit there, in the strangest impasse ever seen. Lena supposed it was disturbingly human to fire at the aliens first and try to make peace second. But it was 1916, and half the planet was gripped in a war, so nerves were long frayed. In the hours and then day that followed, there came the first feeble attempts at diplomacy.

Lena jumped the archival footage forward.

Representatives of most nations—many already in London to discuss the war efforts—came and went, trying to reach the aliens in their various tongues. Each government's agent made assorted demands, bribes and appeals, but, as was plain to see in the footage, none received a response.

The aliens waited for thirty-seven hours until their group's empath, Mind Merge, had assimilated enough of the planet's languages to work out the patterns and nuances of each, and finally began to speak in the dominant one.

Lena watched the disbelief on the crowd's faces when Mind Merge suddenly opened his eyes and spoke in perfect King's English, looking directly down the camera lens, explaining his group's plight. His statements were added to the silent footage in subtitles, and screened for months in cinema houses worldwide.

She closed that video. She didn't need to see the news footage that immediately followed, of the riots and hysteria, religious vigils, and other doomsday predictions that an invasion was imminent. As the months rolled on, every founder became part of a charm offensive and made it their mission to win over planet Earth and its anxious people.

Well, every founder except one.

Lena jumped ahead to the footage of the first global press conference. She pinpointed the dark-skinned woman hanging back, silently watching proceedings with mistrustful eyes, her arms folded, as their leader, Talon

Man, leapt through the diplomatic hoops and amused the throngs with his charismatic routine.

Shattergirl looked unimpressed and irritated to the point of miserable.

Lena snorted. She couldn't blame her. Politics were a cure for insomnia. She skipped forward three months to the most famous footage of all. The day the world's media had gathered at Regent's Park in London for a demonstration of the new arrivals' abilities. One by one, they showed what they could do. It was one part theater, one part silent plea to their new world to allow them to make a home here.

She watched as the rugged Talon Man soared elegantly before landing in front of a tree and whittling at it with the sharp protrusions that ran along his arms and legs.

His movements were faster than the old movie cameras of the day could follow, so he appeared as a blur. When he stepped back, it was a stunningly accurate carving of their host nation's prime minister. The man in question, watching in the crowd, beamed as the media behind him could be seen apparently "oohing" in delight.

Lena shook her head. *Pure circus.*

She ran the video forward again, past guardians with dragon breath and super strength, ones who could melt rocks, or jump a hundred feet. Then, it was Shattergirl's turn. She stepped into the center and, without a word, turned her head sharply to the side, before slamming her hands together in a clap over her head.

Two black automobiles parked on the street suddenly flew into the air above the greened area, smashing spectacularly, raining debris on the grass before them. There appeared to be some sort of startled shout of dismay from two reporters, no doubt recognizing their respective company vehicles, and the faces of the rest broke into laughter.

Shattergirl's expression betrayed nothing as she lowered her arms and stepped back.

In the background, Lena could see furious looks shot at her by several of her group, remonstrating with her silently. She grimly pressed her lips together and stared them down. They broke her gaze and didn't make eye contact for the rest of the segment.

Lena wondered why she'd never seen this footage before. She checked the vid's details. Her eyebrows shot up. Shattergirl's segment had never aired. Huh. Well, with forty-nine other talents putting on a show, the news editors of the day obviously preferred to skip the one unwilling to pretend that this was anything but a debasing dog-and-pony show.

Her fingers tapped her FacTrack and loaded up the video of the day of signing the Pact. It was the guardians' peace deal with the people of Earth. They received a guaranteed safe haven, where they would not be hunted, and the guardians would regulate and govern themselves, and ensure none of their kind stepped out of line.

They were assured, given that a world war was raging, they would be allowed to remain neutral in all human politics, and any country that sought them out for military ends, covert or overt, would lose the services of all guardians within their borders forever.

The guardians agreed, in turn, not to break any human laws except to save a life. They also conceded they would wear special tracking timeslides, alien tech they'd brought with them to Earth, as part of a registry of their whereabouts, updated weekly. And they agreed to always make themselves and their special talents available for the protection of the people of their adopted planet.

It took Lena ten minutes of hunting the crowd scenes to find Shattergirl hidden in the throngs of the clapping, back-slapping world leaders, diplomatic hangers-on, and guardians at the signing. Eventually she spied her, leaning against a pillar, rubbing her temple. She looked like she was thoroughly over everything and utterly miserable.

Lena jumped ahead two years. London. Opening day at the first Facility of a dozen to be set up worldwide to educate, heal, train, and govern guardians. In a stark contrast to landfall, this time the crowd was cheering their protectors' arrival in their city.

She spent another hour studying photo after photo of Shattergirl from news events. The talent's ability to shift large, dense matter effortlessly saw her appear often at landslides, mine collapses, fires, building implosions, and earthquakes.

Many photos captured her profile staring darkly at a horrific sight after having pulled the people to safety. She ignored the thanks of those around her as though they were as ridiculous and pointless as the requests for autographs and photos.

Lena was getting the picture now. Shattergirl did her duty as a guardian, sure, but rarely was she at any of the group photo ops. When she *was* caught on camera at some media or political event, it was always wearing the same pained expression. Lena zoomed in. She had seen this exact look before. Many times, in fact, and not on Shattergirl.

A startling theory formed. She could be way off base... Hell, she probably was.

Lena skipped to the last piece of Shattergirl footage. The video from just over a decade ago that made Shattergirl, until then a virtually unknown guardian, world famous. This was also the only interview with her in all the time she'd been on Earth. Lena hit "Play."

"Shattergirl, Dave Monroe, *The Daily Express.* Do you have any comment on the photos in the paper today which caught you kissing a mystery woman? Are you a lesbian?"

"By what right do you ask me this?"

"As a journalist. I—"

"By what right do you assume to know any part of my private life?"

"Well, the public would really like to know—"

"How does their curiosity give them any rights to my personal business?"

"You're a public figure, a guardian. *And* a founder. Shattergirl, you face scrutiny because you've chosen to be in the public eye."

Her eyes flashed darkly. "I chose *none* of this. Not one part of this was ever my choice."

"But—"

"No! And shame on you for asking."

"Now come on a minute, I—"

"Shame. On. You."

Her parting, enraged glower was flashed around the world and sparked an international debate about what rights, if any, the guardians had to their privacy. Of course, such thorny issues were forgotten by the next month. But for a young Lena, Shattergirl's blunt interview had been the most telling thing any guardian had ever said in public in the past century.

She'd been sixteen back then, in awe, and had damn near cheered Shattergirl putting the reporter in his place. How much simpler things had been then. Before she'd learned the truth about guardians. Before she'd seen how pathetic they really were. Weak. Whiny. Entitled.

Lena considered her options for bringing Shattergirl in. Every instinct told her that with one so smart, the best offense would be no offense at all. Lena's best skill was in getting others to open up to her. To keep them talking and talking, and to slowly bend them to her point of view over days or weeks, while convincing them the decision to return home was all *their* idea. In this area, she was unmatched.

She knew she could swing even this most private and reluctant guardian if she was on her A-game. And really, when wasn't she?

With a cool smile, she turned off her FacTrack and closed her eyes.

Lena dodged an orange-and-white goat on the heat-shimmering tarmac as she followed the disembarking passengers from Air Yemenia's weekly flight into Socotra. The desolate, squat, cream-and-white terminal building looked like it had been dropped in the middle of what could pass as a vast salt plain, bounded by distant purple mountains.

Hot winds laced with microscopic amounts of sand pummeled Lena. Her mouth was instantly sucked dry, and her eyes blinked back grit. She could smell dust on the whipping wind, with a hint of fusty goat. *This* was the Island of Bliss? The longer she was here, the more she wondered why Shattergirl would come to any part of Yemen.

Despite her boss's claim it was only one little island, Lena had now learned the Socotra archipelago had four small islands just off the Horn of Africa, according to the guide book she'd read on the plane. She had ruled out three of the four islands on the way over, as being too tiny or barren to interest Shattergirl. So that just left this, Socotra's main island, as her likely destination. It had enough of a main town for a guardian to obtain supplies, and also enough isolation to hide out, undisturbed, for as long as she wanted.

Lena made it to the front of the queue and placed her Dazr on the customs official's counter, careful to block anyone else from seeing it. The exotic weapon, by law, always had to be declared at airports, but it was also "need-to-know" only. She slid it next to her global authorization papers and waited.

"What is it?" the Middle Eastern man asked her in heavily accented English.

"A Max-fire Dazr. It's a special gun. It shoots a mesh around a person and holds them for an hour to a day, depending on the setting."

"Not that," he grunted. "*That.*"

She followed his gaze to her arm. A curling, deep, parallel set of three scratches spiraled up her forearm.

Lena considered her response. She could hardly say an attack by the mentally unstable Beast Lord. She wasn't entirely sure whether anyone around here had even heard of Beast Lord. Besides, she was under standing orders not to disabuse commons of the notion guardians were anything but cuddly, safe, and, most especially, sane.

She self-consciously lowered her leather cuff that had ridden up, to hide the scars. "A disagreement with a cooking knife."

"Three of them?" Disbelief settled on his face.

She blinked at him innocently, shrugged as though she could barely remember the incident, then offered her most winning smile.

Suspicion now radiated from him. The official made a science of shuffling his papers. "Reason for visit?" he barked.

Lena studied his aggressive body language with growing disquiet. She had talked suicidal guardians down from mountain ledges. She'd convinced one who'd threatened to blow up an entire suburb with his creepy lava eyes to instead go to sleep. She simply explained to him that he was really, so very, *very* tired. And he'd just closed his eyes and curled up and slept, right where he was. Yet some pissy customs officer was looking at her like she was selling him a bag of dead squirrels? She clearly needed a holiday; she was losing her touch.

"I'm a writer," Lena said earnestly. "I hear your island is very beautiful. I plan to give it a big write-up. Lots of eco-tourists will come if I write favorably. That would be great for your economy. And it'd mean more local jobs."

He gave her a cynical grunt. Their eyes locked for an uncomfortably long silence. Finally, he broke the staring contest and stamped her paperwork, shoving it back. "*This* gets you in." He tapped her travel authorization from the Facility that made her untouchable at airports the world over. "Not your words. And, so you know, they don't give these sorts of papers or issue fancy guns to writers. Now go. And get medicine, *sahh*?" he said, waving a finger towards her arm. "Be more careful with your *knives*."

He flicked his gaze over her shoulder. "*TĀLIN*! NEXT!"

Lena swallowed in irritation. It felt like something acidic nesting in her throat given how unused to being doubted she was. She headed moodily for the exit. Definitely needed a holiday.

Lena needed to bum a ride and a group of newly arrived European scientists looked like a good target. It shouldn't be that hard, Lena decided, as the head scientist turned out to be a tall, Slavic woman with considerable charm and bright eyes that seemed to like what she saw in Lena. Or maybe she was just being friendly.

Her name was Larsen. Anna Larsen. Doctor. They were the only two women in the terminal, so that had broken the ice somewhere between the baggage counter and the walk to the exit.

A little mild flirting never hurt anyone, Lena figured, especially if it got her into town without having to face the flea-bitten car rental counter, and a queue to rent a battered vehicle that looked older than Mrs. Finkel. Given taxis were non-existent, she'd suck it up and try a charm offensive.

She gave the scientist a bright smile and mentally flicked through her small-talk repertoire while she examined her quarry. Larsen was blonde. Legs up to her chin, although she'd wisely hidden them from the locals, who, Lena's travel book noted, comprised devoutly religious goat herders, date farmers, fishermen, and a few enterprising types making the most of the eco-tourism boom as guides and trinket sellers.

Like Lena, Dr. Larsen wore a colorful cotton headscarf.

"You come here often?" Lena asked, voice light, as they matched strides.

"Every chance that I get," Dr. Larsen replied, reaching for her backpack. She paused, as though examining her curiously over her choice of words. "And this is your first time here."

"How'd you know?"

"You stopped on the tarmac to stare at the goats."

"Oh. I guess you're used to them then?"

"You get used to a lot of things out here. For example, soon I am to be enjoying a biosystem that has no match anywhere in the world. It is astonishing. "

"You study plants?" Lena asked, as the scientist struggled to gather a second and third bag from the collection area. She stepped up to help. "Where to?" Lena asked, indicating the bags.

"My colleague should be waiting outside for our team. And do I 'study plants'? What a question! What else is there to life but studying plants? Truly, nothing is more important." Her pale eyebrows lifted, daring Lena to disagree, amusement on her face.

Lena shook her head and gave her an incredulous look. "I'll have to take your word on that one," she replied with a laugh. "But mark me down as a skeptic for now."

They reached a white SUV which contained three men who seemed to be arguing across several different languages. Lena hefted Dr. Larsen's largest bag into the rear of the vehicle then stepped back as the scientist put the rest of her luggage in.

Lena looked at her hopefully. "Care to give a skeptic a lift into town?" She rammed her hands in her jeans pockets and grinned.

"That depends. Do you think I could convert you on the road to Hadibo? About how plants are the meaning of life? And that is literally the truth by the way."

"Never know your luck," Lena said easily. "But, seriously, I wouldn't hold your breath. Plants are nice enough, but give me a cold beer at the end of the day, and that's everything I need in life right there."

"A challenge?" Dr. Larsen teased. "Well, how can I miss this chance to convert an infidel. Yes? Climb in."

And so Lena found herself with a quartet of scientists heading to some place called 20 Street in Socotra's main town of Hadibo. The team wanted to stop to pick up supplies before heading off to one of the remote eco-campsites. They were in an animated, nerdy discussion for most of the drive. Lena tuned them out until Larsen, in the front passenger seat, turned to face her.

"We amuse you, do we not?" Her voice was accented, light; the tone curious.

Lena sighed, already over being sociable. But the price for the ride was right, so… She smiled politely. "Not at all."

Well, it was the truth. Boredom and amusement were poles apart.

"Ah, so we bore you with our fascination."

Lena met her eyes in the rear mirror, startled.

"Of course, you are wondering why this dreary topic is so interesting to us. Hmm? So, Lena, do you know what endemism is? Or endemic species?"

"I think I missed that class." She fidgeted and glanced out the window, hoping Larsen would get the hint.

She did not.

"Endemism," Dr. Larsen repeated the word appreciatively as though she was savoring a fine wine, "is a species found in one place only. And this island is bursting with hundreds of such species that never spread to the mainland. A third of the plants here you will never see anywhere else on Earth. Out here you can see giant trees that defy gravity. They have bulging trunks and hang off the sides of steep cliffs. The shapes, the roots, the bark, they look very foreign to Western eyes. Socotra is called the most alien-looking place on earth for this reason. It is our scientific mecca and why we are so very excited."

She paused for a breath and smiled. "Not just us. You should talk to the anthropologists. Many Socotrans ignore Arabic and speak their own tongue, Socotri. It's ancient, and so poetic and lyrical, but it drives us all to madness."

"Madness? Why?" Lena asked in spite of herself.

"It has no written form. Imagine it. Try working out place names when every foreigner phonetically guesses at the spelling, each flavored with their own nationality. The result is that everything here has nine or ten or even twenty spelling variations. It makes all the scientists and tourist operators tear at their hair."

The other scientists laughed in recognition.

"But I'm sure you'll find that out for yourself," Dr. Larsen said. "Occupational hazard? *Ja?*"

Lena's eyebrows shot up.

"I was behind you at Customs. You are a writer?"

"Yes," Lena said tightly. She turned away again to stare out the window and this time Larsen took the hint.

The vehicle rumbled past cream-colored sandstone buildings. The storefronts were crumbling and worn, the streets white with sand, and drowning in rubble and dusty piles of trash.

Market stalls, wooden structures with a few umbrellas and bright sheets pinned up to shield customers from the sun, were lined along the street. Local men, many with headscarves, milled around in their futas, wraparound, calf-length cotton skirts in colorful checked prints. Several women in longer, ground-scraping skirts and blouses stopped to haggle with the vendor selling chunks of pink, freshly killed, goat meat.

A hotel they rattled past looked in better condition. Its old, arched stone window frames reminded Lena of a style she had seen in Morocco once.

Their vehicle came to a stop and the doors sprang open as eager scientists piled out. The smells instantly assailed her—a mix of spices from a nearby eatery, the dark, earthiness of raw meat, rubbish which was getting nosed through by stray goats, and more ever-present dust.

Lena jumped out along with the scientists.

"No sightseeing," Dr. Larsen called to her colleagues. "Get just your essential supplies. We leave for base camp in thirty minutes."

A boy scampered past in worn jeans, rolled up at the ankles, and a white, short-sleeved shirt. He paused to spin around and pull a silly face at the scientists before running off, his clopping brown feet barely staying inside his overlarge leather sandals.

Lena grinned at the back of his head. *Cheeky.*

She tried to imagine the six-foot-tall Shattergirl striding about this chaotic, dirty street, with her regal bearing and aloof, thousand-yard stare. Even hiding herself under a traditional headscarf, Lena couldn't picture it at all. Which made sense. Who runs away to the most alien backwater on earth and then stays in town? No, Shattergirl would be far from here.

"You could continue on with us," Dr. Larsen suggested, as she dropped her own backpack on the ground and locked up the vehicle. "You'll see much more beyond the tourist stuff."

Lena shifted uncomfortably. Her throat constricted at the idea of spending extended time in company. The job was so much cleaner and easier when she didn't have to think about civilians.

"Come," Dr. Larsen goaded her with a smile. "I promise you no electricity, no shower, no bathroom, no phone reception. What is not to love? You cannot write your masterpiece from Socotra's main street. You may as well be back home."

"Maybe later," Lena suggested diplomatically. "I want to get a feel for the area first. Mix and mingle."

Dr. Larsen nodded. "Later. When you are tired of civilization, then you come and stay in the one-billion-star hotel. Out there? Under the heavens? *That's* the real Socotra."

Lena couldn't disagree, but she had work to do. She pulled up the Arabic translator app on her FacTrack, gave the scientist a wave, and headed up 20 Street, hoping that at least some of the locals knew one of the new-world languages and not just Socotri.

She strongly doubted her translation device extended to *un*written languages.

After twenty-eight minutes, Lena knew her instincts had been right. The locals she'd spoken to had looked at her like she had two heads when she showed them Shattergirl's picture and asked if they'd seen her. Only one local woman had said anything useful, and even then it was a tenuous lead at best. Nope, town was not where Lena needed to be.

She ran for the SUV, which was now crammed to the gills with chattering scientists about to head off again.

"So," Dr. Larsen said, rolling down her window as Lena approached. "You feel daring after all?"

Lena shook her head. "That depends. Where are you going?"

"To Mars."

"To...Mars?"

"Well, it may as well be." Dr. Larsen smiled. "We're off to Homhil Plateau. There's an eco-camp there, and a few interesting biodiversity clusters among the *Dracaena cinnabari* that Karl is most anxious to get his equipment on."

Lena stared. "Okay."

"The dragon blood tree," Dr. Larsen said. "Around here they use its red sap as a panacea for medical conditions. If you cut the trunk, it bleeds. Violinists prize the resin for varnish. It is also used as toothpaste and—"

"Sorry I asked," Lena cut in. "But before you go, I wanted to ask about something an old local lady just mentioned. She says Socotra has a protector, a hermit, who lives in the caves, is a bit scary, makes a lot of noise if people intrude into its space."

The car exploded into conversations of various accents.

Dr. Larsen gave her a pained look. "You had to start this debate again? Is it real, is it not? Socotra's Iblis?"

"Iblis?"

"Generically, a genderless devil figure, a smokeless fire. An all-seeing demon." She waved her hand dismissively. "Socotra's Iblis, specifically, supposedly rains boulders bigger than buildings down on people disturbing it. We have trouble keeping guides who avoid the area for superstitious reasons."

"Boulders?" Lena felt a surge of hope. "So it's real?"

"That depends on who it is you ask," Dr. Larsen said.

"Where does it live?"

"Again," Dr. Larsen sighed, "everywhere, nowhere. It's likely not real. A myth."

Lena opened her FacTrack and brought up the topography of Socotra. "Looks like most of the caves are in the middle of the island and some are to the east. So can you narrow it down for me? Where does the demon supposedly make the most noise?"

"Central," came a German accent. A scientist in the back seat behind Dr. Larsen leaned out the window and beckoned to her. "There." He pointed to an area on her map. "Around the Dixam Plateau. Three main caves around there, next to a wadi."

Wadi. Lena thought back to her notes she'd read up on the flight. A valley or ravine.

"Most of Socotra's scientists lose guides around here," his finger shifted left, "and especially here." He tapped the screen near a swirl marked "Marshim Cave" and scowled. "I was trying to get to the area last expedition, eight months ago. Never got close. Too many sudden rock falls. Which was not right at all—the area is geologically stable."

Lena squinted at the sun and tried to get her bearings. "Are you guys going anywhere near there?"

Dr. Larsen shook her head. "No. We're going east. As you can see, you need to head almost due south. I hope you're a good hiker."

"I'm okay." Lena prided herself on her fitness.

"You'll need to be." Dr. Larsen studied her. "It's only twenty kilometers, but it's rugged going once you leave the road."

Lena nodded.

"One more thing." Dr. Larsen leaned forward and gave her an intent look. "If you find this Iblis demon, tell it to stop scaring the *dritt* out of the locals. It's important the work we do and we need their help to do it."

Lena snorted. "But what if this Iblis has a good reason to scare everyone away?"

"What could be more important than science?" Dr. Larsen seemed genuinely perplexed. "It explains everything that we are. Everything we can be."

The other scientists murmured in agreement.

Lena avoided her usual sarcastic rejoinder. If they'd seen half the crazy shit she'd seen—things that defied everything these people thought they understood about the natural world—they'd have to rewrite their textbooks. She exhaled. At twenty-six she was way too young to be this jaded.

Lena fixed a smile and stepped back from the vehicle. "Thanks for the ride in. Happy hunting your endemic, ah, things."

A chorus of multi-accented farewells sounded, and the SUV started and then roared away in a cloud of white dust.

CHAPTER 4

LENA WAS STARING. SHE'D BEEN doing a lot of that the whole way along her journey, but this was insane. The trees were something out of a fevered fantasy-artist's imagination. She passed another twisted monster. A riot of fat, chunky, intricately interwoven branches splayed out like a lace doily topped with spiky green leaves.

She was getting the Mars references now.

Her legs were starting to complain, but she was making steady progress and the scenery was incredible. Finding a waterhole marked on her digital map, Lena detoured there and stopped for a late lunch. "Waterhole" was not even the half of it. A moss-covered natural chute fed fresh water into a clear pool. It was breathtaking.

Lush, giant date palms dotted the area. The stillness was a little unnerving and the air smelled...she paused, searching for the word. *Fresh.* It always struck her every time she returned home how cities smelled of grittiness. Maybe Shattergirl had the right idea. Except Lena didn't fancy living this far from the engulfing heart of a city. She liked being swallowed up into its bright lights. No one noticed her in cities. She liked that rather a lot.

She munched contentedly on the flatbread filled with cooked potato, carrot, onion, and garlic she'd picked up at one of the better-looking restaurants on 20 Street.

She could hear several birds and looked up, catching sight of one. She stopped mid-chew. Okay, vultures were generally creepy no matter what part of the world you were in, but this one was ridiculous. Orange and white—like a bird of prey had been crossed with a chicken. Unbelievable.

Lena finished lunch, packed away her wrappings, and filled her water bottle from the stream. She consulted her FacTrack. Time to pick up the pace.

Flicking to a larger map display, she made a few calculations. She was only about two hours' hike from where the scientist had pointed to on her map. With any luck, the infamous Iblis was exactly who she thought it was—and she could be reasoned with.

And if not? Well, the trek to Mars had been one she'd remember forever.

Dixam Plateau was vast. Rock faces bore stains of brown and purple, along with more of the strange dragon blood trees clinging to any surface, not so much defying gravity as spiting it.

Lena was picking her way along the bottom of a wadi when the first rumble sounded.

She glanced up in confusion. Her study of the clear blue sky was shattered by a loud crash just ten feet away. Rocks suddenly started hailing down out of nowhere, smashing all around her. Squeezing into a crevice in a nearby rock wall, Lena quashed her initial fear and held her breath.

She was pretty sure "rock rain" wasn't a thing, and avalanches didn't come out of thin air. Looked like Iblis had turned up to party. Lena's adrenalin was spiking, and she forced herself to feel calm. When a sense of control filtered through her, she inched the FacTrack off her arm—challenging given her confined space—and slid it into her backpack. Nothing put an overdue offside faster than ID-ing you as a tracker the first second they got a good look at you.

She stuck her head out of the fissure for a better idea of the direction that the rocks were coming from. A boulder the size of a small car smashed a few feet away and she retracted her head swiftly.

"SHIT!" Lena had gone from dodging frostbite and wolf-beasts to flying rocks? Christ, she was getting a workout this year.

That had been so damn close. Lena froze and picked at the thought. Super close. As in *pinpoint* accurate. Which meant it was no accident she was still alive. Heart thudding, she swallowed, and decided to suck it up and put her theory to the test. But if she was wrong?

Well, no one lives forever.

She stepped out of her hiding place, took ten steps, and waited, standing stock still, trying not to flinch as a volley of rocks the size of cows immediately headed her way. At the last moment, as Lena screwed up her eyes, fearing the worst, the boulders bounced harmlessly to the left and right of her, behind, and in front—everywhere except actually on her.

Lena exhaled. Okay. Theory proved. She wasn't about to die today. Her target wasn't homicidal, merely pissed off. And given her rock hurler was clearly controlling the trajectory of her deadly ammunition, this meant she'd almost certainly made first contact with Shattergirl.

Lena slowly began to move forward, plotting a straight line towards the source of the showering boulders. The noise was overwhelming. Rocks smashed, exploded, and crunched around her. Dust filled her eyes, blinding her momentarily as she edged forward.

She could do this.

After five minutes of shuffling, she saw a towering cliff face. Two-thirds of the way up was a flat ledge and, behind that, an inky hole in the rock wall—a cave of some sort. But that's not what held Lena's attention.

A dark shadow stood on the wide ledge, like a conductor on stage, summoning boulders from the rocky floor and hurling them towards Lena with a vicious sweep and slash of its arms.

She stared at the figure in exasperation and put her hands on her hips. "I know you're not actually trying to hit me, so you may as well quit the theatrics," she shouted.

Her words echoed around the valley. For a few moments there was stillness, and then the volley became even more ferocious.

"Give it a rest," Lena shouted again. "I just want to talk."

This time the rocks rained down even closer, and several shattering splinters shot up, far too close for comfort.

"HEY!" Lena bellowed, as one particularly sharp sliver sliced through her sleeve. "I'm not a fucking pincushion. Come on, Shattergirl! Take pity on the *shreekopf!*"

Guardians had the best swear words. This particular word translated into something involving the interbreeding of dimwitted human siblings. The deluge stopped instantly.

"Who *are* you?" The voice was low and indignant, and boomed around the valley before fading out.

Lena exhaled in relief as she recognized it as belonging to her missing guardian. Identity confirmed. She took the pause in being pelted as her chance to sprint for the base of the rock face beneath Shattergirl.

"I'm coming up," she called out as she reached it. "I know you could turn me into road kill or cliff kill or any other kill you wanted, but can you resist until I get up there?"

There was no response. Lena decided to take that as agreement. She wiped her hands on her pants, and studied the rock wall for hand and footholds. Satisfied there were enough, and that her climbing boots were up to the task, she began to scale it.

It was steep to the point of almost vertical, but she'd done enough drills on rock climbing at the Facility to not be daunted. Halfway up, as her muscles were beginning to tremble, there came a scraping sound. She tilted her head as far back as she dared. The toes of Shattergirl's black leather boots now jutted out over the cliff edge.

Subtle.

Lena shifted her gaze a little higher. Shattergirl peered down at her, dressed all in black, in her trademark bodysuit which highlighted her lithe form. The woman's sheer, imposing power struck home. Lena had met plenty of talent before—hard not to in her line of work. They all had a certain something, an otherness to them. That made sense—they were otherworldly, after all. They also tended to be attractive, with their perfect skin and rippling muscles. But there was more to Shattergirl than just superficialities. The waves of power she exuded just from standing still were unnerving.

"I only want to talk," Lena shouted. She found a new handhold and inched higher.

"Don't expect me to listen." The voice was curt and irritated, but at least Shattergirl was actually talking now.

Lena reached for another hold and sliced her hand in a tender place. "Fucking son of a drunken *frakstit* piece of flaming goat turd. Ow! SHIT!"

A strangled noise made her glance up.

Shattergirl was crouched now, like a sprinter preparing for a race, peering over the ledge, a strange, twisted expression as she watched Lena's progress. It took a moment to place the look, so unfamiliar was it on this guardian.

"So my swearing amuses you?" Lena called up, readjusting her hold, giving her hand a quick shake, and ignoring the sting from the cut.

"Maybe clumsy commons amuse me," Shattergirl called down. "Although I've never heard *frakstit* used in quite that way before. Very creative."

Lena smirked. "Thank you."

"So you know," Shattergirl said, sounding almost bored, "I don't talk to journalists. You're wasting your time."

"*Please*—give me some credit for knowing you'd sooner have a colonoscopy than talk to the media."

Another bite of almost-laughter from above spurred Lena to push up another few feet.

"I don't talk to special agents either," Shattergirl continued. "I'm immune to whatever psy-ops scheme your government has cooked up. And it's against the terms of the Pact."

"Sigh-oh…what?"

"It means I don't care whether your sad little nation is about to come under terrorist, chemical, or nuclear attack, or if you have photos of a hospital full of baby orphans who'll die if I don't sign up with you urgently. Take your evil military agenda elsewhere."

"Sorry to disappoint. Not here to recruit." Lena was almost at the top. She blew her hair out of her eyes.

"Just as well. The last agent who tried that ended up in the Baltic Sea."

"Good to know." Lena paused, shaking out one tired hand and then the other. "Hell, I think my arms will be a foot longer by the time I get up there."

"Then your solution is simple: stop climbing."

"Oh, come on, aren't you the least bit curious? I promise I'm not here to sell you magazine subs or discount timeslides."

Lena finally reached the lip of the cliff and, with one last effort, propelled herself over it and rolled, coming to a rest on her back.

Shattergirl took a step forward and bent over her, blocking out the sun. Lena looked up into an imposing six-foot-tall silhouette. She was lean and toned, all straight lines from her hips to her chest, with a black shadow of hair on her perfectly shaped scalp.

At half a foot shorter, Lena, by comparison, was pretty sure she looked like the fittest, shortest member of a gay boy band. (The one on the drums.)

"Oh, now I see," Shattergirl said, face inches from Lena's.

The guardian's voice had far more inflection in person, Lena idly noted. The vids really didn't do her justice. "See what?"

"You're right, you're not military are you? Not with those belligerent eyes."

"My…what?" Lena frowned. What the hell?

"You like to be different? No one tells you what to do? You've got 'insolent' written all over you."

"So much for pleasantries," Lena drawled.

"So, not media, not military," Shattergirl said, ignoring her. "That means you're a different kind of pest. Tell Talon Man he's wasting his time."

"What?" A lash of fear curled through Lena at having been picked so easily.

"Oh, you're easier on the eyes than the last four trackers, I'll grant you that—which isn't hard as you're not one of the males of your brutish species," Shattergirl said, studying her suspiciously. "And I have to wonder why that is."

Brutish species? Rude much? The guardian was peering at Lena like she reeked of skunk, as though her being of the female persuasion was all part of a fiendish plot.

Lena laughed wryly. She sat up, loudly dusting her knees. "You think I'm some sort of Mata Hari secret agent sent by your boss? Here to dazzle you with my overpowering feminine wiles and bend you to my will? Wish my mother were alive to hear that. She'd have 'praised Jesus' if anyone mistook me for having actual feminine wiles."

Shattergirl scrutinized Lena's body with a cool gaze. "Good point," she drawled.

Lena did not react to the mockery. She knew she had a soft butch look. Muscles. Boots. Androgynous to the edge of masculine. So what? Like Shattergirl didn't? She was the freaking poster girl for the sexually ambiguous.

Shattergirl lowered herself even closer, bringing their eyes level. Lena forced herself to return the scrutiny and refused to be baited. She threw in a cocky eyebrow lift.

This resulted in another almost-smile at her audacity, which was quickly chased away when Shattergirl's lips compressed into a thin line. "So why are you bothering me?" she asked. "Because I gave at the office. Repeatedly."

"I'm a writer," Lena said smoothly. "And you are my next story. Before you say no, I do respectable biographies, not newspaper trash. I'm not some media hack."

"You want to feature Shattergirl." The words were flat and cool, not tilting into a question at all. Her lip curled in distaste.

"Yeah. Or is it Iblis the demon, these days? Whatever you go by." Lena shrugged.

"I have no control over local superstitions."

Lena snorted and said lightly, "Sure."

"You wasted your effort climbing up here," Shattergirl said. "The answer's no."

Lena didn't twitch a muscle.

"That wasn't the start of negotiations. Leave or I can arrange a much faster way down."

"If you'd wanted me to be a bloodied wadi stain you'd have flattened me earlier. You weren't even trying."

"That can change."

Lena laughed and reached for her backpack, pulling out a water bottle. "So you're witty? I had no idea."

Shattergirl's eyes narrowed. "How did you even find me?"

"Had a tip-off. I guess not everyone around here buys the mythical demon line. A lot of scientists work on Socotra, for instance."

"Why now?"

"The centenary of landfall's coming up next week."

Shattergirl's lips became even thinner. "So?"

"So, a handful of biography writers have been selected by the Facility to do the bios of all fifty founders as part of a special centenary collector's book." All true. "I'm writing your chapter." Not even close to true.

"Short straw?"

"Actually, I asked for you."

"Why?" Suspicion laced her eyes.

"You're the interesting one. The badass." Lena offered a winning smile.

Shattergirl's nostrils flared in annoyance. "Spare me the fangirls," she muttered, half to herself. "You can leave anytime." She shot up from her crouch to standing, far faster than Lena could react. Her expression was no longer mere disdain, but arctic levels of chilly.

Lena wished she'd thought to tuck her Dazr into the back of her pants. It was a rookie mistake to not have it close, especially around an unpredictable, severely pissed talent.

"Look, I get it," Lena said hastily, spreading her hands reassuringly. "And despite what you think, it's really hard to impress me. I hate people being put on pedestals too. It's a weirdness of our species, isn't it? All I meant was that I like the efficient way you handle yourself. You don't take shit from anyone. That's refreshing given all the bloated egos out there."

Shattergirl frowned. "You know nothing about me. You don't know any of us. We all wear masks."

Lena considered that. "I get that you're private. Who wants the world nosing into your business? I'm the same. I respect that."

"Yet you write about people's private lives."

"It's not like that at all. People only share what they want to. Look, here's the thing, I tell stories. Stories that inspire. Whether you admit it or not, you inspire a lot of people."

Shattergirl gave a cynical snort, but Lena pressed on. "So I'll bottom-line it for you—all the founders are being represented in this anniversary collection. Everyone except you, which is a shame because yours is the only story that really matters."

"Does that line actually work on people?" She gave her a dark look.

"It's not a line," Lena said. "See, the official view is that you should be represented because they can't have the stories of forty-nine founders but not the fiftieth. Unofficially? It's bad when the sole missing guardian is also the only black, lesbian superhero our planet has ever seen."

A sneer curled Shattergirl's mouth. "I wondered when we'd get to that. You think I give a *tagshart* about round numbers? Or ticking some diversity box? Me not being there is Tal's problem, not mine. Now take your pretty words and charming smirk, and go back to whichever festering city you call home."

The wind picked up and Lena adjusted her headscarf, relieved to have its warmth. "Nope."

"What?"

"I said no."

"Do you understand what I could do to you? I could toss you over that ledge by twitching my little finger."

"Yeah, you could. So go ahead."

Shattergirl looked at her uncertainly. "You're suicidal?"

"No. I'm pointing out the obvious—you're not a killer."

Shattergirl gave an aggrieved huff. "I could just fly you to the middle of nowhere and drop you there."

"And what if I got lost? You want my death on your conscience as I wander all over the place trying to find civilization?"

"Fine! Fly you to the outskirts of Hadibo then."

"Hey, I get it. You don't want to talk to me, and I can't make you. But there's just one question I want to ask you first. Just hear me out, and then I'll leave you in peace if you want me to."

"Ask," Shattergirl ground out.

"I saw the unedited footage from demonstration day at Regent's Park. Everyone's abilities put on display for the media."

"I remember it." Her jaw tightened noticeably.

"You were the only person who wasn't shown on the news reels later. Why do you think that was?"

"How should I know? I didn't edit the broadcasts."

"I have a theory. Women back then didn't have equal rights and were treated like pariahs for even challenging the status quo. Then you rock up. Powerful, confident, strong, black. You scared the living crap out of them. Just being *you* was a threat to the establishment. They didn't like the visuals, so you were dumped on the editing floor. Nothing to see here."

Shattergirl's eyebrow slid up. "Was there a question in there?"

"Sure. Here it is—how did it feel being erased from history?"

A sour glare hit Lena.

"That's what I thought. So are you ready to feel that way again? Deleted from the anniversary celebrations and guardian anthology like you don't exist and never did?"

There was a long pause before Shattergirl replied. "It hardly matters this time. I won't be near that spectacle, so what they do to me now is irrelevant."

"That's true," Lena nodded. "So that's the plan? You hide out here at the edge of the world, while everyone watches the big event without you? Oh and 'everyone' includes all the little girls of color desperate to see their hero, all the lesbians, all the women who look up to you, who respected

42

how you held your head high when the media challenged and belittled you for being different. *They're* who need you to be acknowledged, not you. Come on, *you* already know you're good."

Shattergirl said nothing, but Lena could tell she was listening.

"They're the ones who will feel your absence like a slap," Lena continued, thumping the ground. "Because it will be like they don't matter, that who they are isn't even worth a damn footnote in history if you're rendered invisible."

"I didn't ask to be anyone's role model," Shattergirl said in irritation. "Never that." Her fingers curled into fists, and the muscles along her arms tightened. Lena was instantly reminded of the power she wielded. It virtually crackled along her lean form. Shattergirl was simultaneously the most frightening and most aesthetically arresting person she had ever seen. Lena's mouth went dry.

"Yet you *are* a role model," she said. "Look, we both know life will go on if you're not there. The problem is that for the people who struggle to feel good about themselves in a world that sidelines them as 'less than,' your erasure will be *crushing*." She let her words sink in and then added, "That's not spin, that's fact. And here's another fact—all you have to do to stop that is say yes. Right now. 'Yes. I will talk to you, Lena. I will make sure my voice is counted among the fifty.'"

Shattergirl looked at her in distaste. "You manipulate like one of them, do you know that?"

Lena said nothing. It was true. She was "uniquely talented at shaping the conversations and mindsets of people she has just met," as her impressed boss wrote in her first performance evaluation. Most people, though, weren't astute enough to notice when she did it.

"I'm not going back," Shattergirl said coldly. "Make sure to let Tal know that when you two next chat. I will *never* return." She shot an accusing look at Lena.

"I've never actually met him, you know," Lena said truthfully. "And you don't have to do anything you don't want," she added lazily, although she was greatly unsettled by Shattergirl's accuracy. "You have all the power here. But just think about it. Be included—even if it's just this one last time. Use this opportunity as a goodbye to all the commons who care about you if you like."

Shattergirl's glare was even darker this time. Lena wondered if she'd laid it on a bit too thick.

"You're shameless," Shattergirl muttered. But, crucially, she didn't say no.

Lena waited for her to formulate a begrudging agreement—and she would, because Lena had read her mark perfectly. As always. Inherently good people never refused to help.

She always found this aspect of her job disturbing. The fact anyone could be turned so easily, with just a handful of well-chosen words? It was convenient for her, of course, but troubling. This awareness made her hyper-vigilant—always watching and weighing up the words of others for the lie, the con. After all, who knew when someone might turn their psychological games on her?

But without a capacity to trust, Lena also knew the depressing truth—she'd always be alone. It was the price she paid for what she did. Some days she even convinced herself it was for the greater good. Either way, tinkering around the edges of a person's soul was a bleak way to earn a living. Not that she let that stop her.

Lena made a show of putting away her water bottle and adjusting the contents of her backpack, head bent, to give Shattergirl the necessary privacy to come up with her surrender. Lena's deliberately submissive pose was also telling the woman subliminally that Shattergirl had the power in this scenario.

She pulled out her notebook and pen, placing them in front of her, but still didn't look up. Only when there was a sharp, annoyed exhalation indicating a decision had been reached, did Lena raise her eyes questioningly.

Shattergirl glowered at her and waved her hand. "Proud of yourself?" she growled.

Lena shrugged.

"You already knew my answer, didn't you? Profiled me, I suppose? Who are you? What's your background? Psychology?"

Lena opened her mouth to deny everything.

"Don't bother," Shattergirl said. "I don't want to hear any more of your slimy *tagshart*."

"Okay." No point denying it now anyway.

"My relationships are non-negotiable. Don't even waste your breath. But you can ask about the rest. I *may* answer. So...ask."

Lena made sure to hide any gleam in her eyes by studying her notepad. "So—what's your name?" she asked, her pen poised.

"You come all this way and don't know my name?"

"Come on, I refuse to believe you were born with that name." Lena lifted her head. "Shattergirl had to be some bullshit Earth invention. Especially the 'girl' bit. I mean, hell, it's not Talon *Boy*, is it?"

"No. And I haven't been a 'girl' since I was fifty," Shattergirl said.

Wait, was that an actual joke? Lena peered at her uncertainly. She didn't want to guess wrong, so she plowed on. "So...what *is* your name? Your actual name?"

"It's unpronounceable to commons. But my colleagues often shorten it to Nyah."

"Nyah? What does that mean?"

"Daughter of knowledge."

"Your parents valued knowledge then?"

"My homeland is...*was*...a planet focused on the search for knowledge. My parents were scientists. We lived on a continent which was entirely dedicated to various fields of research, so every child got some variation on a science name."

"Any siblings?"

"No."

"Children?"

"No."

"What did you do there?"

"I was trained as a botanist."

"You're kidding. Plants and flowers and stuff?" She stared at her in surprise. "Seriously?"

"Why is that so shocking?"

"I don't know. It's just you're so...so..."

Nyah's eyebrow lifted. "So...what?"

"Kickass."

Dissatisfaction soured Nyah's expression. "Back to that are we? You're surprised I can walk *and* chew gum. That I'm more than just good for slapping rocks together?"

Lena paused. "I never said that. It's just...*flowers*. And *you*. You know?"

"What's wrong with flowers? I was part of a team that grew a certain flower that, when cross-pollinated, could treble crop yields and, in turn, eliminate hunger. On a different continent they grew a hardy grass that, when heated, produced an oil that could fuel our vehicles using only a few drops. Botany vastly improved the lives of my people. You look at flowers and see only pretty blooms. I see potential. Knowledge. And yet you mock it because all your limited imagination can picture me doing is hurling big rocks around."

Lena felt chastened. "Uh, do you miss it? Botany?"

Nyah eyed her coolly. "Very much."

"Oh. Well, why didn't you pursue it here? They'd love you. You're like a living encyclopedia."

"It's not that simple. Scientists love to dismiss theories that don't align with their own, and take apart things they don't understand."

"You think they'd do that to you?"

"I know it. I tried at various times over the past century to offer my services. Initially I was seen as a joke—what could a *woman* possibly understand, especially a strange, dark, alien one? Then I became an object of curiosity to be prodded and poked—my input was entirely irrelevant. Later, when my expertise was seen as valuable, I became a prize to be fought over between several rival universities. But even then, when I had their respect, my dedication to science was dismissed as a hobby while my real job waited."

"Saving people."

"Yes. And it's hard to argue that my being out in the field taking plant samples is of greater merit than saving lives. It's a pity. I miss the collegial atmosphere. The debates we had were always stimulating."

"And superheroing isn't?"

"What do you think?"

"I think you miss being valued for your brain."

Nyah sighed heavily. "I miss *using* my brain." With a frustrated slap to the ground she added, "I was raised to think!"

"Here, we treat you as only worth the sum of your brawn? Or a hobby scientist?"

"Accurate." Nyah looked at her closely. "So, my turn. Who are you really?"

Lena shrugged. "Not sure what you mean. I'm Lena. Lena Martin."

"Lena Martin," Nyah repeated carefully. "Did you study writing formally? At college?"

"No."

"Were you a journalist before you became a biographer?"

"No. I just fell into this job."

"Yet Talon Man tapped you for this important assignment. You, out of everyone on your backward little world?"

"Backward?" Lena's eyes narrowed in distaste. "Are we really so primitive compared to you?"

"Before we landed, you didn't have timeslides, Dazrs, or FacTrak technology for a start. Culturally you were an abyss too. You didn't offer full rights to most minority groups. Even now, some commons yearn for a return to the pre-guardian days when they could demean anyone different to them. Your society is disturbing and, yes, primitive. I'm better off far from it."

"So we're a bunch of primitive apes? Banging sticks together? Is that really how you see us?"

Nyah began to answer and then stopped, suspicion lighting her eyes. "Well, well, aren't you the clever one—changing the subject. Avoiding answering how you got this job."

Lena tried not to show her surprise at being caught out. "It just isn't a very interesting story. I got lucky," she hedged. "Talon Man read my biography about a friend of mine—a teenage yo-yo champion from my home town who turned his success into a million-dollar business. Talon Man said he loved how I took someone average and showed that they were extraordinary in their own way."

"Yo-yos?" Nyah repeated, looking bemused.

"Yes. Evan Young. Have you heard of him?" Lena leaned forward, projecting curiosity and interest.

Nyah stared at her hard. "You know, you remind me of a woman I once knew."

"Was she witty, charming, and hella good looking?" Lena smirked.

47

"She sold pirated vids and knockoff timeslides on street corners," Nyah said, ignoring Lena's joke. "Pethre had a new story for every customer as to why she needed the money. To some she was a sad loner, to others a single mother with four children to feed. She sized up the customers and became whomever they would respond most to."

"You think I'm some sort of a shark?"

"I know you are. I will work out your angle soon enough. Of course, it would save us both the time if you just told me now who you really are."

"How cynical," Lena said. "Do you get that a lot?"

"About as often as you do, I'd bet. Tell me, Lena Martin, when you're not scribbling up a storm, what do you do?"

"Nothing."

"No hobbies? *Nothing?*"

"I'm boring like that."

Nyah cocked her head. "That's twice you've claimed to be boring. Shall we review? You walked into the face of flying boulders without fear. You scaled a sheer cliff in twenty minutes." She pointed down, and Lena had to admit it did look ridiculously steep from where they sat.

Nyah shook her head. "The average common male with good upper-body strength would have taken an hour. Longer, if he had a desk job. You took twenty minutes. Are you *certain* you have no hobbies?"

"The climbing wall at my local gym isn't a hobby. It's a necessary evil to stay in shape," Lena said. "Come on, you think it's suspicious that a writer works out? How paranoid is that? Can you never take anyone at face value? That's a depressing world view."

"Now you're trying reverse psychology? I have to somehow prove my world view is not depressing by believing you? Is that your argument?"

Lena halted, shocked to have been so accurately called out on her manipulations.

"If you're anything like Pethre, you're trying to present yourself as something I want to hear, a reflection of what I value," Nyah continued. "So why do you think I appreciate someone with no hobbies or interests? Or do you feel that I have no life and might respond better if you present yourself as just as woeful? Mirroring, I believe it's called."

Lena's palms became slick with sweat, and she wished she could wipe them down surreptitiously. "I think you appreciate someone who tells the truth," Lena argued. "Which is what I'm giving you. I'm boring. It's sad but true."

Nyah shook her head. "Don't lie to your elders."

Lena twiddled her pen. "Elders? How old are you, anyway?"

"By Earth's calendar? One hundred forty-one years."

"That's ridiculous," Lena deadpanned. "You don't look a day over a hundred and forty."

There was a long pause before Nyah suddenly laughed. She offered a flash of white teeth and a crinkling around her eyes. It transformed her face from severe to stunning.

Lena watched in complete astonishment. She had never seen her look like this. In perusing a century's worth of videos and news photos, *this* smile was entirely undocumented. Lena offered a weak, awkward, half laugh to cover up her shock.

She made a show of flipping the page on her notebook. Staring intensely at the paper, Lena forced that disarming smile from her mind. "I have another question."

Nyah's amusement in her voice faded. "What?"

"Were you all special on your home planet?"

"Special? We aren't special even now. Despite our fearless leader's best efforts to portray us as demi-gods, most of our group bleed when people shoot at us, and we all can die too."

"I don't mean that," Lena said. "I mean were you all super-skilled on your home planet? Able to toss rocks around and fly and all that sort of thing."

"Yes, we could perform these feats on Aril. Were those abilities unusual? No. Everyone had something different they were born with. It's only here that our abilities are seen as amazing. Back home they were seen as useful and incorporated into whatever career we choose. Here they *are* the career." The irritation was back and her frustration seemed to claw at her from a deep place.

"So there you were on Aril," Lena replied, "just one scientist among millions, and then you came here, and for the first time you get worshipped as a demi-god. How did that make you feel?"

"What makes you think here was my first time being worshipped?" Nyah said lightly. Her eyes gleamed.

Lena grinned at her expression. "Oh?" she asked, intrigued. "Were you famous? Did you cure cancer or something?"

"No cures." Nyah rubbed her chin idly. "I was a botanist, like I said. I am just pointing out how much your people assume things. How much you take for granted about the founders, for instance, without question."

Lena paused at the odd statement. Like she was hinting at something. "The founders," she repeated slowly. As far as Lena knew, no one assumed much of anything about the founders beyond what they'd shared with Earth's inhabitants. Which wasn't a huge amount. Talon Man was the most gregarious of the bunch, and it was universally agreed he was a born leader who…

Lena stopped. "Um…what did Talon Man do on your home world?"

Nyah's smile was approving. "What do you think he did?"

"Politician maybe? Diplomat?"

Nyah looked at her in dissatisfaction. "Not even close. Tal was what we call a speed agent, one of the best who ever existed. A speed agent is the equivalent of a used-car salesman here. He slings so much *kineerl* it's amazing he doesn't slide in his own oily puddles when he walks."

Lena stared in shock. "Wait…are you saying you came to a new planet and chose a lousy *car salesman* as your leader?"

"Who else to win over the suspicious populace than one skilled in the art of wooing? As I said, he was one of the best we ever had. He's proved his value in that sense."

"But that's crazy. That's not a leader…that's just style over substance. Why not you? You're smarter than him, right?"

Nyah's nostrils flared and Lena knew she'd scored a direct hit.

"It wasn't that simple. Tal had the right look."

"The right look?" Lena pictured the orange-clad guardian leader with his fake smiles and ready charm. His resonating voice made females weak at the knees, and his enormous online fan base had no equal.

"Must I spell it out?" Nyah asked in dissatisfaction. "His personal attributes matched the characteristics of the caste in ascendancy on your world when we landed."

Lena exhaled. "Caste in ascend…" She blinked. "You mean he's a straight, white male."

"Yes."

"And you aren't any of those things."

Nyah met her gaze wordlessly.

"And so you all had to sit back and take orders from a used-car salesman? Just because he's the pretty poster boy? Sucks."

"It was an adjustment. Especially given the fact the scientists on my world were used to a certain stature."

"In what way?"

"Our political leaders were all chosen from the thinkers—academics, philosophers, teachers, and scientists—because the logic and teamwork traits prominent among these groups were seen as necessary when making decisions for our people."

"So Talon Man, as a speed agent—"

"Would never have come close to a leadership position. His massive ego alone would have rendered him unsuitable."

"No wonder he looks so happy all the time. He's like a pig in mud."

"This has far exceeded his life's ambitions by a hundredfold," Nyah murmured.

"And, meanwhile, you're…" Lena wondered how to say "sidelined" in a polite way. "Um…"

"I'm well aware of how our fortunes have been reversed."

"The world's changed now, though. Would you ever challenge his leadership?"

"What and miss all this?" Nyah asked, waving at the vastness in front of her. "Do you know that your 'most alien place on Earth' is actually the closest thing to what my home looks like?"

Lena took in the purple mountains and eerie silhouetted dragon blood trees with new interest. "Is that why you came here?"

"Well, I can't very well go home, can I? At least here I am free."

There was the bite of bitter bile again. Lena felt her usual dismay creep over her that came with her disappointment in guardians. Overdues always had such massive chips on their shoulders. Only *they* had suffered. Sure, they'd lost their whole world, and that was awful, but it had been a *hundred* years now. How long were they going to haul that trauma around instead of moving on? Humans didn't have the luxury of wallowing for a whole century. They just got on with it, buried their hurts, and faced life because that's all they could do.

Lena sighed. She now realized she had a far harder task ahead than she'd imagined. Nyah clearly wasn't someone easily enticed back to a civilization that she saw as uncivilized by a reminder of the glory days that had never been glorious for her.

"You weren't free before?" Lena asked carefully.

"If you have to ask, then you have no concept of our lives. But I do miss home." Nyah's gaze softened as it took in the landscape.

"Your world must be beautiful then if it looks anything like this."

"It was." Her expression lit up. "We had the Three Moon Seas. That's a spot on the planet where the reflections of our moons would glimmer on the water and give the most stunning effects. We had the rainforest waterfalls. Plants would weep over these waterfalls, their leaves touching the streams, forming a lush green waterslide. There's one like it, not far from here."

"I saw it on my way here. It was pretty."

"It wasn't pretty on our world. It was *magnificent*. The craters of Casterna were stunning too. I could go on, but what's the point? They're all gone. Our planet is dead. Riddled with meteorites, torn apart. Even though we knew they were coming and prepared well, still, seeing it happen…" Sadness washed her face.

Lena tried to imagine how hard that must have been. She couldn't. "Why are there only fifty of you? Where are the rest?"

"Our best minds selected an uninhabited, distant planet that would meet our world's needs. My ship, which was the last to leave, developed a problem and we knew we wouldn't be able to reach the destination. We plotted a new course. Earth was the closest planet which we could reach that had a compatible atmosphere. Unfortunately…"

"It was already inhabited. Yeah. Talon Man told that part of the story a few times."

"Although he left out the bit about what a charming population we found when we landed. Not paranoid or prone to screaming about alien invasions at all."

Lena's jaw worked. "Surely it was better than nothing? And what did you expect from a pre-space flight planet? We didn't know any better. It would have been terrifying. Not to mention you challenged every religious doctrine on Earth by your mere existence."

"True," Nyah said. "It took a lot of adjustments to deal with your people's baser impulses being so close to the surface. We were a peaceful, science-based people. And you were embroiled in a seemingly endless series of wars. Your love of killing yourselves in inventive ways is only bettered by your greedy and mean-spirited natures. The people of Earth make quite an impression."

"*Nice*," Lena said icily, feeling a surge of defensiveness. "You *do* get that you'd all be dead if not for us?"

"Us? You personally saved us then?"

"My ancestors did."

"I actually *knew* your ancestors, Lena. They were uncultured, unhealthy, ignorant, hysteria-prone, racist, misogynistic, homophobic, violent, and borderline xenophobes. It's been such a pleasure sacrificing my happiness for those knuckle-draggers for the past century."

Lena had had enough. Earth wasn't perfect by any means, but neither were the smug guardians with all their endless moaning. They'd come here uninvited, and Earth's people, for all their flaws and initial fears, had been more than welcoming. That was a straight-up fact.

"Your happiness?" Lena asked with deceptive softness. "Let me guess: the woman you were kissing? I notice she's never been seen anywhere near you since you were outed. Did you end things because she was another lowly, uncivilized common? Or did she dump your ass because of your superior attitude?"

Nyah stood abruptly, her eyes slits of anger. "I was wrong. You're not a shark, you're a viper. Leave. NOW."

Lena clanged her mouth shut, furious at her own lapse. She'd stuck the knife in out of pure, petty annoyance, gouging at Nyah's infamous weak spot. Since when did she forget her mission? She stared at the annoying guardian, disconcerted at how a few irritated sentences—hardly the worst she'd ever had slung at her by a talent—had so easily undone her. Lena had to get her head in the game. Nyah looked about two seconds away from hurling her off the cliff. For real this time.

"Well?" Nyah snapped. "I'd go now before you make me question whether I'm truly not a killer."

Lena held up a hand. "For what it's worth," she tried, "I didn't mean to upset you. It's just…that's my world you're trashing. I know we're fucked up at times, but it struck a nerve, okay?"

Nyah gave her a mocking look. "Tell me that you even like the humans you blindly defended just now," she said. "The ones who regarded women, non-whites, and migrants as inferior."

Lena stopped. "Not especially," she admitted.

"And yet you would lash out at me for saying the same."

That's different, she wanted to say. It just was. Only family got to bitch about family.

Nyah raked her with a vicious, pitying look.

Lena wanted to squirm under the scrutiny, but she wouldn't give Nyah the satisfaction. She wouldn't leave either. Hell no, she could sit up here for hours if she had to. At least until Nyah understood that she wasn't giving up easily and the guardian would have to eventually deal with...

The guardian tilted her head back and abruptly shot off into the sky. Lena stared after her in astonishment.

Oh.

Or she could do that.

Nyah's body was almost immediately a blurred, elongated streak, a sign she was traveling exceptionally fast. Sure enough, a sonic boom followed, vibrating Lena's ear drums, causing unsettling rumbling and skittering noises in every direction as pebbles bounced towards earth from the surrounding mountains. Only then did Nyah disappear from sight.

Well.

Lena peered at where she'd been. If that wasn't the ultimate screw-you.

CHAPTER 5

LENA WOKE THE NEXT DAY under a tree that made zero sense and rubbed her eyes. It was like a waxy water balloon had mated with a crocheted tea cozy.

This felt like home for Nyah?

The memories of yesterday's screw-up returned, followed by Lena's crawl of shame back down the cliff to make camp for the night.

Oh yeah, she'd handled Nyah like a pro. The most reclusive guardian in history had finally begun talking, and Lena had jumped up and down on all her soft spots like a petulant teenager. For what? Planetary pride?

Nyah was right—Lena didn't have any love for Earth's commons from a century ago. Hell, she barely liked her contemporaries.

Lena sat up morosely and unzipped her sleeping bag. It was one of the micro ones that rolled up to the size of a brick. More alien tech the guardians had bestowed upon Earth. They had at least been forthcoming with their advanced gadgets. For instance, she vaguely recalled from history class that everyone used to have something called "watches" before the guardians showed up. These ancient devices were apparently just time tellers that had none of the interactivity of even a basic timeslide. Why bother?

Lena stuffed her sleeping bag into her backpack and rose, unkinking her muscles that were still sore from yesterday's hike and cliff climb. She strolled over to a nearby stream, stripped, and had a rudimentary wash. Lena glanced at the sky as she toweled dry. It was gray, and the darkening streaks of cloud looked ominous.

She quickly dressed, hunted around for some sticks for kindling, and ambled back over to the stream again. A few fish slithered past as she contemplated her breakfast options. A ration pack full of granola bars and various other Facility-issued supplies were crammed in her backpack, so

Lena could afford to leave the local wildlife in peace for now. Besides, if today went anything like yesterday, she'd probably be dumped at Socotra's airport from a great height before she got her greeting out.

With that sobering thought playing pinball around her head, she tossed her kindling in her backpack and slung it over her shoulders.

It took a little less time to scale Nyah's cliff on this attempt as Lena knew where all the handholds were, having mastered an ascent and a descent by now. By the time she reached the top, she wasn't entirely surprised to see the imposing guardian standing there, watching, her eyes hooded. Her stance was aggressive, but her expression wasn't radiating fury as it had been yesterday.

Lena rolled over the edge, splaying out in a heap at Nyah's feet as she caught her breath. When she focused again, she was caught in a glare.

"I'd thought you'd gone for good." Nyah's voice was dripping with acid.

"You hoped, you mean?"

"Yes. What else is left to discuss?"

"So much."

"Doubtful." Nyah turned and headed back inside her cave.

Pensively, Lena watched her leave. No invitation had been extended for her to enter what was essentially Nyah's home, so she drew herself up into a cross-legged position and evaluated her options. The wind whipped around the ledge so she tightened her scarf as she decided.

Time for the big guns.

She cracked open her backpack, took out the kindling, and set about making a small fire. It wasn't protected up here, so she was forced to use her body to block the worst of the wind. Lena took out a plastic container, her water bottle, and a tiny tin pot. She placed the pot gingerly on a tepee of sticks, then filled it with water. The fire might have been on the pathetic side, but it did heat Lena's pot. As she warmed her hands over the flames, the water gradually came to the boil.

"Are you trying to smoke me out?"

She turned to find Nyah watching her from the mouth of the cave.

"Because you'll need a considerably bigger fire for that."

Lena smirked. Undeterred, she rattled the container which held ground beans. "Want a coffee?"

Without waiting for an answer, she cracked the lid, pulled out a mug, and measured a spoonful into it. She made the drink and stirred vigorously, hearing Nyah's footsteps near.

This was the guardians' drink of choice. It was one of the few things that could make any of them weak at the knees. Lena knew most of them used to grow these beans in their homes the way humans might pots of herbs. The handful of beans the founders had brought with them to Earth had been carefully cultivated and turned into a well-kept crop on the fourth floor of the Facility. Only Talon Man and a few of his chosen ones were even aware it existed. Plus Lena. The Facility's gardener kept her well stocked in exchange for a small, regular bump in his account balance. It had been her secret weapon with taciturn overdues for years.

Sure enough, Nyah's nose twitched and her face shifted to surprise and recognition. "Where did you get *klava*?" she whispered reverently. She sank to her knees and leaned closer to it.

The wash of scents was heady. Lena hadn't found a direct Earth comparison, but it smelled to her strongly of a sort-of coffee with undertones of cinnamon and chili. For guardians, the rush was a euphoric high because it mixed the beans' alluring, addictive flavors with something they believed was long gone: their world, Aril.

"I have my ways," Lena said casually, holding out the mug to her. "I thought you might like a taste of home. You probably need this more than me."

Lena had developed her own fondness for the potent stuff, but she wasn't wasting the precious brew. Nor was she screwing up again with this target.

Nyah reached for the steaming mug, hand trembling, and paused for a moment as though not quite believing what was in front of her. Her fingers curled around the white enamel and she lifted the mug to her lips. Instead of drinking, though, she inhaled deeply and uttered a low hiss. Her eyes fluttered closed and, finally, she sipped. Slowly.

A swallow came, and then a soft, pleased moan that was completely unexpected.

"Um...rain's coming," Lena said abruptly, tearing her gaze away from the intensely private moment. Her cheeks burned at that low, evocative sound, and she peered up at the skies. "Clouds are pretty ominous, right? Might throw it down soon. Get real wet out here, huh? Way up here?"

Nyah didn't answer, so Lena settled for picking at the seam of her leather cuff like it was the most interesting thing she'd ever seen. Out of the corner of her eye she saw Nyah eagerly swallow the rest of the brew and return the mug to the ground in front of Lena. She did it reverently and slowly, like a reluctant temple offering.

Her gaze flashed back up to meet Lena's. "All right," Nyah said, voice low and hoarse. She looked appreciatively at Lena, then gestured at the mug. "That earns you more discussion. But this time if you mention...*that topic*...again, I *will* toss you over the edge. Do you hear me?"

"Sure. No problem," Lena said contritely. She reached for her backpack to get her notepad and pen out, and felt Nyah's gaze still on her, studying her face.

"Are you of this faith?" she asked suddenly, pointing to the headscarf.

"No," Lena said, pulling out her writing gear after a wriggle, and placing it in front of her. "Me and religion don't see eye to eye. But 'when in Socotra...' and all that. It's also good for keeping off the wind. Pretty chilly this high up."

Nyah leaned forward and touched the scarf, pausing as though waiting for an objection. Finding none, she slid it off Lena's short hair and studied her face more closely. Her scrutiny shifted back down to Lena's cuff and toughened boots, well-worn from spending months at a time in the field on assignment.

"Not exactly Earth standard are you?" she drawled.

"Normal is overrated," Lena shot back.

"Yes," Nyah said, replacing the scarf carefully and sitting back on her haunches. "On that we can agree."

Their gazes locked and Lena felt a flare of mutual understanding. Nyah rose and walked to the ledge facing the wadi below. She lowered herself down, dropping her legs over the edge, then turned back to look expectantly at Lena—a silent invitation—before resuming her observation of the landscape.

"It's peaceful here," Nyah said evenly.

Lena joined her, dropping her notebook to the ground beside herself, and mirrored Nyah's pose, leaning against one arm, resting her other hand on her thigh. It was something she'd figured out early on as a tracker—copying body language fosters an artificial sense of kinship. It leads to faster breakthroughs.

Lena stopped cold. She just did this by rote now, she realized with surprise. Hell, she barely even noticed when she was manipulating people these days. It was second nature. When had she stopped relating to people like everyone else? When had she forgotten how to even have a normal conversation? Did she no longer even care?

Lena deliberately altered her body language and felt a tiny burst of satisfaction.

Apparently she did care.

"Before we begin," Nyah said coolly, studying the horizon, "your turn."

"What?"

"I did all the talking yesterday. So talk."

"I'm not the one being interviewed. I'm boring, remember."

"So you keep saying. I thought about it last night. Somehow you have managed the rare feat of getting me discussing myself. For you to have achieved that, there must be more to you than what you present yourself as. I want to know what that is. So, tell me your story and then we will resume your interview."

"I don't feel comfortable talking about myself." Lena wasn't lying. She'd never felt at ease baring any part of herself. The truth was that she wasn't any good at interpersonal stuff. She might excel at putting others at ease and drawing them out, but she had yet to work out how to turn the mirror around.

"Well now, isn't that a coincidence?"

Lena flicked her gaze to Nyah. "How could I ever be interesting?" she asked. "Especially compared to you?"

"Let's find out. What's your story? Start with this." She waved her hand in front of Lena's check shirt and jeans. "Why this look? I know it's not just practical. You wear it like a uniform."

Lena wondered how to answer that. She mentally flipped through all her usual stories, the ones she rolled out on cue whenever anyone got too chatty. She had so many personas. So many lies. Any would do, really.

"Why *not* this look?" Lena finally replied, dispensing with them all. "It's unusual."

"Is it?"

Nyah tapped her wrist cuff pointedly. "You know it is."

Lena shifted uncomfortably under her drilling stare. "This is what I wore as a teenager and felt comfortable in. Never felt a need to change."

"I see. And does your family appreciate your display of rugged individuality?" The tone was faintly amused.

Lena narrowed her eyes. "Let's just say my mother never gave up hope I'd find my inner girly girl. How about you?" she asked suddenly. "What did your family think of your look?"

It was a deceptively daring question. Nyah's appearance had been a source of much discussion on Earth—her failure to conform to traditional female stereotypes had been duly noted by all the pearl clutchers, commentators, and radio shock jocks. Nyah had never been drawn into answering any of them.

"It's clothing," she said with impatience. "I find it aerodynamic and functional. What other point is there? Now can we talk about why we're even doing this exercise in futility? Going through the motions of you getting to know me? You don't actually care, do you? You're not even really a writer. So tell me, what are you?"

"If you think I'm a liar," Lena asked, "why are you allowing me to talk to you at all?"

There was silence as Nyah turned back to study the horizon. "I'm not sure."

"Really?" Lena lifted her eyebrows. "I've never heard any guardian say that."

"How many of us have you met? You do get around for a humble writer." Lena fell silent. *Crap.*

"Tell me Lena, what's a Dazr? I mentioned it yesterday. Few commons have ever heard of it as it's a weapon to bring down a rogue guardian. Yet you show no curiosity at all in something new. I find that hard to believe in one so smart."

"Smart?" Lena repeated. She offered a crooked smile. "I think I was allergic to school."

"What has school got to do with a person's worth or intelligence?"

Lena looked at her uncertainly.

Nyah tilted her head. "Regardless of your education, or lack of it, what I see is that clever brain of yours whirring furiously, cooking up lies." Giving Lena a hard look, she pointed at her wristband. "Here's an easier question—will you take this off?"

Lena reflexively covered it with her other hand. "Why?"

"Why not?"

Lena's pulse jumped. What the hell could she say now?

Turning to peer off into the distance, Nyah said flatly, "I'll save you the effort of lying to me again. It hides the mark of Beast Lord. I saw the injury when you first came over the ledge yesterday and your cuff slid up."

"It was a cooking accident," Lena said, wincing internally at how bad that sounded.

"You don't cook," Nyah told her certainly and turned back to eyeball her. "You *camp*. It's second nature to you. You made that fire as expertly as any survival expert. In the same way you scaled a sheer cliff at remarkable speed. You have no desk job, Lena Martin. You don't even own a desk. Do you?"

"So I'm fit and I like camping. So what?" Lena shrugged.

Nyah stared her down. "But the biggest giveaway? Your second question in our interview."

"Second question?" Lena was mystified. What on earth had she asked? What was she supposed to ask? Did writers always ask the same thing? Why hadn't that come up in her research into biographers?

"Question one, 'What's your name?'" Nyah said, sounding bored, as though she was reading a list. "Every writer worth that title knows that question two is always 'And how do you spell that?'"

Lena's heart dropped to her stomach. Shit. That made sense.

"So I ask again," Nyah said, gaze steely, "who are you? Really?"

"A writer," Lena said firmly, and shot Nyah her most convincing look. "And if you'd actually let me get to the end of the interview, I would have asked you for spellings, specifics, the whole bit. Why would all writers do their jobs the same way?"

Nyah studied her so carefully that Lena wondered if she might have actually won a round.

Finally, the guardian answered. "No, you don't write, you manipulate people, and with a great deal of skill. Although I don't think you were lying about disliking school, were you? You have charm enough to cover the cracks, but your speech patterns give you away. Did you even pass English? Or did you learn it all on the street?"

Shock stabbed Lena at the not-entirely-crazy guess. Her notepad was suddenly snatched from her side before she could protest. Nyah flipped through the pages and Lena glowered at her. Lena's palms immediately slicked with sweat, and she felt the pit of her stomach clench.

She knew what her handwriting looked like. Large, childish, letters. Badly spelled words. Shame flashed through her at the thought of being ridiculed by this woman, a scientist no less. Someone she'd looked up to once, a long time ago, before she'd realized the sheer worthlessness of having heroes. Especially heroes like guardians.

Her hands, resting on her knees, closed into tight fists, as she waited for Nyah to mock her as her school peers had so often done. Instead, the notepad was returned, and gently laid beside her.

Nyah said quietly, "I see."

The sympathy was crushing.

"You see nothing," Lena ground out.

Nyah's smile contained a knowingness that made Lena's fists clench even tighter with anger.

"I'm not stupid," she said hotly. "You think you have me all worked out."

"I never said you were. And, if you remember, this discussion came about because I just wanted to know who you are…and we both know who you definitely *are not*."

This time the mockery was back in spades.

"Drop it," Lena said darkly. "I mean it."

"Why? Afraid I'll stumble on the truth? Dig up the real woman under all the lies? Or maybe it's not you, so much as how you grew up. Tell me, Lena Martin, I want to know all about your mother…"

"SHUT UP!" Lena scrambled to her feet and was dismayed to hear her words echoing around the wadi below. "My life is not yours to pick over."

"And yet mine should be?"

Lena walked back to grab her backpack, and rammed in her notebook. She needed to not be here right now, and losing it in front of the talent was unacceptable. Not again. Not after last night. Nyah was pushing every button she had, and doing it with ease. She was making Lena look like a fool and unraveling her, picking her apart, seemingly at will.

Lena paused. Wait, was *that* what this was? Payback? She tightened the straps on her bag with vicious jerks as she turned the idea around in her head.

"Leaving so soon?" Nyah asked, the condescension coating her tongue. "But we've barely scratched the surface. 'So much to discuss,' I believe you said."

Yep, Lena got it. She was being carved up by a fucking master. She'd be almost impressed at the tables being turned if she wasn't so damned rattled.

"Another day," Lena said, voice straining, her hands ghosting down the taut canvas of her pack that she'd tightened until it choked. Losing her temper was *not* part of her mission. She had to get back in control, and she couldn't do that right now under those sharp eyes.

"But we barely got to know each other." Nyah's drawl became even more pronounced as her amusement leaked out. "What about discussing the latest fashions? Music? Or the girls we like?"

Great. The woman's perceptiveness clearly had no weak spots. "Another fucking day," Lena hissed through her teeth. She slid the pack on her back.

"Such eloquence. Did you pick that up at writing school?"

"I can see why your girlfriend dumped your smug ass." The insult slipped out before Lena could stop it.

However Nyah's expression didn't change. "And I can see that you have no one at all in your life. Unlike me, it's not by choice, is it? You never let down your guard, do you? You probably manipulate everyone 24/7 until no one wants to be anywhere near you. Can you even recall *how* to speak the truth? Do you even remember *what's* true anymore?"

Lena looked directly at Nyah, feeling her rage stab at her anew. "It's so easy for you, isn't it? Shit-hot, scary smart," Lena said with a snarl, wishing she could hide how much Nyah's words had sliced into her. "But if you think you're better than me because you're a scientist from some fancy, evolved world, and I barely got through school, then that just makes you an asshole. Actually you're worse than that. You're just a bitter, failed guardian in hiding who lost her edge and can't deal with life. At least I *try* to engage with the world. What's your excuse? 'Sorry, can't be bothered. You can all go screw yourselves?'"

"I *did* help for almost a century, or did that slip your mind?" Nyah said archly.

"Under sufferance though, wasn't it? You *lowered* yourself to do the right thing, didn't you? And now you're over us. What happened? You get bored? Were we too embarrassingly adoring for your lofty fucking standards? The worst part is that you *are* as good as you think you are. None of the other guardians have your level of powers. So you know you can make a huge difference, and yet you refuse. That's not even cold. It's just pathetic."

Nyah's jaw clenched. "Life advice from a trained manipulator? I'm honored."

"Insults from a coward?" Lena shot back. "Hey, maybe you're right, Earth doesn't need to know what Shattergirl thinks about anything. Because Shattergirl isn't *worth* the hero title."

"Ah, yes," Nyah said silkily, "I was waiting for that, the 'you're not worthy' speech. Do you *really* think I care what a scheming tracker thinks of me?"

Lena froze.

"You truly thought I didn't know? Someone who manipulates like a speed agent and can virtually run up cliffs like you do can only be one of Talon Man's elite trackers. You're exactly who he loves to hire because you're just like him. You fling pretty words around that twist people and tie them up in knots until they do whatever you want. You have no shame."

"You're just jealous because he's the leader of your people when you think you should be." It was a wild guess, but Lena felt a stab of satisfaction when she saw a small twitch in Nyah's face.

The guardian's lips pulled down into a snarl. "How little you understand."

Lena shook her head sharply. "I understand that guardians have every advantage, and all they do is bitch and moan about how hard it all is. Get over yourselves. God! You're such a freaking disappointment."

Lena bit her lip, appalled that had just slipped out. Any hope Nyah wouldn't see the comment for the weakness it betrayed was dashed when the woman cocked a mocking eyebrow.

"I *disappoint you*? Oh, let me guess, you loved me once, didn't you?" she suggested, leaning closer. "Had my poster on your wall? And when I was outed, were all your fevered teenage fantasies realized? Your heart burst with pretty pink pride?"

Lena gave a careless snort, but was dumbfounded at how scarily close to the mark she was. Her heart thudded painfully at the memories of years she'd rather bury in a deep hole.

"Then what? I didn't say exactly the right thing? I wasn't the proud role model you so badly wanted? I *failed* you?" Nyah mocked. "I'm so terribly sorry, Lena Martin, that I wasn't living my life *for you*. You know what's most ridiculous? On my world none of us was viewed as special. Here, the adulation is bad enough, but there's also an expectation to represent this label or that group. Why? Just because we have a few unique skills? Does that even make sense?"

Lena eyed her morosely.

"What's wrong, my manipulative tracker? Your favorite hero let you down?" Nyah taunted.

"God, you're so full of shit," Lena ground out. "You say it's the hero-worship stuff you hate, but the truth is you just don't like being held accountable to anyone but yourself. You hate your responsibilities and obligations to our world—which fits because you hate us so much."

Nyah laughed coldly. "Ah, yes, well done. *That* must be it. You've figured me out." She clapped slowly. "Now give Tal and his cronies my best, and pass along my regrets for his ego-stroking ceremony. Goodbye."

The finality of Nyah's tone brooked no further discussion. Lena felt the wall between them now as though it stretched a thousand feet high. She had just been comprehensively shut down. And even if the guardian was interested in sparring some more, to what end? They'd just go at it until their throats were dry, neither giving an inch.

Lena had to admit that, for the first time in her life, she'd met her match. Well, been thrashed might be a better word for it. Worse, their encounter had gone so badly that she had learned nothing at all new from Nyah that she could use, and had gained no leverage with which to manipulate her. Instead, she had been eerily, accurately profiled, forced into an angry outburst, and, when Nyah had been finally done with her, sent packing.

She swallowed. It was hellishly unnerving being this bad at something Lena prided herself at being brilliant at. She couldn't even say the experience had been educational. Lena mechanically shouldered her backpack. It'd been like tap dancing with a nail gun.

Speaking of guns, she supposed she could pull a Dazr on her target. But the guardian's sharp eyes were watching for it, anticipating. Did she ever miss anything? Lena already knew that answer. Besides, even if Lena was faster, she couldn't bring herself to go so low with an adversary so worthy. Her ass had been handed to her on a plate, and she was going home.

Without another word, and studiously avoiding glancing in Nyah's direction so Lena wouldn't see any triumph, she lowered herself over the ledge and did not look back.

CHAPTER 6

THE FIRST FAT DROPLETS HIT when Lena was halfway down the cliff. Then, like a tap bursting, the skies opened up and threw down a torrent. Her face was soon numb from the pounding, icy rain, and her fingers struggled to find purchase on the rocks. Lena squinted up, blinking, and could make out darkening, purple skies. Looked like more than just rain, but a nasty storm brewing. Just great. What an absolutely freaking great end to a shitty morning.

Almost as soon as she'd had the thought, the wind picked up and began curling around the face of the cliff, like giant fingers plucking at her. Her solid but small frame repeatedly lifted and slammed against the rock wall. It took everything she had to stay attached.

Her muscles trembled as she reached down with her foot for the next hold. Her boot hit a smooth, slippery patch. Another gust of wind, stronger than the last, tore her legs to the right. She swung her weight in the other direction to compensate.

Lena impacted solidly against the cliff, gritting her teeth against the pain, mercifully finding a new protrusion for her foot. She looked up, just as a rock the size of a toaster bounced and skittered towards her. Lena ducked her head, its tumbling weight missing her by inches as it grazed her backpack and continued its descent. She swore softly. She had to get down, *now*. Anything had to be better than this crapshoot.

It had been almost forty-five minutes, and her muscles were cramping up. She peered down. Still barely past halfway. Her fingers, almost white from the pressure of hanging on, quivered from having to support her weight.

Another searing gust tore across the cliff face, again threatening to rip her from it. She rammed her feet onto their holds, her left boot scrabbling for a moment before settling.

The pain in her arms had gone from an aching throb to a searing objection at being held for such an extended period. With a growing sense of dread, Lena knew she could hold on for only a few minutes more.

At that sobering thought, her mind wandered to dark places. If she tumbled to her death, would Nyah bother collecting and dumping her body somewhere for the authorities to find? Or would she toss her out to sea just so she didn't have to look at it?

The logical part of her brain, the part which knew how all her targets ticked, reluctantly conceded the answer—underneath everything, Nyah was a good and decent person. She'd been a guardian for a century despite hating it. So, she would do the right thing.

That thought gave her little comfort.

The rain became heavier. Lena peered around at the various cliff faces jutting up from the wadi and wondered at the shimmer she was seeing. All along the ridges, water was starting to trickle from the top, creating hundreds of mini waterfalls. It would be pretty if it wasn't so alarming. She glanced down and realized the ground, far below, was moving. Worse, the churning water seemed to be rising rapidly.

She gritted her teeth.

Lena had now lost feeling in her icy fingers. Her arms were spasming, and one boot kept slipping off its hold. In the eerie daylight darkness she could no longer see where to put her other boot.

She shivered uncontrollably as another gust of rain shuddered through, tearing off her headscarf.

"ARGHH!" she shouted into the wind as she watched it disappear, and felt marginally better for it.

She reviewed her options—take a chance and keep trying to inch down to a ravine that was flash flooding. Or...

Lena contemplated her Dazr. It had a grappling hook setting, but she was old school and didn't trust it at the best of times. Maybe it was an irrational fear, but what if the electronic rope powered down and blinked off mid-climb? That thought was frightening enough, but when wind and water were in the mix, it seemed risky as hell. Still, it had to be better than nothing.

If she could reach her Dazr, maybe she could do the one thing that made her stomach curdle—get back up the cliff and beg a guardian's hospitality to ride out the bruising storm in the safety of her cave. The same guardian who, less than an hour ago, she'd just insulted, called a coward, and needled about her girlfriend dumping her ass.

She was *so* screwed.

Lena swung herself until her backpack twisted to one side. It slid halfway down one arm, its bottom now resting on her thigh. Using her teeth and nose, she nudged the buckle open after a few attempts. Wind howled in her ears as she leaned forward, desperately hoping her calisthenics had shifted the Dazr from the very bottom of the bag.

A gleam of polished metal caught her eye, and she almost wept with relief. She took a deep breath, clutching her holds as tightly as she could at three points, and rammed her hand into her bag, pulling the Dazr out. She thumbed the setting to "Hook." Her other arm was screaming in agony at supporting so much of her weight. Then one foot began to slip.

Now or never. She pointed the gun to the top of the cliff and smashed the trigger as hard as she could with her finger. Blue light arced upwards, twirling around itself, forming a solid rope, and then, at its end, it morphed and shimmered into a claw. It sailed over the ledge above, coming to a rest. She gave it a tug, tapped the "Lock" setting on her gun, and waited as the claw scraped and shuddered, retracting back towards the edge, seeking an anchor point to grip. It settled on something out of sight which she hoped like hell was solid. She tested it with a mighty jerk. To her relief and surprise, it held.

Lena shrugged and twisted her shoulders until her pack returned to the center of her back and, after a pause to gather her courage, put both hands on the Dazr, clutching it in a death grip. She thumbed the "Retract" button and sucked in a breath.

There was a bounce, then a split second's pause, and then she was shooting upwards. The alien tech made it seem easy. This felt so simple. She'd been hauling ass manually up cliffs for years when she could have been...

CRACK.

Whatever boulder was holding her hook in place abruptly shifted forward, and fear rocketed through Lena as the rope jangled and jerked suddenly, swaying her wildly.

"HOLD ON!" she screamed at it.

A fresh gust of wind pushed her sideways. Then the boulder pinning the hook came into view as it began to inch forward towards her. The Dazr's blue rope suddenly flickered. A warning flashed on the screen: "Anchor point unstable."

"I know!" she hissed at it in disbelief. "Fuck it, I can see the damn rock moving!"

The shifting rock finally found the cliff edge and, to Lena's horror, began to drop directly towards her. Simultaneously the electrical rope disappeared with a soft warning beep…and that was that.

There was nothing but air.

Lena tumbled backwards, staring up at her boots in disbelief. Her traitorous Dazr fell from her grip, spiraling on its way to the wadi floor.

The sensation of silence was what surprised Lena most, not the fact she was about to die. Her brain seemed to block out everything else around her apart from the stomach-plunging feeling of free fall. A roller coaster with no bottom.

So. This was how it was going to end.

Time slowed and warped. She pictured her funeral. No one to mourn her. Her boss would probably have to turn up—although she didn't know if Bruce Dutton even liked her. For a microsecond she strained to work out whether he did, and decided probably not. Maybe Mrs. Finkel would miss her. A brief image of fatty Bernstein flashed into her mind.

So much for poignant last thoughts.

But there would be no one else. It was true. Just like Nyah said. Lena Martin had no one.

With that depressing thought, her mind emptied, and she willed the end to be painless and instant. That was pretty likely, given the huge boulder she'd dislodged was bearing down on her from above too.

If the fall didn't crush her, it would.

Something streaked past her. Then a waterfall of rocks was falling around her, as though something enormous had exploded above her. The eerie silence was replaced by the ferocious roar as all the elements suddenly crowded in on her. The howl of wind returned as her torso jerked and her arms were gripped painfully.

She was shooting upwards.

Wait, what?

She was shooting upwards!

Adrenalin and shock coursed through her as she tried to make sense of it. *Nyah!*

She'd been about to die. It had been inevitable. Instead, she could feel another pounding heart next to her own and smell a faint *klava* scent from the pursed lips next to Lena's wet cheek.

Every part of her felt weak from relief. Her arms ached from where Nyah's fingers dug harshly into the flesh. Water coursed off Lena's face, and she shut her eyes to keep it out. She could hear thunder, and a brilliant flash of lightning seared her eyes through her lids.

There was a sudden shift midair that startled her into opening her eyes. They were falling. The sound of a shuddering intake of breath against her skin was even more unsettling.

"Air pocket," Nyah said grimly. "Hold on. Correcting."

The falling stopped, and Lena's stomach lurched chaotically as they were now hurtling at breakneck speed back up, and then over the cliff edge. Then she was lowered outside Nyah's cave. Lena's legs did a comical little wobble the moment they touched solid ground.

"What the hell were you doing?" Nyah demanded in irritation as she stepped back immediately. Clearly touching Lena for even that long had been unsavory. "You should have been halfway out of the wadi by now. Instead, I find you flapping about from my cliff like a flag. You didn't even get to the bottom?"

Lena didn't answer as she was busy wriggling her toes in her boots to verify this was even real. How was she even alive? Lena ran trembling fingers through her hair, slicking it back, out of her eyes. Then she smiled as a crazy, giddying elation hit her. "Actually, I'd have gotten to the bottom in, oh, three seconds flat if you hadn't shown up."

Nyah gave a disdainful snort. "True. And you're welcome."

"Thanks," Lena muttered as Nyah's snide tone reminded her of all the acrimony from their fight. She hated feeling in anyone's debt, especially Nyah's, but she didn't want to start round two either. She didn't have the strength for it. Her shaky legs felt ready to drop her. "How long do the storms around here last?"

"The usual storm systems last a few hours. However, the after effects of them can be felt for a day or so."

"Shit." Lena shivered.

Nyah looked out at the weather grimly. "But this isn't a usual storm. Judging by the air pressure shifts and insanely fast wind speeds, we're getting licked by the edge of a cyclone. I experienced similar weather conditions during Iiesar Tashabalaan."

"Say what?"

"It was a cyclone. Come inside," Nyah sighed. "You're soaked, and it's too cold to discuss in the middle of a storm."

Lena followed her into the darkness, her pupils taking a few moments to adapt. Rocky formations of rare beauty concertinaed across the high cave ceiling, creating the effect of a natural cathedral. She gave a low whistle. "Wow."

"I know," came Nyah's disembodied voice from ahead. "Why do you think I chose it?"

Lena stepped past a pair of buckets that were catching water dripping from the overhead stalactites. Nice. Water was sorted for the next few days at least, given how much the buckets had already collected.

"This way," Nyah said, leading her into a central chamber.

A fire was flickering in the middle of the area, and Lena gratefully knelt before it, warming her frozen hands. Her eyes darted around the rest of the cavern. It was neat and ordered. A pile of tinned food on makeshift shelves sat along one rock wall. Stacks and stacks of books and journals were beside those. She squinted. Pretty much all science related. Plant bibles. Botany guides. *Figures.*

A roomy cot, snugly lined with pelts and with a folded blanket on top, sat in one corner. It was a pretty cozy set-up, if cave chic was your thing.

"Iiesar Tashabalaan is what the locals called Cyclone Chapala," Nyah said, rooting around for and then tossing her a rough towel. "Dry your hair first," she ordered, sitting opposite her in front of the fire.

Lena obeyed, feeling instantly better as her head warmed up.

"It hit in 2015 and was the second strongest tropical cyclone in history out here. Winds were 150 miles per hour. It flattened Socotra. The air out there now feels much the same. It's not going to be pretty when the worst of it goes by. I suspect it will be much, much worse in fact."

"How bad was it last time?" Lena began to relax, the fire warming her as relief flooded her body. She dried her hair quickly, then slung the towel around her neck.

"Five hundred homes flattened. Thousands evacuated. And that wadi you were heading for? It became a roaring river. I came to see whether you'd been swept to your death or were about to be, and found you still stuck on the cliff. Your mountain-goat reputation is taking a bit of a battering."

"It was slippery out there," Lena mumbled. "I couldn't climb down at my usual gallop."

"Mm."

"So does this happen often? Just…BAM! A cyclone comes out of nowhere?"

Nyah shrugged. "We're so far off the grid and out of the news loop that large weather events can sneak up without warning." She glanced towards the cave entrance. "The whole island will know how dangerous this one really is in about an hour or so."

Lena frowned. "But you're the only one on Socotra who knows it's going to be really bad, right?"

"So?"

"So—you have to warn them it's coming! People have to be told to seek proper cover." Alarm filled Lena at the thought of the vulnerable locals.

"No."

"No?" Lena stared at her in astonishment.

"I'm retired," Nyah said, her tone mocking. "Remember?"

"But the people! They're at risk—and all you have to do is tell them it's going to be as nasty as before. Come on! Do you really hate us so much?"

"I already explained it won't be 'as nasty,'" Nyah said in a measured tone. "It will be far worse. The winds are already considerably stronger, and it's not even made landfall yet."

"You're just going to do nothing? What are you so afraid of that you'd prefer to cower in here?"

"Are you quite finished?" Nyah's voice was sharp.

"Not yet," Lena said hotly. "Look, if you don't care about anything else, I know you care about science. At least save the scientists who are out in the eco-camps. They'll have no protection at all—they'll be blown away. I know where they are. I can show you," Lena reached for her FacTrack, still buried in her backpack.

"No," Nyah said coldly. "I'm not going anywhere."

Lena stared at her in complete confusion. "Why not? You saved *me*."

"A move I'm rapidly starting to regret. Now stop moving away from the fire. You're still soaked. It'd be a wasted effort if I saved you only for you to die of pneumonia."

"God forbid you broke a sweat for nothing."

"Exactly," Nyah said. "It'd be inconvenient as hell."

Lena didn't speak for some time, lost in her thoughts, trying and failing to understand the contradictory woman. What was her game, anyway? She'd save Lena but no one else? Was she so deeply stuck in her comfort zone that she didn't ever leave it?

"Any more *klava* in there?" Nyah asked, breaking her reverie, gesturing at Lena's bag.

Lena dug into her backpack. She tossed the small container to her. "This stuff is addictive. You know that, right?"

"It won't kill me," Nyah said lightly. "There's much more dangerous *tagshart* out there. Like trackers, for example."

Lena snorted and resumed clawing through her backpack, looking for some dry clothes to change into. "And cyclones stalking defenseless people." She pulled out a pair of thin socks. Well, it was a start. She deftly replaced her socks and saw, out of the corner of her eye, Nyah turn sharply to look at her.

"I saved your life."

"That took less than a minute. And it would have taken you five minutes at most to warn the town and another two to get to the scientists." Lena lay her wet socks on a rock near the fire to dry.

"You think a random person could just sidle up to some scientists and claim that she sensed that the air currents from three thousand feet up matched those of a cyclone, and they had to take secure cover urgently? Assuming they didn't recognize me, they'd look at me like I was delusional. And if they somehow did recognize me out here in the middle of nowhere…" She frowned at the thought. "I will *not* take that chance."

She put some water on to boil and measured out *klava* into her mug.

"So that's what this was?" Lena peered at her. "You don't even try because it might blow your cover? Shit, I could figure out a great story for you. They'd never think you were a guardian."

"Oh yes, because you are so very good at lying, aren't you, Lena?"

"You don't actually care about commons at all, do you?"

"If I didn't, you'd be busy decorating the wadi floor right now."

"Then why not try?"

"You wouldn't understand."

"Yet more cryptic crap? You're so annoying." She glared at the flames.

"At least I don't manipulate others." Nyah stirred the mug vigorously.

"And I don't cause deaths I can easily prevent," Lena said. "I try to help at least."

"I did!" Nyah snapped, slapping down the spoon. "I did. Last time. During Iiesar Tashabalaan. I tried."

Lena shot her a doubtful look but said nothing.

"I'm not invincible," Nyah added with a dark look. "Far from it."

Shaking her head, Lena said, "I know that."

"Do you? Really?"

Waves of frustration came off the other woman. Lena studied Nyah as the guardian sipped her *klava*. Her face was tight and angry. There was deep disappointment there too. And something else. Embarrassment? "What happened?" Lena finally asked. "Last time?"

"Nothing. It was pointless. They didn't need me."

"Trying to save people isn't pointless. Of course they needed you."

Nyah's expression darkened. For a long moment Lena thought the conversation had ended until Nyah's head suddenly lifted. "Last time I knew there were thousands trying to get to safety. You felt us drop suddenly when I was saving you today?"

Lena nodded.

"It was the same then. The air turbulence was volatile. One minute I'm at three thousand feet, the next one thousand. The shifts are unpredictable in a cyclone. I could see where I wanted to fly, but as hard as I tried, I couldn't get there. It was exhausting. It felt like I was being thrown about in a tumble drier, over and over. I might be able to fly, Lena, but I can't defy a cyclone. It was insanity to even try."

"Did the people…" Lena swallowed.

"As I said, it turned out they didn't need me." Nyah gave a hollow laugh. "Seriously, they really didn't. All of them lived. They know their island better than I do. There was only one person who came close to death when lightning struck nearby. And that was the only person foolish enough to risk being in the middle of a cyclone in the first place—me. So, lesson learned. Never again."

"But…"

"No." Nyah stared at her intently. "I am not immortal. Lightning scorches guardian flesh as easily as yours, as I was reminded that day. I am also not bulletproof or gale-proof or anything else. All I can do is fly, Lena. Fly and throw heavy things. That's it."

"Oh."

"It was risky even saving your life just now. The air pressure dropped suddenly twice on the way down, once while I was shattering that boulder you'd displaced and again on the way up. I very nearly dashed us both to death against that cliff."

"Oh…" Lena repeated, and the memory of the lurching sensation she'd felt during her rescue returned. The thought she might have been saved briefly, only for her and Nyah to be hurled to their deaths moments later was chilling. "I had no idea."

"No," Nyah said. "You didn't. You just assumed I'm some egocentric, alien freak immune to the forces of nature who willfully chose not to help."

Lena felt ashamed. "Thank you," she said, earnestly this time.

Nyah watched her for a few moments, and then closed her eyes as she drained the last of her drink. "I still haven't decided why I risked my life for you. A tracker."

"Because when it comes down to it, you're a good person. Even if I'm not."

Nyah placed the cup on the ground. "Do you actually believe that?"

Lena hadn't expected that question. She'd just said it because she was sure it was what Nyah thought—more mirroring behavior. She kept doing it without thinking these days. But *did* she believe it? Lena hesitated. "I'm not sure," she finally admitted.

Nyah merely nodded, and the edge of her mouth curled into the hint of a smile. "That's the most honest thing you've ever said to me. Perhaps there's hope for you yet."

CHAPTER 7

IN A SMALL NOOK PAST the main cavern, Lena changed into dry clothes and then returned to lay her wet things on rocks near the fire.

Nyah, who had retreated to her bed, eyed her black boy shorts, bra, jeans, shirt, and socks laid out. Lena half expected a snide comment about how she wasn't running a laundry but Nyah said nothing, returning to her *Handbook of the Yemen Flora*.

Lena stretched out on her sleeping bag and reviewed her day so far. It had gone from explosive to terrifying to death-defying and now sort of weirdly tedious. She was exhausted yet wired, her mind leaping from one abstract thought to the next with dizzying speed, trying to make sense of a muddled mess of experiences.

She considered how long she'd be stuck in here for. That flash flood had been as impressive as it was sudden. How long would there be a river down there?

Lena remembered where her Dazr had ended up. Damn, she'd have to submit a DT7-10 Lost Equipment Report when she got back. Great. Wherever it was, it was swimming with the fishes now. Or the fissures. She snorted softly to herself. She rubbed her hands over her face, pressing the heels into her eye sockets. Hell. She must be delirious if she was doing bad word puns.

She missed hotdogs, Lena suddenly decided, dropping her hands to her stomach. And Mrs. Finkel's meatballs. She was as skilled at whipping up those as she was disastrous at making coffee. Whenever Lena had returned from an away assignment, her neighbor would bring around a ceramic dish bursting with rich, bold Italian aromas, covered in a cloth that she would whip off like a magician's scarf.

Lena knew feeding her was just an excuse to reminisce with her about the good old days on the news desk or her beloved granddaughter, Diane.

But Lena didn't entirely object to the company or the conversation—after all, the meatballs *were* very good.

Her thumbs drummed her stomach, and she strained to work out how far away the storm was now. But it was impossible to tell. All she could hear outside was the distant roaring wind, a perfect wall of white noise. She shifted her focus to the cave.

Drip, drip, drip.

Trickle. Trickle.

Lena turned her head, scanning the walls. Where did the water gather that slid down various unseen fissures in the cavern? She had heard it trickling in several places before but where did it go? Would it flood in here if it rained too much outside? No, that wasn't likely. Nyah had already been through one cyclone here. She'd hardly make her home in a flood zone.

Nyah. Her eyes slid to the left to observe her contrary cave-mate. At least Lena was no longer fighting with her. That was an improvement. And she had saved Lena's life, which gave the guardian an automatic free pass on everything today. Still, Lena was greatly unsettled over their no-holds-barred confrontation earlier. That was a nice word for what it really was—a brawl. They'd both been vicious and had drawn blood, but only Lena's had showed.

It was uncomfortable being so near someone who'd effortlessly done that to her. Lena's control was usually much stronger. How had she made herself vulnerable? How had Nyah uncovered her weaknesses so easily? How had Lena let her see them in the first place? She was usually so much better at this.

She worried her bottom lip with her teeth at that thought, and stared at Nyah reading on her bed. It had been an hour since they'd last spoken. Lena didn't usually crave conversation, but she hated oppression more. Feeling trapped. There was literally nowhere else to go.

"Good book?" she asked.

"Adequate. Although what commons don't know about botany would fill a much larger one."

Lena considered that. Was it frustrating being unable to share her superior knowledge? What had Nyah said? She missed the collegial atmosphere. It was more than that, though. Her eyes had burned with regret when she'd uttered those words.

Lena wondered if that meant she was lonely. Intellectually at least, if not emotionally.

"What?" Nyah muttered, not shifting the book from her face. "You're staring."

How did she do that?

"Are you lonely?" Lena asked suddenly. She blinked, astonished at herself.

"Are *you*?" Nyah shot back acerbically.

"Too busy to be lonely," Lena said glibly. "Always on the go."

"Mm. So many guardians to harass, so little time? And what of when you're not busy making our lives miserable? When you're home in your bed?"

Lena considered that. "I enjoy my own company. Don't you?"

"Immensely." Nyah slapped the book closed. "Why all this concern about my social life?"

"It's my brush with death talking," Lena suggested, not entirely sure herself. She propped her head up on one hand. "Are you really retired? Or is it temporary? Like a vacation?"

"A vacation," Nyah said with a derisive snort. "I'll let you know when I have my first one."

"What do you mean?" Lena looked at her curiously. "Why don't you take vacations?"

"Have you ever actually read the Pact? Or considered what it really means to be a guardian?"

Lena had, in fact, read the Pact. It was part of her induction on the first day on the job. "Sure, I've read it."

"Did you see the bit about how we're slaves to commons for life?"

"Slaves to…? What the hell? That's not in there." Lena sat up indignantly.

"Isn't it? Hmm. Would *you* like to work for three hundred and sixty-five days a year, always on call, and have no say in it? What if you were required to be on your best behavior in case you brought shame on your colleagues?" Nyah tossed her book away from her. "How would you like to be seen only as an exotic oddity? We can never let down our guards. We can never relax and just be ourselves. We're always watched, videoed, tracked, and analyzed, and what one of us does, we are all judged for. We have all the responsibilities and none of the rights of commons. Our lives have never been our own."

Lena picked through the outburst, not sure she agreed with much of it. Guardians had rights, what was she on about? She frowned. Nyah's eyes narrowed as she studied Lena's face.

"You doubt me? Why would I lie?" Her lips twisted in distaste.

Lena combed some stray hairs behind her ears with her fingers, trying to work out what to say. Of course she doubted her. Because guardians were entitled, and didn't know what a hard life really was. Bitching because they're watched and adored? All famous people go through that, guardian and common alike. Why should Earth's superheroes expect anything less? Lena didn't say it, though. That whole "saving her life" business had earned Nyah some space to run her mouth off without Lena's sarcastic retorts. For today. Well, an hour at least. So she bit her lip.

Nyah's expression darkened as she realized Lena's continued silence was not, in fact, agreement.

"Do you know that if we run or...what is that revolting term you trackers use? Splat?" Nyah said, her voice rising in irritation. "If we dare to die in a public place while saving commons, we are made invisible, while your tracker friends become complicit in pretending to the world it never happened. All to keep the myth of our invincibility and our perfection. But it's worse if one of us has a mental breakdown. Do you know what they do to us if we crack under the pressure?"

Oh shit. *That.* Lena broke eye contact. On that topic, Nyah had a valid point.

"Ah, I see you do. But that wasn't your question, was it? You want to know why don't we get vacations? Simple. It's because even if we try to have one, wherever we go in the world, whenever something happens nearby, we're expected to drop everything and help. That's a clause in the Pact, by the way—render assistance at all times. And the problem is your planet *always* has problems. So if we help, we never get a break. If we don't help, people die. We have to live with the guilt of doing nothing. So, inevitably, we always help and then burn ourselves out. Haven't you noticed the rate of guardian breakdowns lately? Or is that something else you choose not to think about?"

Lena had, in fact, noticed the spike. All the trackers had—these days there was plenty of overtime to be had for a tracker who wanted extra cash. But she was startled to realize she never thought much about *why* it was happening now. She blinked at Nyah in surprise. Was she saying that the guardians were all just severely burnt out? Even the mad ones like Beast Lord? All because they'd never had a decent few days off in a hundred years?

Her frown deepened. Talon Man had to be a complete fool not to know that running his workers into the ground would blow up in his face. Was this a joke? Because this smelt like some grade-A bullshit.

"Why aren't the guardians demanding changes to protect themselves then?" Lena challenged. "Hell, if you did it in the media and made a big fuss, they'd probably agree to change the Pact to give you all mandatory time off or something."

"And be forced to admit we're less than perfect?" Nyah gave a bark of laughter. "Tal would love that."

"Well, why don't you do it in-house? No commons have to know you're on vacation."

"*We'd* know," Nyah said sharply. "Don't you understand by now what it is to wear this uniform?" She tugged at her outfit in aggravation. "We're your protectors, and we are *always* on duty. We can't see something and walk away."

"So *that's* why you're hiding out here?" Lena asked. "You decided to get far away, in a place where not much happens, so no one knows you, and they won't ask for help even if it does?"

"That's one reason, I suppose. I also need to not be around commons anymore. I've done my time. I have come to the conclusion your people are not worth my effort. In short, I'm done."

Lena wanted to roll her eyes. This again? "Come on, are we really so bad? Is our adulation really that traumatic?"

Nyah studied her coolly. "Be careful of questions you can't handle the answers to."

"I can handle it," Lena said. She meant it. Seriously, how much worse could a guardian's life be compared to what she'd gone through? Nothing she'd heard had made her think they understood real pain, beyond what sounded like the struggle of working too hard and facing constant fame.

"How interesting," Nyah said sarcastically, "a liar in search of the truth."

Lena exhaled sharply, willing her tongue to stay silent. She was done being goaded so easily.

"So quiet now," Nyah noted, and her tone became sly. "Don't hold back on my account. Your railings in defense of your little planet are always entertaining."

Lena cocked an eyebrow. "You know this is ridiculous, right? You, out here, hiding away at the end of the world from every person on the planet? That is completely insane."

"Why? It's my choice."

"You're so much better than this. Look, I get the need for a vacation. You all sound overworked and badly needing a break, and that is shitty as hell, I agree. But retiring? You don't get to withdraw your unique skills. It's a waste. A terrible, stupid waste of a rare talent. And we both know it."

Nyah suddenly was on her feet and stalked over to where Lena sat. Her imposing height was as acute as a threat. "The point *is*," Nyah said coldly, "you and the human race shouldn't get to tell *me* how I live my life. *That's* the biggest waste—me, living a life dictated by others just because I can do a shattering party trick. You think it's insane I'm out here? Insanity is thinking that being Shattergirl was ever any kind of life."

"But you're so good at it!"

"Yes, I am. So?"

Lena stopped, uncertain.

Nyah dropped to a crouch and met her eye with a flinty gaze. "It's not like I'm the only one of my kind. Others will fill the gap I left."

"But it's...a shame," Lena said lamely.

"For you, maybe. I'm fine with it." She rose and returned to her bed, snatched up her book, and resumed reading.

Lena stared after her, confusion washing through her. She'd always been so sure about what was right regarding guardians. They were given a safe harbor in exchange for putting their talents to good use protecting humankind. All their material needs were met. They were adored. Who wouldn't want that?

But...what if...what if some of them despised it? It was a confronting thing to get her brain around. She tried to imagine any life that was not of her own choosing. It felt stifling.

"Okay," Lena muttered in a reluctant concession.

"What? Was that acceptance?" Nyah asked, not looking up. "Is it a sign the apocalypse is nigh?"

"Funny." Lena shivered and shifted a little closer to the fire. "No. I just get it a little better."

Nyah's book snapped shut again and she peered at Lena over it. "How long have you been a tracker?" she suddenly asked.

"Five years."

"Are you any good at it?"

"The best." Lena didn't bother to hide the pride in her voice. It was the only good thing in her life.

"I see. So you excel at hunting, lying, and twisting guardian psyches?" There was a speculative look on her face rather than scorn.

Lena eyed her, bemused. "That was just work."

"Your work was my life," Nyah said sharply.

"I know. I just hadn't fully thought about it from the guardian perspective. And come on, it's not like you make your perspective known to the commons, is it?"

"I'm well aware. We're all so perfect and idolized. Teenagers collect our trading cards. Tell me, did you do that? Have my trading card?"

Lena scowled. "You love the idea I might have worshipped you as a kid, don't you?"

Nyah eyed her with amusement. "I like confirming a theory. Which one was it? Action Shattergirl? Or the Platinum Issue Exclusive Shattergirl. A hologram. I shimmered when you turned the card."

Lena narrowed her eyes. No, she hadn't been able to afford the platinum card. But she had owned the action one. It had been a highly treasured possession. She still had it somewhere in her stuff. "Why do you want to know? We were all kids doing stupid stuff once. Then we grow up and get a clue."

"So you got a clue about me," Nyah suggested. "Do tell, what did I do wrong?"

"Where to start," Lena said with a snort, deflecting the question.

Nyah didn't seem offended, merely curious. "And are you so perfect?"

"Far from it." Lena fiddled with her cuff. "We're all fucked up underneath, aren't we?"

"Essentially. So tell me, what has your life been like so far?"

"Why?" Lena was suspicious now. "Why are you asking me all this?"

"I'm tired of thinking about what it is to be a guardian. You say you understand me a little better? Now I want to better understand you."

"But why?" Lena repeated. "You know trackers aren't interesting. Hell, we don't even officially exist. Did you know they even advertise tracker jobs as something else and only admit once we've got the job what we're really doing, *after* we've signed non-disclosure contracts." She shook her head. "Kinda funny when you think about it. You're in the most visible job on the planet; I'm in the most invisible one."

"I said I wanted to understand *you*. Not your job. I am well aware of how trackers ply their trade. We will be stuck here for a while, so we may as well find a way to pass the time. So...Lena Martin...what has your life been like so far?"

Lena debated what to tell her. She could lie of course, but Nyah seemed to have an inbuilt bullshit detector. She wondered what it would be like having an actual conversation with someone about her life. The thought was just too...ugh. A world of no.

Lena was met with an even stare. She supposed sharing a few of the basics wouldn't kill her at least. Who was Nyah going to tell, anyway?

"Dad died before I was born," she said, finally. That was safe enough. She had no feelings on that topic one way or another. "Obviously I don't remember him."

"And your mother?"

Cold water shot through her veins. Not safe. Not safe at all. Lena steeled herself. "She's dead now."

"I'm sorry."

"She was sick a lot of the time, so it's probably better for her." Lena's stomach lurched and she rushed in. "I didn't *want* her to die, though. I don't mean that."

"I knew what you meant."

"Okay." Her palms were slick so she wiped them down her thighs. She knew Nyah saw the nervous habit, and her heart rate picked up again.

"What was wrong with her?" Nyah asked, not unkindly.

"The doctors never knew." Lena shook her head. "They were morons."

"Why do you say that?"

Lena scowled. "Tell me about your girlfriend."

The silence was as long as Lena had expected.

Finally Nyah spoke, the familiar annoyed edge back again. "I don't talk about that. You know that."

Lena said nothing.

"You could have just said the same, that you don't talk about that topic." Reproach laced Nyah's voice.

Lena rolled onto her back and said grimly, "Yeah. But now you know exactly how it feels to be asked."

"All right."

The fire was warm and the conversation dried up. Lena relaxed once she realized that was the end of the grilling. She closed her eyes. Just for a moment.

Lena awoke groggily, shocked to find she'd fallen asleep. Aromas nearby made her hum appreciatively. Nyah was at the fire, stirring something in a pot. Something sublime. Her stomach rumbled. That breakfast granola bar had been hours ago.

"Time is it?" she asked, her tongue thick and dry, as she sat up.

"Welcome back. It's almost six."

"PM?" Lena started. She took stock of the glorious smells. "What are you cooking?"

"Dinner."

"God, you're hard work," Lena said tiredly, struggling to sit up. "What *exactly* is dinner?"

"It's a sort of risotto concoction I fell in love with in Italy. I've compromised for local conditions and limited cooking utensils, but the flavor's essentially the same."

"Italy?" Lena asked curiously. "I thought you protected the Americas?"

"Yes, that didn't mean I didn't see other parts of the world. It was after the earthquake in Milan six years ago. The guardians asked for all spare hands. I volunteered. It's my specialty after all."

"Rock shifting. Yeah." Lena's mouth was watering as more smells wafted under her nose. "Although I'm guessing cooking might be another specialty."

Nyah's eyes sparkled. "Perhaps. My father loved to cook. He passed his knowledge on to me. Of course, we didn't use the ingredients you have on this world. I adapted."

"Was it hard? Adapting?"

"Obviously." Nyah dipped a spoon into the liquid and tasted. She added some seasoning and resumed stirring. "I can't imagine anyone adapting easily to losing their world, all their loved ones, and moving to another, then begging for resettlement as stateless refugees. Can you?"

"Talon Man did."

"Yes. That's his nature. He seized an opportunity when he saw it."

"Why's he still in power? I know his orders about what happens to the guardians who have breakdowns. And I know the overdues that are brought back get put on short leashes, monitored for the rest of their lives. Why the hell do you all put up with it? The guardians should overthrow his bullying orange ass."

Nyah's lips thinned. "As long as he's so popular among the commons, no guardian will challenge him. And before you ask, no, I never want to be in charge of an organization dedicated to governing the thing I despise most—being a guardian."

"But what if the public learned the truth? About guardians and Talon Man?"

"It won't. You signed a non-disclosure agreement, didn't you? Every common at the Facility has."

"Yeah."

"It's iron-clad," Nyah said. "A young nurse who worked with the guardians who'd had breakdowns challenged her NDA about forty years ago. She failed in her court case—which was heavily suppressed. Her destroyed reputation and being bankrupted was a consequence that Tal greatly enjoyed. All Facility medical employees got the message loud and clear. There have been no further challenges. Now everyone accepts that it is what it is."

"Even you?"

"I did raise these issues many decades ago with the other founders. They didn't want to challenge the status quo in case it backfired and the masses got angry. They didn't want to risk losing all their rights and what little freedoms they have just to unseat Earth's most popular guardian. It's futile to argue with them. I tried, but they were too afraid. So that's the end of it."

Lena watched Nyah stirring vigorously, her mouth in a grim line. The injustice of the situation screamed for a resolution. The way things were wasn't right. She thought hard.

"Can you stop thinking so loudly," Nyah complained as she tapped the spoon on the side of the pot. "I can virtually hear your brain grinding its cogs from here."

Lena's head snapped up as Nyah rubbed her temple, looking thoroughly disagreeable. And there it was again. That expression. So familiar. Lena stared, recognizing the look for what it might be. Surprise, elation, fear, and distaste mingled as she considered the ramifications. Had her fleeting first suspicion been right? With a thudding heart, she wondered how to broach the awkward subject.

"My mother," Lena eventually said, almost choking out the words, "suffered from terrible migraines."

A startled look flitted across Nyah's face at the introduction of a topic Lena had comprehensively shut down as off limits bare hours ago.

"I commiserate."

"It's why I thought the doctors treating her were idiots. She had these crippling headaches, 'worse than childbirth' she would tell them, but they kept trying to find environmental factors. Well, when they weren't doping her up with drugs."

"You don't think it was environmental?"

"It had to be genetic."

"Oh. Did her parents have this medical condition, too?"

Lena shook her head.

Nyah paused in her stirring. "So what makes you so sure?"

"We moved a few times. We've lived country, city, everywhere in between. She had it her whole life. It wasn't environmental. My earliest memory was her clutching her head and crying in pain."

Sympathy laced the Nyah's features. "What set it off?"

"People. Their thoughts."

The guardian abruptly stopped what she was doing, and that was the moment Lena knew she'd been right.

Dark brown eyes bored into Lena's. "What?" It came out like a shocked hiss.

"People. Being too near them," Lena said quietly. "She could...we never told people, they wouldn't believe us, but she heard people's thoughts. They hammered away at her, some days worse than others. Crowds were the worst."

Nyah dropped her gaze, focusing with a scary intensity on the pot. She didn't resume stirring. Just stared at it. "Who was it?"

Lena stared at her in complete incomprehension. "What do you mean?"

Nyah looked at her in surprise. "Never mind. Did your mother ever get past it? Find a way to make the pain go away?"

"Yes. She did."

"How?"

Lena didn't answer immediately.

"Well?" Nyah asked again, impatiently. "What did she do?"

"Why do you want to know?"

"We're just talking."

"No, we're not."

Nyah shook her head. "I'm not sure what you're getting at."

"I'm getting at the fact that you and my mother had this condition in common."

A gamut of emotions crossed Nyah's face, and Lena saw the truth behind her blustering words. "We... What! No."

"Your expression in all the old vids? It's the same. Identical. Even the way you hold your head and try to make the pain go away. Always in crowds, and the degree to which you look in misery is always dependent on how many people are around you. It's a direct correlation. And I swear, it's like a mirror reflection, the way you and my mother looked when the pain was at its worst."

"I don't get migraines." Nyah said, voice tight.

"Not anymore," Lena suggested. "Not out here, far from people. Right?"

Nyah didn't reply. Her grip on her spoon looked tight enough to crush it to metal filings.

"It's also how you knew the other trackers were coming for you," Lena said. "And the scientists encroaching. You heard their thoughts from miles away. But not mine, right?"

Nyah glanced at her sharply. She wrenched the spoon from the pot, tomato juices running down the handle, and laid it flat. She took the pot off the fire with precise movements, but Lena could see her shaking hands.

"Before your mother, did anyone else in your family have this ability?" Nyah asked. Her expression was scarily intense. It made Lena uneasy.

"No. Just her. It's a pretty crappy skill you both share."

"It's not a skill." Nyah said sourly. "It's a curse—unlike the few guardians who were born with it and have mastery of it, it's one I only acquired when we landed here. None of my people know why. Suddenly I went from having peace to enduring human thoughts crowding my head. They drown all other thoughts. It's disturbing to know the petty, base, and dark imaginings of your species. Especially the impulses of younger, testosterone-filled males and those you call rednecks. It was quite an education." Her revulsion was written all over her face.

"No wonder you hate our people so much," Lena whispered.

Nyah didn't answer. She put a lid on the pot to keep it warm and eyed her. "I *do* know why I allowed you to stay here, even knowing you were a tracker. It's because you were the only human I've ever met who does not leak their thoughts. I need to know how you block being read. And I especially need to know how your mother found a cure from her curse."

"No," Lena said, feeling queasy and gross. She stared at her hands, shocked to find them trembling, and curled them into tight fists. "I can't do that. You'd need my life history for that. And I'm private."

"*Private*," Nyah repeated incredulously. "I'm not asking for prurient reasons. I *need* to know."

"I know that!" Lena cried. "You want peace from humans? A way to silence their thoughts that drown you and crawl around in your head? I *know* that. I get that. But I won't tell you." Lena unclenched her fists and tried to force herself to calm down.

"Lena, somehow you, alone, have a rare skill among billions. Just tell me how you do it?" Nyah's brows were drawn darkly together, and a frustrated edge crept into her voice.

"No. You don't know what the cost is. It's too high."

"The cost?" Nyah repeated flatly. "Ah. Now I see." She regarded Lena stonily for a moment before adding, "I'm prepared to pay whatever the price."

Lena stared at her in dawning realization. She felt numb at the implication. "The hell? You think I'm holding out for money?"

"Some prices are not monetary," Nyah said, her voice cool. "I am open to hearing any proposal. I assume you wish me to go to that anniversary ceremony? Correct?"

"You think I'm *blackmailing* you?" Lena could barely contain her shock.

"*Is* that the price?" Nyah pressed her, distaste coating her features.

"No," Lena snapped. "No, it's not the price! And screw you for thinking I'm so mercenary. There *is* no price. There never would be. I meant the cost was too high for *me* to pay." She stood. "I'm going t-to stretch my legs."

"Lena…"

"No! I think you've said enough. I can't even look at you."

CHAPTER 8

LENA HEADED FOR THE BACK of the cave, desperate to put some distance between her and Nyah. Anger pounded in her head in a matching, staccato beat to her feet pounding along the cave floor. Of all the fucked-up, crappy things to say. Lena had a bunch of flaws, Christ, a truckload of them, but blackmail was not one of them. Especially not over something so close to the bone as this. Something that had the power to snap her in two if she wasn't careful and didn't watch herself to make sure she didn't slip back. Her rage at Nyah's heartless, ignorant allegation rose anew, and she picked up the frenetic pace.

Lena followed the narrowing path, wondering where the twists and turns led. Sounds of running water began getting louder, so she headed toward them. A shaft of light drew her attention, diverting her, and she discovered an opening, little better than a wide fissure, which she turned sideways into and squeezed through.

She emerged on the far side of the mountain, on a ledge protected from above by a small, jagged overhang that kept the worst of the rain off. Stubborn stubbly bushes clung to the cracks on the ledge, shaking under the high winds. Lena squinted into the distance. In the strange, not-quite darkness, she could see more mountains below, studded with clumps of spiky green plants. As she stared, she realized she was really seeing hundreds of dragon blood trees, bent almost in half by the wind, their trunks invisible in the half light. Wrapping her arms around herself, Lena shivered at the sheer unrelenting force of the wind, only too aware of how vulnerable she was to its fury.

Hours ago she'd fallen off a mountain, for God's sake. She should be dead. It was hard to still get her head around that. She *would* be dead, if not for Nyah.

The rage that had been knotting Lena's insides seeped out of her, little by little, at the memory of her rescue. She exhaled shakily, suddenly feeling weak after being drained of fury. She dropped to her haunches, leaning back against the rock wall, and smoothed her hands over her knees and calves, again and again, trying to get her emotions back under control.

The irony was that at work they thought the great Silver had no emotions. Out here, though, it was as though she barely knew herself; everything was so close to the surface. She'd felt more anger, uncertainty, doubt, humiliation, and pain in the past two days than she had in the past two years. What the hell was happening to her?

There was an eerie light over Socotra—the clouds parted briefly and then swallowed the sun once more. The skies returned to brooding black, with a brown, angry smudge where the sun should be. The wind swirled and changed, flinging a brief burst of rain at her. She pressed herself back harder against the mountain, shaking with cold, but not ready to retreat inside yet. Not ready to resume *that* conversation.

Lena couldn't tell Nyah her story. Her life was as messed up as it came. She'd taken years to recover. But she'd gotten herself together. Found a job and thrown herself into work to the exclusion of all else. She'd honed her skills, learned the secrets to knowledge and control. She'd built up a good intelligence network across the various Facility operations worldwide, and had eyes and ears everywhere.

Outside of the office, away from that bureaucratic, political world that hid all the guardians' imperfections and secrets, she'd turn into someone else entirely: a ruthless, empty tracker who reveled in the chase and the win. Over the years she'd become addicted to the thrill of winning. No guardian's story was too sad or too awful for her not to use it to score another winning notch on the board.

Their stories never bothered her for long. And, yes, she definitely knew where the broken guardians went all right, after trackers brought them in. The unstable ones such as Beast Lord? They'd be twenty-two subfloors down by now, doped up to their eyeballs indefinitely. Never to see daylight again.

Carefully enhanced and edited images of them at various distant, unspecified disasters would be drip-fed to the public for the rest of their days, maintaining the illusion they were still off doing hero work somewhere far, far away. They did that for the splats too. As far as Earth's people knew, the aliens that walked their planet were immortal.

Lena's wet fingertips dug into the thin layer of dirt beside her, scraping and heaping it into a small mound. She turned up a rock and flicked it into her other hand, before batting it lightly from hand to hand. The repetition helped her think.

The faking of heroic deeds wasn't new. They'd been doing their digital sleight of hand for longer than Lena had been alive. Hell, they'd been doing it with Shattergirl too, now she thought about it. No wonder she hadn't realized the guardian had been missing for eighteen months. The Facility was all about maintaining the illusion. They were damned good at it. But did she care?

That was the question. Lena polished the rock against her jeans, cleaning it as she considered the ugly decay and muck in her own life.

She'd made a concerted effort in her career not to think too hard on certain things going on in the periphery of the Facility. Besides, technically, she shouldn't even know any of this. She had decided not to dwell on anything long enough to have an opinion. Nothing she'd heard whispered on her network had been enough to give up a career, hell, a life, which held her only purpose for getting out of bed.

There were occasionally stories of a few trackers developing a conscience and letting some of their targets run. She hadn't given them much thought either. They were replaced soon enough. Besides, why would she care what men and women unable to do their jobs thought?

Naturally, no such rumors ever swirled around Silver. Hell. No.

The wind bit at her now numb face as Lena acknowledged an unsettling truth. She had never really been bothered enough to ask certain, deeper questions. The guiding principle she'd lived by was that the best trackers didn't wonder whether the talent had a reason to run or fret about what might happen to them on their return. Whether it was right.

The best trackers didn't doubt. Lena had worked out years ago that to be the best, she needed laser-like focus. They wanted a tracker? She gave it everything. She didn't question what she did, or its impact on her. She'd never for a heartbeat wondered whether it was worth the cost to her as a person. She told herself she didn't need friends to prosper. She didn't need anyone.

Sure, she admitted sometimes, in the darkness in her own bed, that maybe, just maybe, it'd be nice to be connected with someone. To actually have a lover she could trust. Someone to share stories and days and worries with. A woman she could enjoy a beer and a laugh with after work, and shoot the breeze. A woman who *got* her. Even just for a little while. But that couldn't happen because that wasn't who Lena was.

Because Lena Martin didn't trust anyone.

She threw the rock with all her might, almost wrenching her shoulder. It sailed over the ledge, disappearing from view. She rubbed her suffering arm. Trusting people? No. That wasn't her at all.

Besides, Lena told herself, thudding her head back against the hard rock wall, she was fine with how things were. Once the storm passed, it'd be a new day. She would consider the assignment over, pretend she'd never clapped eyes on Shattergirl, move on, and need never face such troubling thoughts again.

Because doubts were the real enemy. You lost focus, you were no longer the best. Doubts were like the past; they could turn the strongest person into a shell, and she couldn't face that. Not again.

A memory curled into her brain before she could stop it, and suddenly she was back *there*.

Dread filled Lena and she squeezed her eyes tightly shut, willing this not to happen now. Tears pricked her eyes and she repeated in her mind on a loop, "Not now. Not here. No."

The wind was howling, and she no longer cared if it swept her from the ledge. Another gust, more powerful than the last, ripped around her, threatening to do just that. It made her whole body shudder.

"You know, there are easier ways to die," a voice said beside her.

Lena stiffened, her eyes flashing back open. She hadn't even heard Nyah approach.

"In fact, if you're going to offer yourself up as a sacrifice in a cyclone, you're making me wonder why I bothered saving you earlier."

Lena stared sullenly into the bruised skies. "It's in your job description. That's why."

"Much as I hate to admit it, that's true. So what do you see in those angry clouds? What are you thinking?"

Wasn't that the question? She was suddenly too tired to bother with any more clever little answers, always neatly side-stepping the truth. Her reserves were shattered.

"I'm thinking about who I am as a human being. And all the ways I am not a worthwhile person." Lena tilted her head towards Nyah and added flatly, "I don't believe we've been properly introduced. I'm Silver."

There was a silence and a sharp intake of breath behind her.

"You're...*her*."

Lena looked away, unsurprised at her visceral reaction. All guardians had heard of the infamous, ruthless Silver, the world's top tracker. She was as bad as a curse to a guardian on the run.

"I'd like to say pleased to meet you," Nyah said coldly, "but that's a lie."

"Don't blame you," Lena said, shutting her eyes. The rock wall felt nice and cold against her warm head.

"You're the one they say has never been beaten."

Lena's lip curled in derision, and she fluttered open her eyes. "Actually you did beat me," she said tiredly. "Before the storm started. I was heading home, about to report you as untraceable. Congratulations." She gave a hollow laugh. "You broke my winning streak."

"I see."

Lena could hear the shuffle as Nyah edged closer. "Do you even like your job?"

A sudden brightness made Lena squint, and she marveled at a fork of lightning on the horizon. It was beauty and devastation combined. "Being the best means something to me," she said flatly, suddenly wondering if that was even still true. "You should see me when I'm really in the zone. I can talk anyone into anything. It's all about winning. Nothing makes me feel better."

At the prolonged silence, she turned to find Nyah studying her, not the storm.

"*Nothing*? That's sad."

"I suppose. Actually what's sad is I'm a winner who hates everything and everyone. I've come to the conclusion out here that I'm a lousy human being."

Nyah's reply was sardonic. "Well, I hate everything too—*including* my job. You at least like yours."

Lena said nothing for a moment. "It's not that I like it. I just like to win. The feeling I get from that is why I do it. Especially since I never won shit as a kid. I lost the life lottery, but won in the end."

"You wanted to prove them all wrong."

"Yeah." Lena stared at the rain. It was getting heavier. "I think... somewhere along the line I stopped caring about the things that matter. I look at you...you stopped caring too. So much so that you even walked away from everything. But the big difference is, you never lost your compassion."

"You don't know that."

"I do," Lena said. She glanced up at the hooded eyes watching her. "You carry on like you're so confident and smart and better than us all, but I look into your eyes now and you know what I see? A fraud. You're full of shit. You still think we're worth saving, don't you?"

"That's just the thing, I don't."

"I don't believe you," Lena said. "You saved me."

"It was a reflex."

Lena scoured her face, wanting to see the lie for what it was. She was stymied when she couldn't read her expression at all.

"You're desperate for that not to be true, aren't you? I warned you about the masks we wear. I meant it when I said I don't want to do this anymore."

"I hear that, and I understand needing a break. A long one. Hell, a year or two, even. But I really don't get giving up on everything, on life, all of it, *forever*. That's such a long time. I know you felt forced into this hero thing, but the Pact was supposed to be a *fair* deal. It was never meant to hurt you. It was only meant to ask a small price for us giving you a new home."

"I'm well aware of the debt owed," Nyah said sharply, "because the people of Earth never let us forget it. Every day, in big ways and small, they reminded us that we would be dead without their generosity. But it's a debt without end. How much is enough?"

"I don't understand."

"How much blood will commons extract from us before they agree we've paid our dues and should be allowed to be free? And when will our opinions not be sorted into guardian or common? Alien or human? Will we always be outsiders?"

"But you don't even like commons," Lena said slowly. "Why would you want to be considered one of us?"

"It would be nice to not always be singled out as 'other.' It'd be nice not to be me. Alien. Different. Special. Someone to point at."

Lena studied her in surprise. "*You* just want to be average? To blend? Come on."

"I'm *tired*," Nyah snapped. "I know you're just a common, but don't you actually get that?"

"I do. But that's too easy. Come on, we're *all* tired. We all think there's gotta be more to life than the daily grind. But you just gave up on life. You! Who's so strong. What's the real reason? I don't buy that you're just tired of it all."

Nyah joined Lena in leaning against the rock wall. She held Lena's gaze. "I warned you that you wouldn't want to know the truth. I meant it."

Lena didn't flinch. "Try me. I'm so done with all the *tagshart* right now, including my own. I'm sick of the lies I tell and the lies the world tells me. I think, right now, I have never wanted anything more than hearing the whole truth. So, will you share it? Your truth?"

Nyah searched her face. Finally, she nodded. "Let's go back to the fire."

CHAPTER 9

NYAH PLACED A PLATE OF food in front of Lena. "You should probably eat first," she said.

Lena wondered what could possibly be so bad that Nyah assumed she'd lose her appetite after hearing it. She didn't ask. Instead, she picked up a fork. The risotto was delicious, but Lena ate it quickly, anxious to get to the point. They didn't speak, and Lena felt a heaviness behind Nyah's solemn eyes watching her.

Pushing away the now empty plate, Lena looked up. "I'm ready."

"I wish I had been." Nyah brushed her thigh with her hand, a gesture that looked almost nervous. Lena felt a dusting of fear spider along her nerves at the sight.

"When I first arrived on this world," Nyah began, "I knew nothing of a people so close to their primal emotions as your people are. On my planet any feuds tended to revolve around science and be intellectual in nature. Never things such as gender or skin color or who we love."

"We can be petty at times," Lena said uncomfortably.

"No, it's not petty," Nyah said darkly. "It's deadly. The way your world treats differences as a threat is chilling."

Not everyone does that, Lena wanted to protest. But taking one look at Nyah's haunted, dark features, she didn't speak.

"I had only been on your world a few years the first time I saw it," Nyah continued. "I came across a man with wild black hair, skin darker than mine, and terrified eyes. He looked right at me, right *into* me. He couldn't talk he was so frightened. He'd spoken to a young, white girl, asked her her name, and the townsmen hadn't liked it and claimed he was up to much worse. They were tying the noose when I arrived. Forty of them. Forty grown men, against one young man."

"A lynch mob?" Lena felt ill. "What did you do?"

"They were flung up to the top of the tree they were planning to use. It was a *very* high tree, so it terrified them all."

Nyah stared into the fire. "But I could hear their thoughts. The way they regarded their victim. The disgusting things they thought about me. It was a level of hatred and revulsion I had never experienced in my life. I was unprepared for it. The echo of what I heard that day followed me for years." She rubbed her temple. "Fear and loathing filled my brain. I had nightmares for months."

"Did the police do anything when you reported them?"

A hollow snort sounded. "I didn't need to report them. The sheriff was among those clinging to the tree, trembling, and screaming for vengeance."

"Hell. I'm sorry," Lena said sincerely.

"Why? You didn't do it. Nor did you light a garment factory on fire in South America. I saved twenty-four impoverished workers that day. Fifty-eight more died when the ceiling collapsed because I couldn't get to them in time. The best part was how the newspapers blamed me for spreading the fire due to my 'excessive flying speed.' They didn't want to say that the prominent businessman who ran the factory had been cutting costs on safety. The asbestos from the ceilings got in my lungs. I usually heal rapidly. Not from that, though. That took months."

"I'm...that's awful."

Nyah studied her hands, knotted tightly in her lap. "That was nothing. It's not the fire that haunts me. I heard their screams. The dying workers lived inside my head. I heard their final thoughts. Can you imagine what that's like? To feel all their lost dreams, lives wasted, regrets for children they'd never see grow up, loved ones they hadn't said 'I love you' to before they left for work that day. After that I never wanted to go near a fire again."

Lena couldn't imagine something so horrible.

"I see inside people's souls, Lena," Nyah continued. "I see what no one ever should; what only the gods they believe in should."

"Is that why you quit?"

"No. But time and again, after decades of seeing lives cheapened and injury deliberately inflicted, I asked myself, why should I be a slave to those who don't value life or each other?"

Lena's stomach sank at the brittle way she said it. "Is that really how you see us? *All* of us?"

"What I see is a species that judges me for factors beyond my control and yet is surprisingly obtuse in facing its own malfunctions. Do you know that sometimes I hear people wishing I wasn't touching them, or wanting to debase me in disgusting, perverted ways, at the very *moment* I'm saving their damned lives? That sort of thing ate away at me."

"Some of us are stupid, violent, and cruel," Lena said tightly, hands curling into defensive fists, "but what about the innocents? Surely they're worth it?"

Nyah ran her hands over her scalp, pausing at her eyes, drilling the heels of her hands into them as though wishing an image could be ripped from them. "These innocents you speak of—to hear their thoughts is torture of another kind. Little ones crying for their parent or a favorite teddy bear or pet. Broken hearts, crying for the dead. The sick grieving their lost vitality. The frail and elderly their youth. I hear their voices in my mind, laid over and over, like sad, endless whispers. They rustle around my head like fall leaves."

Lena's hands uncurled. "Sorry" seemed so inadequate, but she said it anyway, stumbling over it, the word sticking awkwardly in her throat. There needed to be a bigger word.

Nyah studied her, eyes unreadable. "What are you sorry for though? Do you even know?"

"I'm sorry for all the ways we've failed you as a people."

"You think this is about me?" Nyah asked, sounding appalled. "How self-absorbed do you think I am? Your people haven't just failed me. You have failed yourselves and your planet." Nyah stood abruptly. "Come with me."

"Where to?"

"I'll show you exactly why I have no time for your people anymore."

She gestured for Lena to stand. Lena did so uneasily.

"But the storm? Is it safe?"

"No, it's not *safe*," Nyah said, biting off the end of the word. She began striding toward the cave's front entrance. "But your education is necessary. The cyclone's shifted west now. And we're going to head east."

"But where?" Lena repeated and scrambled after her.

Nyah ignored the question. They reached outside and Lena was almost ripped from the ledge by the gale. Nyah quickly clamped a hand on her bicep and pulled her firmly against her torso. "Ready?"

"No." Lena's heart began to thump in a mix of fear and adrenaline.

Nyah said grimly, "Good answer."

And then they were airborne.

"Have you ever been to hell?" Lena remembered she'd been asked that question once. By a social worker, years ago, when she was a teenager. The question had stuck. As had her answer. "Don't be stupid. Hell isn't real."

She was wrong. So utterly wrong.

Lena yanked her shirt up at the collar over her mouth to stop from gagging. Her eyes were watering, and her hair and skin now reeked of acidic chemicals.

Baotou, Inner Mongolia, Nyah had called this place. It had been their fourth stop on what Lena was starting to think of as a tour of hell.

In the distance was a giant, crouching factory complex that spanned as far as the eye could see—a single Chinese, city-sized corporation swallowing the entire 180-degree horizon. Row upon row of cooling towers and discharge chimneys clawed at the bleak skies, belching out grey and white smoke, like some dystopian nightmare.

But that was nothing compared to what was spread out below them—a lake oozing with thick, black sludge.

"What is it?" Lena asked, barely moving her lips beneath her shirt.

"A tailings pond. It contains all sorts of toxic chemicals, acids, and radioactive elements. The price paid for the next phone or gadget upgrade. This used to be pristine farmland."

The smell scratched at her throat, making Lena gag. "I never buy any of that crap," she muttered.

"Well, that makes it all okay then," Nyah said dryly.

"I didn't do this," Lena said, desperate to get her to understand.

Nyah glanced at her as though she was missing some obvious point. Lena gritted her teeth in annoyance.

"I am showing you what matters to your world. What humanity values most."

"This isn't us. That's crap. This isn't what we value most."

"No?" The tone was faintly mocking. Without another word Lena was pulled tightly into Nyah's chest and catapulted skyward.

They touched down in the middle of a rundown city street lined with cardboard boxes. It smelled of sweat, dirt, cigarettes, and urine. She recognized slogans and names on the boxes. They were in America.

"Now we're at the epicenter," Nyah said, "although others might disagree."

"Epicenter of what?"

"There used to be a factory around here that had jobs for thousands before they were offshored. That simple act, a flourish of a pen on a piece of paper, ripped the heart out of the whole city."

Nyah's eyes scanned the streets, blinking against a fierce wind. "The workers who stayed failed to find new work and the economy died. Now a second generation has been born into poverty, never knowing a family member with a job. Some were born alcohol or drug addicted. Some sell their bodies for food or drugs. Gangs sprung up. You stand here for long enough, and you feel it. Waves of it. We're at the epicenter of the absence of hope. I find that it spreads from here like a spiderweb, not just from where we stand, into the surrounding streets, but from one generation to the next. This, for me, is the exact beating heart of human despair. I feel their worthlessness like a clammy hand pressing at my throat. No one here has hope. No one has dreams. They're all shells of what they once were, ghosts of what they could have been."

A chill wind whipped around, flipping up the cardboard flaps revealing that the boxes weren't empty. People *lived* here. Lena saw feet, like rows and rows of dirty matchsticks. She saw smaller feet, too tiny to belong to adults, in the boxes as well.

Lena rammed her fists in her pockets feeling the bleakness settle around her like a cloak, turning over Nyah's words. So many feet. So many broken dreams.

"So," Nyah said, "tell me again what your world values most?"

Lena couldn't look at her. "Not this," she muttered. "We don't want this."

"Really? And yet, here it is."

Lena bit her lip.

Nyah suddenly stiffened beside her.

"What is it?" Lena asked.

"A car just crashed a street away," she said, squinting, as though trying to work out exactly where. "Someone's...trapped. She's so afraid."

Lena wondered what Nyah would do. Didn't she say she was retired?

Nyah exhaled heavily, resignation crossing her features. "Well," she said dryly, "duty calls." She glanced at Lena. "I can't bring you along. It'd raise too many questions."

"I know. Go. I'll find you."

Lena skidded around the corner, keeping an eye skyward to see where Nyah was heading. When the guardian angled back toward the ground, Lena put her head down and sprinted. She emerged onto a street empty of cars but filling with onlookers. Fifty so far and counting. Nyah was nowhere in sight.

A driver had lost control on a bend and punched into a pillar just inside a building's parking garage entrance. Above the garage sat a multistory residential building. The demolished pillar clearly had been a support column as the cracks from where it once attached to the brickwork were spidering upwards into the apartment building. The whole structure was tearing itself apart before their eyes.

The wedged car now had the weight of a barely supported building starting to crush its roof. Beyond the cascading bricks and dust came high-pitched cries from the driver.

Lena shuddered at the frightening sounds and peered up. The building had several balconies and one, three floors up, was only hanging on by a single strut. Rubble was raining down now. A deafening crunch sounded as the whole structure shifted suddenly along the spreading crack, dropping a few inches.

The woman's screams were more desperate, buried somewhere deep inside the mess. Lena could only see the square taillights of the car now. Her brows knitted together. Where on earth was Nyah?

Dust rose, more bricks fell, and the crowd surrounding the area thickened. The building stuttered again, offering a low moan like a pained old man, and the shrieks from the car became more terrified. Suddenly the car lurched back a few feet toward the road, screeching as its roof scraped along the garage's ceiling that pinned it. Part of the brown trunk could now be seen.

Its movement was not enough to free it. Hundreds more bricks showered from the higher levels. A window creaked opened on the top floor. A shadow passed by it.

The driver's cries were much louder and the crowd began to shout assurances.

"Ambulance is on its way."

"Police called."

"Hang in there!"

"Don't move."

"Are you hurt?"

The car lurched again, its back doors now outside, and this time, through the debris, Nyah could be seen standing beyond it, almost obscured. Lena could see her arms outstretched. Her mouth was a line of grim concentration, her brows pulled into a fierce frown, as she propelled the car out of its prison with the sweep of one arm, while pushing back the weight of the half dozen floors above her with her other straining arm.

The crowd screamed its recognition.

"A GUARDIAN!"

"HOLY SHIT, LOOK WHO IT IS!"

"I NEED MY CAMERA."

"SHATTTTTERGIRL!"

Nyah's eyes snapped shut and she grimaced.

Lena stared at the incredible sight of one woman literally holding back the world from crushing her—not to mention a mangled car in front of her.

As the crowd grew louder, their thoughts, emotions, fear, and excitement mounting, literally closing in on her, Nyah's shut eyes tightened.

"BE QUIET!" Lena shouted. "You have to let her concentrate!"

They ignored her, and some began to press forward.

"Move back!" Lena called out again. "Look at the building! It's cracking in half!"

"Shuddup," one man hissed, holding out his battered phone. "And move over, you're blocking my shot."

"You wanna die trying to get that?" Lena glared at him. "Cos this building's coming down the moment she gets that car out. Look at it, it's barely holding together as it is. She's the only reason it's not rubble now."

Trembles and tremors were rocking the building on its foundation each time the car inched back toward the street. Lena's gaze flicked back to the open window a few levels up. A small girl's head popped up.

"Oh hell," Lena groaned. "No."

The child crawled over the window ledge, dropping onto the now drunkenly swinging, barely attached balcony. There she sat, uncertain what to do next, one small fat fist holding the strut of a thin rusty balcony rail.

The crowd saw her too, and began screaming and pointing.

"SHATTERGIRL! THERE'S A CHILD!"

Nyah's head whipped around toward the crowd in confusion, but there was no way she could see anyone above her from inside her crumbling tomb. Chunks of concrete suddenly rained down on her as her attention shifted, and her arm waved abruptly to deflect them away.

The car moved another foot, now two-thirds of the way out, its roof almost completely shredded. The strain of manipulating it while holding back the building seemed immense. Lena could see the extent of Nyah's effort in the snarl of her now-bared lips and the grimace on her face.

A dozen people had rushed over to the balcony, shouting to the girl, some holding out their arms. They were well inside the footprint of where the building would crash when it finally lost cohesion.

"GET BACK!" Lena shouted. "IT'S NOT SAFE!"

She ran over and tried pulling them back, grabbing fistfuls of shirts, jackets, blouses. A few retreated; most did not. The man filming on his phone turned to her. "Fuck off. This is my payday. It'll make all the news feeds."

SCREECH.

The car abruptly shot clear ten feet and safely out into the open. The entire building shuddered. It bounced the balcony with the child on it, which snapped its final strut.

The girl fell. The crowd screamed, and two men rushed toward her, arms outstretched. Lena shut her eyes, focused hard, and dropped all her mental barriers and repeated only one thought: *A girl is on the balcony out front, falling.*

The world went dark.

Lena opened her eyes, coughed, and sat up. A four-story building was now a grey, dusty pile of bricks and cement, wrought iron spikes from the formwork jabbing at the skies. A fire engine's siren wailed. A woman was crying. Lena turned toward her. Oh. The woman in the car. Some bystanders had wrenched the door open and were trying to calm her down. She had a bloodied face, and looked dazed and shaky, but otherwise unharmed.

"You okay, lady?"

She looked up into the eyes of the man she'd warned to stay back. He shifted his gaze back to his phone, giving it an annoyed shake, but it was a cracked mess. So much for his big scoop. She glanced behind him and saw everyone staring at her.

"What happened?"

"It collapsed on you," the man said. "We saw the guardian swoop up to get the kid so we ran back as the building came down. But you were just standing there with your eyes shut. Didn't even move. Then...BAM! You got blown backwards and now we got this. A huge motherfuckin' pile of bricks."

Lena swallowed, tasting grit. "Where's Ny... Shattergirl?"

He shrugged. "In that somewhere." He pointed to the rubble pile. "But they can't get killed can they? I mean guardians don't die? Right? I've never heard of it."

Lena scrambled to her feet, opening her mouth as panic coursed through her. "NYAH?" she shouted, earning confused looks. She focused and thought urgently: *Where the hell are you? You'd better not have gotten your ass killed.* She ran towards the rubble and began tossing rocks back.

"What in hell are you doing, woman?" the man called. "And who's Nigh-uh?"

"Don't just stand there!" Lena shouted back. "Dig! Ny... Shattergirl could be hurt." She glanced back and saw many in the crowd gaping in astonishment.

"Are you an idiot?" he hollered. "She's a *guardian*."

"But she's not invincible."

Members of the crowd looked at each other, then back at her, unconvinced.

"It's true!" she shouted. "They bleed too. Come on. We have to help, have to...shit!"

There was a roar as the mountain of rubble suddenly erupted with a writhing tornado of broken brick and debris. A dust-coated Shattergirl burst into the open before them, holding a small girl in her arms.

A woman cried and ran forward. "My baby! Oh lord, I didn't know! I didn't know she was inside. She was supposed to be with her daddy today." She flung her arms out, tears streaking down her face.

Nyah handed the girl to her and looked around the crowd. She paused on Lena, her eyes narrowing, scanning her dust-covered, torn clothing. If Lena didn't know better, she'd say she looked concerned. Their eyes locked for a moment, then Nyah's face became blank. She turned her back to Lena, scanning the debris. Professional mask duly welded on.

You're fine, right? Lena thought, staring hard at her back.

Nyah paused, turned to one side, looking at no one in particular, then gave a tiny nod.

Relief flooded Lena. *Meet me where you first landed?*

Nyah didn't respond this time, but Lena didn't need an acknowledgment. She backed out of the crowd, trying to stem her irritation as she saw people rush up to Nyah, waving paper, pens, and phones. She'd just risked her life, and all they wanted was a prized pound of flesh to claim.

"Spare me the fangirls," Nyah had growled to her the day they'd met. Lena felt a stab of sympathy for her now. It was obscene in a way. But this was hardly new for Nyah, and Lena knew she could handle herself. She glanced back at the crushing, suffocating press of fans and tried to imagine facing that every day for a hundred years. She couldn't.

"I love you, Shattergirl!" one excited woman's voice called. "Can I have a selfie?"

Lena paused in distaste, whipping her head around to see Nyah's reaction. They didn't know her at all.

At that moment, Nyah glanced up and their gazes caught for a beat. Lena shook her head slowly. *This is insane.* Nyah's eyes dropped, as she murmured something to the man closest to her, who was waving a pen in her face.

Lena darted away, zigzagging through the alleys, and, five minutes later, reached their landing point. She was only there a minute before Nyah slowly descended from the air, looking as regal as a goddess. And how the hell had she gotten all the dust off her? Had she looped the city at the speed of sound or something?

Lena focused on putting her mental barriers back up, building a wall between them.

"A pity," Nyah said, with a small smile as she touched the ground. "I was becoming accustomed to your voice in my mind. Especially all those sarcastic rejoinders you never share with the world."

Lena shot her a wry smile. "Well, I discovered early in life that the world doesn't appreciate my biting wit."

"Oh, I wouldn't say the whole world." Nyah's expression tightened and she glanced down at her side. She lifted her tunic and Lena gasped at the darkening patch across her ribs.

"You said you weren't hurt!" Lena said.

"I only cracked them. They'll heal soon. Probably an hour at most." She gritted her teeth, then gingerly slid her top back down.

"How did it happen?"

"I picked up the girl and turned to see the building about to land on your head, and you were in your own trance. I had to propel you out of the radius with everything I had—which would have knocked you out briefly. By then the building buried me and crushed my ribs. I used my powers to create a small bubble of resistance and waited for the shifting to stop. I heard you call."

"I'm glad you're okay," Lena said, suddenly feeling foolish. Maybe the man was right. Nyah was a guardian. Born to survive. Lena shifted her feet. "It was amazing, by the way," she admitted. "Seeing you at work. Sorry about all the clingy commons."

Nyah's eyebrow lifted in amusement. "Are you, Tracker Martin, actually admiring a guardian? What's the world coming to?"

Lena scowled, folding her arms. "I wouldn't call it 'admiring,' exactly."

Nyah's eyebrow lifted even higher.

"You know, you'll sprain it if you keep that up," Lena said pointing at her arching brow. "And just take the compliment will you?"

Nyah shrugged. "But it's what I do."

"I get that in theory, but seeing it for myself? It's something else again. You know?"

"I know." Nyah sighed. "And that is the problem. I'm too good at what I hate." She held out one arm and looked at Lena pointedly until she stepped closer. "Come on—I would prefer to not be here anymore. This place is too depressing to linger too long."

Before Lena could comment, Nyah torpedoed them off into the skies once more, a swallowed half grunt her only concession to her injury.

They cleared the city, traveling faster than they had before, and the longer they flew, the more withdrawn Nyah appeared.

"What's wrong?" Lena asked. "You saved that driver. Not to mention me. Shouldn't you be a little happier?"

"But I didn't save the old man being mugged two streets away. I didn't stop the teenager vandalizing some street signs as we speak. I didn't help the woman who just fell down a flight of steps and broke her hip. I prioritized the loudest pain of the one, but that doesn't mean I can't still hear the many."

"Oh." Lena couldn't even wrap her head around that. Her heart clenched at a thought. "Is our planet just a never-ending series of hellscapes for you? Is that how you see it?"

Nyah gave her an unfathomable look. "Actually I prioritize shades of hell too."

"That's… Christ, Nyah." She swallowed. "So can we go back to Socotra now? I mean are we over our hell tour?" She'd rather have asked if Nyah could drop her straight back to her apartment so she could crawl into a ball in bed and forget the past twenty-four hours. But her backpack was still in Nyah's cave, along with her passport and an extremely expensive, company-issue FacTrack.

Nyah gave her an appraising look. "Not yet. There's one last thing I want to show you. And, for the record, you haven't been to hell just yet."

Lena shuddered and shut her eyes.

They were sitting on the roof edge of a random tenement building in a downtown city. Lena hadn't asked which one. What was the point? It looked like just another boarded-up, rundown, black spot, like so many in the world. She could tell by the cars they were still in America, but not much else.

Nyah's customary confidence had dissipated. Her shoulders were slumped, and her eyes held none of her customary spark. Lena wondered what this place signified.

"Why are we here?" she asked lightly. She tried a joke. "What's this city done to you lately?"

"Look at the tallest buildings," Nyah said quietly. "Pick them all out for me. And then tell me what they all have in common."

Lena stared at the glass edifices on the horizon emblazoned with familiar logos. "They're all banks."

"Yes," Nyah said. "This is the god your world worships. This is what your kind deems most important. Banks, corporations, money. I have learnt that on this world you use people and love things. That is why we see broken humans, yet efficient strip mines. Shattered people with suffocated hopes, next to shiny, soulless towers of greed. On Aril wealth was never a goal. We embraced ideas. The better the ideas, the more standing you had. Here? It's the men and women in those buildings in thousand-dollar suits who are worshipped."

"So you're here to tell me our economic system is all wrong?" Lena looked at her in disbelief. The topic made her all kinds of uncomfortable.

"No," Nyah said, sounding tired. "That's not why we're here. It just occurred to me now while we were here anyway. I suppose I was delaying. But we're actually here for this." Her hand dropped uneasily to the building they were sitting on. "*This* is why. This is why I walked away from everything."

Lena took a closer look at where they were. The apartment building was worn out, with a rusty tangle of fire escapes and crumbling red brick. She counted. They were fifteen levels up.

"We're here because of Lucy. That's who I.... I saved a little girl from throwing herself off this very building," Nyah said, her voice bleaching of all life. "She was right here, sitting beside me, when I talked to her. She was only eight."

"Eight?" Lena gasped. "Why would she want to do that?"

Nyah's face became still. "She told me that her daddy did secret things to her from the time she was five. Things that hurt her and made her bleed." Her eyes filled with a dark anger. "And while he did these things to her, he told her that she was nothing. Not special. Not a thing anyone would ever want. He said that she was lucky he was there to bother with her. Lucy believed him with all her little heart. She had a beautiful soul, Lena. I could hear it. In her thoughts. She just wanted to be a good girl. And she believed to her core that she was dirty, unlovable, and broken."

Lena's eyes filled with tears and she squeezed them shut, wishing she couldn't hear the words, or the heartbreakingly empty way Nyah delivered them.

"I sat up here with her for three hours, telling her all the ways her life could be amazing if only she believed. I told her she wasn't broken, but beautiful. And she touched my skin, so like her own, and ran her hand down my face, as if daring to see the truth in it. And then she nodded. I made her believe." Nyah became unnaturally still, her eyes fixed on the smaller buildings below.

"That's good, right?" Lena whispered. She reached for Nyah's hand and gave it a squeeze. The other woman's fingers lay unresponsive under hers. Lena felt a tremble in them.

"Her father's dark thoughts were a blackness I could feel even from up here. Lucy's mother knew what was happening too, but she didn't want to lose him. I felt those fearful, selfish thoughts. She *knew* and she let that happen."

Nyah inhaled sharply and one hand curled into a fist, so tight her knuckles went white.

"I confronted him. Told him if he touched his daughter again he'd never walk straight, let alone sire another child. I felt his terror. I made a report to police and Child Protective Services. They agreed to investigate. Said they'd make very sure it was looked at, top priority, because I had asked personally." She shook her head. "When you're a guardian, people do what you tell them. Always. So I assumed…" She looked ill and then gazed at Lena helplessly. There were tears in her eyes.

"I was busy with a rockslide in Argentina after that… It took a few weeks to clear and get all the survivors out, so I didn't follow up immediately. Those officials had looked me in the eye and said they would make Lucy their *top* priority. I believed them, of course, because I was Shattergirl, damn it, a perfect, glorious superhero in the eyes of the commons." She gave a cynical, cold laugh. "And people always do what I say. By the stars, I was so arrogant."

"Did they? Help her?" A sense of dread curled into a ball in Lena's stomach.

Nyah looked away. "Three weeks passed. They were so busy. Nothing happened. Her father obviously thought I was long gone, and returned to his abusive ways. Lucy believed I'd abandoned her. I promised her it would get better and yet nothing changed." Nyah shook her head. "She's right, I did fail her. I did."

Her voice shook. "So she came up here again and did it quietly, all alone, so no one would stop her this time. Lucy left a note weighted down by an old brick, as cracked as she felt. The note said: 'Please tell Shattergirl I'm very sorry.' I still have the note, tear stains and all. I see her face at night. *Every* night. And I hear the memory of her voice whispering in my head that day we spoke. Do you know what her thoughts were? 'You're wrong, Shattergirl. I am nothing.'"

Lena stared in horror at the drop below. That poor little girl.

Nyah brusquely wiped away a tear.

It was a tragedy on every side. Worse than that. Lena's stomach was churning, and she felt cold, sick, and disgusted by everything. To think she had ever had the conceit of thinking her life was worse than a guardian's. This hell Nyah had gone through would have broken her for good if it had been her. She scrambled to her feet.

"Get me out of here." Her voice was raw and rough with unshed tears.

"You see now?" Nyah asked, rising slowly and holding out her hand. Shame colored her features.

"You couldn't have known." Nyah wasn't wrong in assuming her request would be honored. Lena had seen people do anything for a guardian. *Anything.* Her confidence hadn't been without basis. "It isn't your fault."

"Isn't it? I should have done something more to her father. He's in jail now, I made sure of it, after she died, but I wish…I wish many dark things."

"Then that would make you a killer. And you're not."

"Some days I think that's a shame."

"Nyah," Lena said softly.

Without another word, the guardian wrapped an arm around Lena, and hurled them both into the sky.

CHAPTER 10

WHEN THEY MADE A HARROWING, wind-swept landing back on Socotra, Lena pushed off against Nyah, and almost sprinted inside the cave, desperate for distance from the horrors she'd experienced, and, by proxy, the person who'd opened her eyes to them. She didn't get far, her burst of energy suddenly seeping from her. She dropped to her knees beside the fireplace, too shaky to walk, and unsure what to do next. How long had they even been gone? Half a day? Felt like a year.

"I'm sorry," Lena said, as the guardian's footsteps strode across the cave floor. "For everything you've gone through and the terrible crap you've had to live with."

"It wasn't my intention to make you so upset."

"Of course it was," Lena said wearily. "But you're right. You're right about our world and its fucked-up priorities. And you're right to be angry at what we forced on you. I don't blame you for running after what you've seen. I'd also hole up in some cave at the end of the world and toss anyone who came to recruit me into the Baltic Sea. Hope his ass drowned."

"Well," Nyah said with a long pause, "I didn't *exactly* drown that agent in the middle of the Baltic."

"But…" Lena frowned trying to recall their first conversation. "I thought…"

"There was a ship nearby," Nyah admitted.

Lena stared at her helplessly. "How do you live with this? These thoughts in your head, going around and around? I couldn't. It's inhuman expecting someone to cope with that for a day, let alone a hundred years."

"But I'm not human, remember." Nyah lowered herself down to sit beside her. She expertly relit the fire. "Which means no one cares what we go through. We're just expected to do our jobs without complaint. Every single day." There was no self-pity in her voice, just resignation.

"Fuck them all then," Lena said fiercely. "I mean it."

There was a pause. "So do you think an overdue can be just left to run?" Nyah asked. "Whatever happened to the legendary Silver—no guardian left untracked? No hesitation or doubt. Always gets her prey?"

"Fuck her too."

"You know what this means?"

Lena lifted her head and saw amusement in her eyes. "What?"

"You're not the awful person you think you are."

"You'd be wrong about that."

"Oh?"

"I'm pretty screwed up. There's a crap-load of things I've done that I'm not proud of. I'm ruthless at what I do. Hell, I'm little better than a machine." She swallowed. "But now I've seen...*that*. Now, I have...I have *doubts*," Lena said with a harsh whisper that felt wrenched from her.

"Doubts," Nyah repeated quietly. "So you do have compassion."

It would be so easy to accept that. Absolution from the most haunted and hunted guardian who'd ever lived. The words, surprisingly gentle, felt like a caress. It was undeserved. Lena couldn't accept them. Nyah didn't know the truth about her. If she did, absolution would be the last thing she'd offer.

"I need to get some rest," she said abruptly.

"Lena..."

"No."

"It might help to talk."

Lena didn't reply. She lay on her side, on her sleeping bag, facing the fire. The silence dragged on, her back taut, as she waited to see whether Nyah would press her.

Instead, there was a cautious "All right."

She closed her eyes, shutting out the superhero, and heard the shifting of grit on the cave floor and retreating, booted footsteps. The creak of the bed told her where Nyah had gone, and it allowed Lena to feel safe enough to risk opening her eyes again.

She stared into flickering flames that should have warmed her. Instead, a sickness spread though her that left her washed out and clammy. So much had been stirred up that she wasn't sure she could shove it back inside ever again.

Lena was so damned tired of her past. Reminders of it loved to sneak up on her, ambush her, and stick its claws deep into her. She closed her eyes tightly. No matter what Nyah thought, Lena was damned sure she didn't have much of any compassion left in her. Nor did she deserve any from others. Simple fact: some people were beyond help.

Hours later she woke to the sound of a howling wind just outside the cave. "It's back," she muttered softly. "Worse this time."

Nyah's cot creaked behind her. "Yes. I told you the storms around here take days to dissipate. So much ocean to power them."

Lena rolled over to look at her. "How long was I asleep?"

"Five hours."

"Did you get a nap too?"

"No."

"Don't you ever sleep?"

"Not much."

"Guardian metabolism? Like how you all heal super fast?"

"No. I just don't like the dreams that come with night."

Nyah's face was neutral, like she'd just said night skies are black. But her words hit Lena like a slap. She felt all the memories of their day flooding her, and she resented them. She didn't want to know the things she now knew.

She glanced around to distract herself. "We need more firewood."

"Yes, but not right now. It's not safe outside."

"Can't you just fly in a different direction like before and get some?"

"That storm is directly outside now. You'd be hauling me back to Tal in a body bag."

"Oh." Lena examined the fire, which had shrunk to half its size. "Are we rationing wood then?"

"Mm."

Lena shivered. "Okay."

Nyah sighed and stood, snatching up a blanket from her cot and walking it over to Lena. "I swear you're such a fragile species." She held out the woolen spread.

"Yeah. Pretty much pathetic on every level." Lena took the soft grey material with a grin.

"That was a fast capitulation." Nyah sounded amused. "Where did your defiant defense of your people evaporate to? I thought you were going to poke my eye out when I first declared you all unworthy of saving."

Lena gratefully wrapped the blanket around herself and patted the sleeping bag beside her. "Turns out someone explained our flaws in vivid detail. Thanks for that," she said, unable to keep the accusing edge out of her voice.

Nyah lowered herself to the ground next to her. "Would you have rather not been told?"

Lena wanted to lie. Badly. But there was something about Nyah that made her feel slimy whenever she did. "Probably," Lena admitted. "It's depressing knowing what you know. I feel shredded, inside and out. How did you get up each day for work knowing the voices of Earth's victims and assholes would be shoved in your head without permission?"

"How did your mother cope?"

Lena swallowed. "It's not the same thing." She huddled tighter under her blanket and picked at it with a finger and thumb. "All she had to deal with was me. She didn't go out much. You have the weight of a planet's expectations so you have to face a lot of people. Sooner or later you get an entire population's thoughts rammed into you."

"I've had a century to get used to it. And a century to know when to say 'enough.' But now you understand? There's not a pretty word or clever tactic you could ever use on me to change my plans on staying here."

Lena rubbed her eyes, as the memories of sitting on that terrible rooftop came back. How could she *not* understand? "I get it. I do."

If she'd expected a gleam in her eye at Lena running up the white flag, she would have been disappointed. Nyah merely nodded.

"Is there any *klava* left?"

Lena pointed to her backpack.

Nyah extracted her stash of coveted ground beans and prepared a mug. They watched in silence as the water boiled and she poured it.

"It's all that's left," Nyah said, glancing at her. Her gaze dropped and she studied the steaming brew for a moment, then passed her mug over to Lena. "Here. You look like you need it more than me."

Lena hesitated a second before taking it, recognizing the words as those she'd once offered to Nyah. She raised questioning eyes and was met with a steadfast gaze. Lena drew the mug to her lips and sipped.

It was pleasing and smooth, as always. And while she didn't get the high that guardians experienced, she appreciated it. "Thank you," she said, exhaling. "I mean it. Thanks."

Nyah didn't reply, leaving Lena to sip it in silence.

After a few minutes, Lena studied the drink and looked up. "How come you didn't know Talon Man was growing this stuff? Didn't your guardian buddies tell you?"

Nyah's expression darkened. "They're more colleagues than anything else. Photo-op partners at best. It doesn't exactly shock me they did not share this with me."

"Really?"

"When we are required to gather en masse for events, I turn up. I see them then. Those who were on my ship were in the sales, craft, or manual labor trades. We never had a lot in common."

"Oh," Lena said. "They aren't friends? Or even scientists?"

"No."

"So you not only lost your world, but anyone to talk about your interests with."

"I did."

"I must be a poor substitute for your scientist buddies."

Nyah snorted softly. "Actually, do you know what I miss most? A colleague would have a theory. Sometimes, just for the challenge, it would be deliberately ridiculous. We all took great delight in trying to prove it, despite it being outlandish. The intellectual thrust-and-parry was so involving and stimulating. It was…"

"Fun?"

Nyah's smile was slow and beautiful. "Satisfying."

"So now you're bored out of your brain, stuck with someone like me. You know, I'm just smart enough to see how that could be frustrating," Lena said with a self-deprecating grin.

"Intellectually stunted you may well be," Nyah teased with a haughty eyebrow lift, "but I never said I was bored. That was my point, Lena. For some reason I don't find you a poor substitute. If anything, I haven't felt this challenged in decades."

Lena's mouth fell open. "Bull."

"It is no lie. Why *are* you so interesting? I could have tossed you back in town dozens of times, but I haven't. Why is that? I don't understand."

"Because you can't read me," Lena suggested. "Mystery is always way more interesting."

"If that were true I'd find my fellow founders interesting too. I don't. They're tedious and baffling. So who are you, Lena Martin, that you should intrigue me? And a tracker no less?"

Lena rubbed her wrist cuff self-consciously. No one ever found her intriguing. Even Mrs. Finkel found her merely curious, like a puzzle to be solved. "I think you're just tired of hiding out here for so long without anyone to talk to," she suggested.

"Oh, that must be it," Nyah said sarcastically. "Anyone will do." She leaned back and her gaze slid languidly across her. "Tell me, what were you like as a girl?"

Lena shrugged. "Small and young."

Nyah waited.

Lena hesitated, wondering whether Nyah was trying to read her. She quickly ran through her favorite ice cream flavors, butterscotch brittle, lime, raspberry. Sometimes pineapple. But it was really hard to get pineapple. There was that one place in Hawaii that had...

"Oh, don't worry—I can't read your thoughts. Whatever mental gymnastics you do to keep me out are still working. Besides, I'd prefer to hear your thoughts voluntarily." She studied her intensely. "Were you sporty? No, that would have involved interacting with others in teams. So were you the watcher? Always on the outside looking in?"

Lena looked down. She hated remembering those days. No, she wasn't the damn watcher. She was too busy wanting to disappear into the ground. Her memories of those dark days were of drowning, not even wanting to get out of bed. Hating everything about herself was the only thing she excelled in.

Lena's eye fell to the last mug of *klava*, still held tightly in her hand, and a warmth at Nyah's generosity surged through her. The other woman knew she would never get to enjoy the drink ever again. Lena could not lie to her. So, for the first time in years, the truth tumbled out.

"We were poor and it showed," Lena said, fidgeting at the memory. "My mother was in too much pain to keep a job. I was barely at school. One principal sent a social worker around to check up on us. I still remember the tone of her voice. Asking over and over if I was fed, if Mom neglected me, how often I had to look after her. I was so humiliated, but it was way worse for Mom. She cried for a week. It made me furious at everything. I hated everyone. Although that wasn't new."

Lena fiddled with the blanket ends. "I was always the weird girl at school that everyone made fun of. I didn't fit in, I was awkward and broody and androgynous looking. By the time I was ten, I discovered climbing trees. Hiding in the branches. Spying on the world from up high. Away from it." *Safe.* "Trying not to get stuck at home with Mom and her sadness. One day I got the kid across the street to give me a haircut. A buzz cut. Well, you can guess how that went down. 'Freak' was the nicest name I got called after that."

Nyah's eyes narrowed. "And what did you say to those unevolved bullies?"

"I couldn't really disagree. I mean, hell, I looked in the mirror and there I was—this gangly, skinny, messed-up outsider, with sunken eyes and pronounced cheekbones and freaky hair and no interest in any of the things they were into. I also wore these crap hand-me-downs. So, you know, I couldn't argue. I just took it."

"I see."

"I'm sure on Aril being different was some fascinating new scientific thing to be studied. Here, the worst thing you could be at school was different. It's tribal, and I didn't fit in anywhere. I pretty much hated life and everything in it."

"Sounds bleak."

Lena's lips pressed together. "Not my best years."

"So what happened? You obviously survived. Prospered even. World's top tracker and all."

"I survived because one day something incredible happened." Lena's heart thudded as she recalled the moment. Like a light going on.

Nyah looked at her with interest. "Oh?"

"Those paparazzi photos. Of you with that beautiful woman. You, looking at her the way you did. The way you touched her face, it was obvious what you were to each other. So from that moment I didn't feel so alone. I mean, if one of your people—a founder even—could be like that, like me, maybe, just maybe I wasn't such a total freak. I know it sounds ridiculous now. It wasn't to me, not back then."

A shadow crossed Nyah's face. "Those photos were an invasion of my privacy," she said in a low voice. "They ruined *everything*."

"I know." Guilt needled her. "Your interview shredding that reporter? Don't worry, we got the message. But the photos still changed my life. I went to school the next day not caring what I got called. I didn't care because now I knew I mattered. Because…because there you were. Standing tall and unafraid, larger than life, not taking crap from anyone. So I thought, screw the bullies, I'll do the same. And that was when life started getting better."

There was a long silence. Nyah's scrutiny was like the edge of a razor blade. Lena wanted to squirm. Instead, she forced out a small laugh. "Ah, so I guess thanks are in order. For, you know… Saving teenage me. Even if you didn't know I existed. Thanks anyway."

"You really don't want to thank me."

"Why not?"

"Because I'd have let all the teenage Lenas in the world struggle rather than have those photos out there. I'd have gladly abandoned you all if it meant my life stayed as it was."

Lena blinked at the bluntness.

"This shocks you? I know it sounds selfish. It was. I was. But I just wanted my privacy and my chance at happiness. It wasn't a lot to ask. I was robbed of both in an instant. I will never forget my anger over what I lost that day."

"You mean *who* you lost," Lena said tentatively. "Your girlfriend. Right?"

Nyah stared at the fire grimly. "She never wanted to be in the public eye. She was a beautiful, creative, shy artist who valued her solitude. Her greatest love was being apart from everything, just immersed in her own world. I did everything I could to protect what we had. I went to great lengths to keep her hidden as she wished. But I'm me. It was inevitable it wouldn't stay a secret forever. And when the world's media landed on her doorstep, she couldn't cope. She loved me, but it wasn't enough. I wasn't worth her world being torn apart. I don't blame her. I blame them." Nyah retreated into her thoughts. The fire reflected in her brown irises.

"I'm so sorry. For you both."

"Now you see why the news feeds that made your teenage self so thrilled made me want to destroy every camera on the planet."

"Fair enough too," Lena said grimly. "Hell, if I'd known you back then, I'd have probably offered to help. I still could. Trust me, I know some pretty interesting people in crime and punishment. And I have a *really* creative mind."

Nyah looked at her in surprise.

"What?" Lena asked. "Come on. Two heads are better than one when it comes to a bit of vengeance planning. Did you get as far as figuring out the best method of torture for the asshole photographer?"

Nyah cleared her throat and mumbled something.

"What?"

"I said 'maybe.'"

Lena looked at her gleefully and rubbed her hands. "It's a start. Shame you have no booze here, because we could have an awesome fantasy revenge party. I already have a few thoughts to kick us off on how to make his life miserable. After all, you have mad skills just waiting to be used."

Nyah rose abruptly and walked to the far corner of her cave. She returned with a dusty crate. "I was saving it for a good cause."

Lena grinned at the half dozen bottles of wine in the crate and promptly emptied out the dregs of her klava into the fire.

"Good," she said firmly, thrusting her mug forward. "Let's get the party started."

Hours had passed, the exact number of which was still buried somewhere in Lena's booze-fogged brain. She was merrier than she could remember being in years, and Nyah definitely looked a lot more relaxed. Not to mention, supple, liquid, and smoking hot.

Lena tried not to focus on that, and, instead, cleared her throat and reviewed their list. "Okay," she said, as though reading the minutes of a meeting. She squinted at her notes and wondered why everything seemed to be written in fuzzy duplicate. "To recap our, um, thingy…" She frowned. "I've forgotten its name. Crap!"

"It's at the top of the page," Nyah said helpfully, tapping it. "You wanted to call it 'The Vengeance Manifesto.'"

"I did? Wow, that's a great name."

Nyah's eyes gleamed. "I concur. Continue."

"Right, so we agree that topping the list of best method for, ah, revengifying the diseased paparazzo turd who ruined your life, is to throw his car up onto his house. Right? Preferably by way of his pool. So drown it, then toss it."

"Apparently," Nyah agreed, taking another sip of wine. She looked vastly amused.

"I voted you do it with him in the car, so he'd be screaming like a little girl, but you said no." Lena pouted.

"Be more fun to watch his reaction as his car's threatening to roll back down and squash him, don't you think?" Nyah countered.

Lena snapped her fingers, or attempted to. "*That* is an excellent point. So…in conclusion…photographer on ground, drowned car on house." She ticked the item with gusto. "Okay, time for another shot. *Screw the paparazzi!*" Lena threw back some more wine, draining her mug then refilled it liberally. "*Screw life-ruining,* shreekopf *commons!*"

"I don't think 'wine shots' are an actual thing," Nyah observed, although she dutifully swallowed each time Lena did. Nyah peered into her mug and gave it a swirl. "You know, I think this was a good vintage once, but my taste buds stopped noticing about two bottles ago."

"Booze is like that," Lena said cheerfully. "Okay, so next item. We gotta mention the highly commend-ded-eds on the short list. My personal favorite is that we spread the word he has an alien disease only obtainable by fucking alien farm animals."

"Even though we brought no farm animals, alien or otherwise, with us," Nyah pointed out.

"Pfft," Lena said. "The world doesn't know that."

"Fairly sure it does," Nyah said, eyes sparkling. She waved at Lena's list. "But, by all means, continue."

"Then you killed my freaking awesome idea of photos of him in fluffy pink handcuffs dangling naked from a flag pole. His nasty ass on display to the world."

"It was a logistical issue," Nyah said. "Wouldn't he just slide down the pole?"

"Hmm. True." Lena's brow furrowed. "Hadn't thought of that." She chugged more wine. "I think your idea of dropping him off at a polar ice cap is kinda cool."

"No pun intended."

"Huh?"

"Never mind."

Was Nyah laughing? Lena squinted at her. Must be a trick of the light. "But there's no humiliation factor. Your problem is you're too freaking nice." She thumped Nyah earnestly on the back in solidarity. "And that is no good when planning evil payback."

"Good to know."

"Exactly! The punishment's gotta fit the crime. And that bastard stole your love life. *Oh my god*, why did he do that?" Lena asked, suddenly overcome by the enormity of the question and the attendant horrors done to this woman. "Humans are such assholes."

"Uh huh. How much have you had to drink now?"

"Just getting warmed up. Oh, hey, you're swaying!"

"I'm not the one swaying."

"Oh, then why…" Lena crashed to the ground, confused as to how she had even come to be standing. "What were you saying? Or were you thinking something loudly and I just read your lips?"

Nyah's mouth twitched. "If you must know I was thinking that this is the least enraged I've felt towards the paparazzi in years. So, thank you. This is surprisingly cathartic."

"But we haven't *done* anything yet!"

"The object is to enjoy the fantasy, not actually do it."

"Is it?" Lena couldn't remember. The early stages of this planning operation were lost in the mists of that rather delicious sauvignon or three. She did vaguely note that this was why she never drank. Ever. You lost control when you drank. You blurt things. Not good when you're in a top-secret profession.

"I don't date anyone," Lena suddenly announced solemnly. "Tried it. Hated it. The women all want me to open up and bare my soul, and I don't do that for anyone." Lena blinked. *Shit.* Blurting things out like *that*.

"You don't like trusting people," Nyah clarified. Her eyes seemed kind. Like she knew things about Lena without her having to explain.

"Yeah," she exhaled in relief.

"But you trust me," Nyah said. "You told me things you wouldn't have if you didn't trust me."

"You started it," Lena grumbled. "Being all honest and shit." She picked at her jeans with her thumbnail. "I'm not sure why I told you all that. It's not *me*. But you made me somehow. You're like a truth serum."

Nyah shook her head. "It's not me either," she admitted. "I'm not sure why I told you about my girlfriend. I've never told a soul. Why *did* I tell you?" She looked genuinely perplexed.

"People always tell me stuff," Lena admitted blearily. "It's a skill. You were right about me. I manipulate people. I'm the worst."

"No. You were honest, and I told you anyway. I can't figure you out."

"S'okay," Lena said emphatically. "Don't feel bad. I can't figure me out either. I've lost myself in all the lies I tell. Some days I wake up wondering who I am under all the mounds of *tagshart*."

"But not today."

"Nope. Today I'm the stone-cold, honest chick. Who's also kinda drunk. So for the record, I'm a lying, scheming, semi-literate hothead."

"And I'm a coward," Nyah said dryly.

"I didn't mean that," Lena said, suddenly teary at the thought Nyah might believe her earlier criticisms. She grasped her hand, *so soft*, willing the guardian to understand the depths of her powerful, admittedly booze-induced, regret. "It was crap. Shooting my mouth off. I was just angry when I said that."

"Because you wanted your friends to live, and have me warn them," Nyah said. "The scientists you spoke of?"

"They're not really my...I mean I barely know them. But they seemed worthy, you know? Not like me—hell, the world goes on turning with or without me in it. But they're so full of energy and excitement, talking about their research endi...epend...epidemic thingies and hope for science and the future. And it's not too often I meet people like that. Most people I find are pretty shitty as a whole."

"Isn't that my line?" Nyah's smirk was kind of lopsided. But then again so was Lena's head.

"Yeah," Lena gave her a sloppy smile and added almost cheerfully, "You hate us all as much I do. Maybe even more."

124

Nyah chuckled. "Do you think we'll ever reach a point where we don't dislike people so much?"

Lena gave that some intense thought. "Of course. It only takes meeting *one* amazing person. Right? Only one, and boom…it's all changed."

"Just one? How do you figure?"

Lena nodded. "White crow theory."

"White crow?"

"Yep. You only need to see one to prove they exist."

"Ah. That seems scientifically sound. So do you think you'll ever meet one?"

"Already have," Lena said and nudged Nyah pointedly in the ribs. "Not sure how you keep doing this to me. That's twice in my life you've given me a reason to stop hating the world." She lowered her voice to a stage whisper. "You're, like, a *really* bad influence."

Nyah seemed amused. "Well, it's apparently what I do."

"Yeah." Lena abruptly looked away. She stared at the fire, feeling morose. "Truth is, I think I may hate you for it. Like, part of me enjoyed hating everyone. It kept me warm being that smug about everyone. I liked knowing they're all cynical and fake. Fits my world view." She glanced at Nyah. "So can you stop being you? It's way better when I don't see white crows."

"What if I promise to do something cynical and fake every day to restore your lack of faith in humanity?" Nyah's eyes danced with mirth.

"*Please*, you couldn't even nudge me over a cliff even when you worked out I was a tracker. My faith in your inhumanity is a little thin." Lena gave her a withering look.

Nyah laughed then, a low, rich sound that was so unexpected and warm that Lena laughed with her.

"Wow!" Lena said, "I love your laugh. It's beautiful. But then you're totally beautiful."

Nyah rolled her eyes. "And you're seeing me through wine goggles." She paused and studied her. "You are like no one I've ever met. And I've lived for one hundred forty-one years. So that's high praise."

"Well, I'd say that's impressive, all right," Lena agreed. She smiled broadly as a brilliant thought occurred to her. "So if I kissed you right now, would that be a terrible idea?"

At Nyah's surprised look, Lena quickly added, "I mean it wouldn't have to mean anything. Just two lonely people stuck in the middle of a storm. Two people saying 'fuck everything.'"

"Two people taking comfort?" Nyah clarified.

"Guardians need comfort too," Lena said firmly. "More than lousy trackers. Maybe more than anyone else on our world. I know that now. I'm really sorry I never saw it before."

Lena leaned forward and pressed her lips against Nyah's. Her heart thundered in her chest, but she was too busy noticing how soft Nyah's lips were. And how, after a few, agonizingly long moments, Nyah kissed her back.

CHAPTER 11

Nyah woke at dawn, just as she always had from the moment she'd first come to this strange planet. Earth would probably never feel like home to her; she had only one home, and that was now pockmarked and dead. But after last night, she felt less dismay toward her adopted world. That was new.

An odd noise made her turn her head. She almost laughed as she spotted Lena snoring softly in her sleeping bag, where Nyah had inserted her last night when the other woman had been barely able to stay conscious. She would have an exceptionally sore head when she woke.

Nyah observed the tracker closely, making the most of the freedom to do so without her watchful eyes challenging her at every turn. Strong and fierce, this was a woman who had determination, fear, bravado, and wariness all wrestling furiously inside. She recognized these things all too well. Nyah's gaze slid to the muscled biceps, and then to Lena's hand, curled under her chin, clenched into a fist that occasionally tightened, twitched, and flexed.

Was Lena fighting her demons even in repose? Or was it the guardians she hunted in her sleep?

Rising, Nyah slipped on her uniform and boots, then padded out of the cave, pausing as she passed Lena. Beside her lay the wine-blotched list marked "The Vengeance Manifesto."

Nyah resumed her path, her smile broadening, as she recalled the events of the previous night. Honestly, Lena had been adorable in her own fiercely loyal way. Not that Nyah would ever admit that. But having someone so outraged on her behalf felt unexpectedly warming. It had been a long time since she'd had someone in her corner. She hadn't realized how long until last night.

For the first time in years, the memory of Isabella sending her away with a teary "I'm so sorry, Nyah" no longer made her insides clench with fury, hurt, and despair. Somehow, Lena had done that. Somewhere between four bottles of red and one not entirely surprising kiss, she had taken out the stinger that had poisoned Nyah for years. She'd been well used to its dull ache. Looked forward to it, even. Her righteous indignation and that dark, warm burn of bitterness had propelled her to the ends of the world, seeking escape from humanity and all she hated about it.

It had brought her here, to a place as close to home as she'd ever found on Earth. An escape that had given her mind peace from the thoughts of others. So, for that, she'd never regret her rage at losing Isabella. But now the worst of the burn was gone. And wasn't that a surprise?

Outside the cave, Nyah propelled herself easily into the skies.

Her feet touched down a few minutes later on the thin, sandy stretch encircling her favorite freshwater lake. It was inaccessible by land due to sheer cliffs on all sides, which, at their peaks, jagged up into the skies like shards of glass, giving her complete privacy. She stripped and waded into the still, aqua waters, allowing her body time to adapt to the chill.

The water felt incredible sliding across her skin, but for once it did not give her focus. Instead, two questions kept coming up: What had possessed Lena to kiss her? And what had possessed her to kiss her back?

Nyah ducked her head under the waters and re-emerged, sliding onto her back, floating. She supposed that lonely people in storms sometimes do things they regret. Or, a mischievous voice whispered at the back of her mind, things they don't regret at all.

Well, there was that.

Lena was beautiful. Others might not see her that way—those whose focus was on superficialities or the way women were "supposed" to look. They were blind. For Nyah, Lena's strength, determination, and sheer physicality were most impressive. She had been remarkable to watch on that first day, scaling a sheer rock wall that would have daunted most humans. And Lena's nimble mind, even though Nyah had picked apart all the lies, had been entertaining when it wasn't infuriating. Her eyes, though, were the thing. Shadowed, pained, wary, curious, and cautious. There were layers to her that had drawn Nyah deeper in and made her want to understand who Lena was.

Nyah closed her eyes as she drifted. She was really a sentimental old fool—in every sense. Still, it felt a relief to be around someone whose uncensored thoughts weren't thrust on her like vendors waving fruit at a market bazaar. But Lena's worth was far more than that. Having someone as emotionally guarded and selective as her look at Nyah with grudging admiration meant more than a planet's worth of adoring fans. Although her admiration was considerably less grudging when she was drunk, Nyah noted with amusement.

Flipping onto her stomach, she breaststroked easily back to shore and waded out of the water. She grabbed her pile of clothes, knelt before the lake, and began to wash them. As she worked efficiently, her hands a blur, Nyah smirked, wondering how enamored the people of Earth would be of their heroes if they saw them doing their laundry. There was nothing sexy about washing day.

Finished, she used her powers to mentally force every drop of water from the now clean garments. She dressed again, and glanced up, noting the position of the sun.

She'd do a quick unofficial patrol of the island to see how it had coped with the storm, especially the eco-camps the scientists favored. She would have done it anyway, but Lena's fears had made it a priority. After that, she'd see how her highly entertaining, vengeance-planning guest was faring.

Nyah froze when she realized how much she was looking forward to that. This was faintly ridiculous, getting sidetracked by someone who'd be gone by day's end.

Even a cute someone with vengeance manifestos and soft lips. She shook her head at herself, and shot off into the sky.

The eco-camps appeared to have missed most of the storm, and Nyah made sure to stay out of sight as she spied a team of scientists on Homhil Plateau going about their business. She'd already checked four other encampments, and aside from a pair of shredded tents and someone's torn flannel shirt winding halfway up a *Dracaena cinnabari*, it appeared she'd been right when she told Lena they hadn't needed her inserting herself inside a volatile cyclone. Being scientists, they'd probably been tracking the weather event for days.

Last thing to do before heading back was an ocean run. Nyah liked to keep an eye out for pirates who plagued the waters off Somalia and sometimes strayed too close for her liking. Myths about a sky demon who protected Socotra kept most of them clear of its shores, but some tested their luck from time to time.

The wind was picking up and starting to buffet her when she saw what appeared to be a fishing boat. However, the flash of weapons at the hips of sailors proved their only intended haul was science and tourist vessels. A small dinghy towed behind the stern was another sign. Poor fishermen rarely had backup plans. A tendril of fury curled through Nyah. She would put them out of business before they could choose their intended victims.

She shot upwards, turned, lined up her quarry, and torpedoed towards the boat, gathering as much speed as she could.

Her strike was silent. The creak of the mast shifting on its mountings was the first clue that alerted the crew to her attack. They rushed to the deck, looking around, shouting at each other, gesturing at the splintering mast. No one had yet looked up.

Nyah just needed a few more seconds to press home her advantage. She channeled her powers forward beyond her outstretched arms, like an invisible string between her and the mast. Her hands squeezed into tight fists as the mast abruptly shuddered and stuttered, and she focused on pushing it straight down. It smashed through its base and began to jackhammer itself into the deck below.

Cries of fear filled the boat and the crew ran about comically. Three were already unlashing the dinghy. One was hanging on to the mast as though he alone could prevent it moving.

From behind a barrel, a young deckhand, barely twenty, suddenly jumped out, eyes white and wide, as he spotted her and shouted to her in a foreign tongue. She didn't need to understand his words because his primal, fearful thoughts jagged across her brain like a knife: "I KILL YOU!" He pointed a rifle at her that seemed almost bigger than he was. He screamed to her, drawing all eyes on the boat, as he took aim.

Nyah roared in fury, a sound she made as grotesquely alien and frightening as she could. It shattered the still air. Fear and panic from the crew flooded Nyah's mind, but she'd been anticipating that.

The deckhand dropped his rifle in terror. There was a sharp crack. A piece of wood flew off the mast. Pain sliced through her, and she registered the connection between the two events a second later. She'd been shot.

The deck was now fully impaled by the mast which she'd pushed through the vessel like an apple corer. The remaining crew fled for the dinghy. With a detached gaze, Nyah watched the men scrambling for their lives, as the two ends of the vessel folded up, like groaning, wooden origami.

Suddenly Nyah realized she was going too fast. Her brain had wandered and her reflexes were shot to hell. Literally. She snapped herself around so she was feet first and, as the rapidly submerging, wobbling vessel came rushing up to greet her, she bounced heavily off it with an almighty, splashing THWACK, before rebounding back up into the skies.

Touch-and-go guardian style.

The impact shuddered up her body and jarred the wound at her side. Nyah bit back a cry and turned sharply for home. She waited until she was well out of sight of the pirates before she reached for her side.

It was wet.

She looked down to find red coating her fingers. *Oh.*

CHAPTER 12

LENA AWOKE WITH A DESERT-DRY mouth and a pounding head screaming blue bloody murder. Christ, she knew there was a reason she didn't drink. She glanced around. The cave was empty but the fire was now blazing merrily. She was in a sleeping bag that she had no memory of crawling into, and felt one notch above death. Give or take a notch.

Lena slid out of her bedding and rummaged about for her toothpaste, toothbrush, and a bottle of water. As she brushed, still barely awake, she absently thought of Nyah, and a jumble of strange, warm, and haphazard memories overwhelmed her.

They'd been drinking last night, toasting stupid vengeance schemes, and…things got blurry after that. Wait. Her eyes flew open.

Oh, shit, shit, shit.

She spat out her mouthful of toothpastey water and swore. She hadn't actually…because that would be *nuts*. Lena had…kissed…Nyah. As in Shattergirl. Her target. A guardian. The most standoffish, intimidating, and scary-smartest one of them all. And, not to forget, her childhood hero.

And Lena had just up and *kissed* her.

A hysterical laugh burbled up. "God no," Lena moaned. She panicked as she desperately tried to clear out the mental cobwebs. What on earth had happened next? Nyah had leaned back, giving her a half smile, and said something about Lena being tempting but not sober.

They were "both unsober," had been Lena's apparently brilliant retort. "Doesn't that that cancel things out or something?" she'd asked hopefully.

Nyah's look had been of genuine surprise. "I thought you knew. Few guardians are affected by alcohol. Oh, it's relaxing and pleasant for us, but the intoxicants don't affect us at all."

Lena groaned as she digested that memory. She'd been making a fool of herself all night. Nyah had been humoring her. This just didn't get more embarrassing.

Her face was hot when she rinsed, stashed her toothbrush, and slung a towel over one shoulder, pocketing her soap. Plucking her now-dry underwear off the rocks, Lena headed towards the back of the cave. She'd heard water trickling out there yesterday and was anxious to see if she could find its source and wash a layer of dust off her.

Lena passed the fissure she'd stopped at the previous day and this time kept going. Not far beyond that she discovered several small pools being filled by water running down the walls. It wasn't much, but it'd do the job.

She stepped out of her clothes, shivering in the cool air, and bathed as best she could in a body of water little bigger than a wading pool. It was refreshing at least, although her sore head protested the temperature shock.

She dried off quickly, feeling a lot fresher, and pulled on her clothes, trying with difficulty to forget her humiliation at throwing herself at Nyah.

Upon returning, she dropped her belongings beside her backpack, then headed for the cave entrance, wondering where Nyah had disappeared to so early. She was conflicted about how she felt about seeing her. On the one hand it was Nyah, whose company she had come to greatly enjoy. On the other hand, it was Nyah, before whom she had made a complete idiot of herself.

The searing orb of torturous red light that was the rising sun smacked her in the head. Lena shielded the rays with her hand. At least the skies had cleared, and she got her first good look at the damage the cyclone had wrought. As far as the eye could see were flattened or uprooted trees. The wind was still whipping about and she shivered, missing her scarf. She'd have to get a new one when she passed through town today on her way to the airport.

She sat. A distant flash in the sky caught her attention. *Nyah.* Drawing her knees up under her chin, she watched, rapt, as the blur passed behind the jagged peaks. The figure soared suddenly in an updraft and tumble-turned gracefully, mimicking a champion swimmer changing direction.

Lena stared pensively. In her entire life she had never done something so reckless as kiss this woman. Everything she'd ever done since becoming an adult had been about maintaining control. It was a simple rule she had followed all her life, and it had kept her safe. She couldn't believe her drunken idiot self had acted on her attraction. That was it—she was officially swearing off alcohol for life.

She nibbled on her lower lip. The more she thought about it, the more she realized Nyah had let Lena down gently last night. And now, too, this morning by making herself scarce.

With some effort, she forced the humiliation from her mind and moved to the edge of the outcrop for a better view. Nyah was exceptional to watch. Totally wasted out here, of course, hiding from life. However, Lena understood now. She rested her chin on her fist as she watched Nyah float for a moment, as though deciding her next direction.

It wasn't fair to ask any more of her. The woman had suffered and a part of her had died. It would be cruel to force her to go back to her old life. If anyone had earned retirement, it was Shattergirl.

Nyah changed direction, then darted off to the east. In the way super-speed flying tricks the eye, it looked briefly as though her entire body was stretched like a vivid paintbrush slash before she disappeared out of sight.

Mesmerizing.

She sat, watching where Nyah had been, long after she was gone. Lena was a lost cause. The sooner she was out of here the better. This, whatever this was, was not in her job description.

She stood, dusting down her pants, and went back inside the cave. She should pack. Lena had her answer on Nyah's whereabouts. The storm had cleared. The airport, presumably, had reopened, which meant she'd be out of here by tonight, winging her way back to civilization.

The thought didn't excite her as much as it would have even a day ago.

She sat on her sleeping bag, sliding her toiletries and clothes into her backpack, then rinsed out her mug and tucked that away too. Her eye fell to her notepad, and the scrawled "Vengeance Manifesto."

Lena stopped and read their increasingly outlandish theories. Alien farm animals? Even Nyah had been unable to hide her smile at that one.

A pang of regret struck her at leaving so soon, just when she was starting to see the real woman. Someone whose company she really enjoyed. Lena shook herself. She'd always known this job was as temporary as the rest. Yes, she'd score a goose egg on it, her first fail, but then four other top trackers had also struck out, so it wasn't too unexpected. Sometimes trackers didn't win. Just the way it went.

She paused. She'd never forget *this* talent, though. That had been a revelation, knowing she would miss Nyah. It was an unfamiliar sensation, bonding with someone, sharing things she never had with someone so opposite to her. Lena wasn't sure what it meant.

She stoked the fire, mulling over her uncertain, drifting thoughts. The wind picked up outside, and after a minute the rain started again.

Before long Lena could hear pings of it hitting the buckets Nyah had left out, and the sound of running water as it flowed in all the hidden channels in the cave system. It sounded lighter this time. So just regular rain then, not the end-of-times stuff again. Even so, she hoped Nyah didn't hang around up there too much longer.

There was a whoosh and thump outside. Speak of the Lycra-clad devil.

"Hey," she called out, turning. "I …" Her words died.

Nyah was clutching her side, blood oozing between her fingers. Her face was twisted into a grimace.

"What happened?" Fear lanced through Lena. Her heart sprung into her throat.

"I did a sweep to assess the damage from the storm when I saw a pirate boat," Nyah said. "They sometimes use the islands around here for cover or to attack the vessels near Somalia. From time to time I remind them Socotra's off limits when no one's around to see me."

Nyah peeled off her top, wrenching it over her head with a pained groan, dropping it to the floor, leaving her clad in a black sports bra.

Lena gasped at the size of the wound on her bloodied side. "Did a bullet do *that*?"

"Looks worse than it is. Grab the medi-kit." She pointed to a white box near her bookshelves. "It was just a lucky shot. The little *tagshart* dropped his rifle in a panic when he saw me coming. It went off when it hit the deck."

Lena quickly found the medi-kit and popped the lid. Nyah sat on her cot and waited while Lena shuffled through the contents.

Nyah peered at her. "There's a…"

"Pressure bandage. I know." Lena sat beside her. She pulled out the white package, putting it to one side. "Is the bullet out?"

"It was never in. It only nicked me. I saw it embed into the mast."

"Good. Don't move. I need to get sterilized first." She washed her hands in a sterile gel then dug up a bottle of saline solution. "Gonna sting," she warned, wrenching the lid off.

Nyah didn't flinch as Lena poured a liberal dash of liquid on the wound on both sides to clean it. She ripped open an antiseptic wipe to finish the job, then positioned the bandage. She was sticking it down neatly with extra tape to be sure it would stay secure when she felt eyes boring into her.

"What?" Lena asked, not looking up, her fingers still pressing hard, checking the gauze was holding.

"You've done this before," Nyah said, sounding curious. "Many times, I'd wager."

"Getting myself banged up is one of the perks of my job." She grabbed a nearby water bottle and rinsed the blood off her hands, then snapped the medi-kit closed. She gave it a kick, sliding it towards the back of the cave again, and turned to face Nyah. "Have you got a spare shirt or something? You need to be warm."

Nyah inclined her head towards a crate, and Lena strode over and popped its lid. A neat pile of black, identical supersuits greeted her. "Seriously? Nothing but black?" She dug deeper. "Not even any casual wear? Just your hero outfit?"

Nyah shrugged. "It's aerodynamic."

"I could loan you one of mine, but you're half a foot taller than me."

"It's fine. I prefer that."

Lena shook out a uniform top and eyed it critically. It was black, with thick, padded shoulders, and expertly stitched ribbing around the ribcage that gave Nyah a sleek, perfect, muscular silhouette. In so many ways, *this* was what the commons worshipped, a manufactured god.

Her fingers slid along the material, bumping over the ridges that created the impression of a hyper-being. Lena glanced at the woman before her. She had never seen her not encased in her sculpted armor. In her sports bra and leggings, she was still lean and angular, but less imposing. Smaller.

She met Nyah's gaze and could see in it trepidation. Wariness. About what? The lie of her enhanced suit? Did she wonder whether Lena thought less of her, knowing the truth of what lay underneath it?

Because Nyah still oozed a power that came from her alone. It was in the angle of her head and the shift of watchful, all-seeing eyes. Her body, stripped of this suit, seemed more leonine than stylized muscle. Lean cat, not mountain lion. Smaller, yes, but even more beautiful. Nyah had nothing to feel self-conscious about. Lena wished she could tell her that, but since the humiliation of their kiss, she knew it would sound like something else. So she held her tongue.

Lena's thumb bumped the rough thread of the silver Facility logo embedded above the uniform's left breast. She studied it. A tiny rocket inside an oval. As her fingers traced the insignia, Nyah's breath hitched.

Startled, Lena's head snapped up. Nyah's lips were pressed tightly, her eyes fixed on Lena's fingers. Lena quickly removed her hand from the logo, wondering if she'd committed some faux pas. She let her eyes trace the rest of the material, pondering this manipulation that turned Nyah into someone else. Something else. It held so many layers, meant so many things: armor, branding, camouflage, intimidation.

"Why do you still wear your uniform?" Lena asked, handing her the tunic. "Couldn't you have found something else aerodynamic since you left the Facility?"

"I've never *not* worn it." Nyah looked down at it in her hands. "We don't take our uniforms off except to clean them. I haven't even thought about wearing something else. We just don't."

Lena picked apart her words. The rare use of the word "we." This was more than a uniform. It was a symbol for a fellowship of survivors, as well as what she was still tethered by.

But why keep something branded by the hated organization she so desperately wished to flee? It made no sense.

"Why don't you give yourself permission?" Lena suggested. "To take it off and leave it off. How can you ever become Nyah while wearing Shattergirl's uniform?"

Nyah hesitated. "It's not that simple."

"No?" Lena sat beside her and gently said: "Maybe it's time to move on? You act like you've left the Facility and your hero self behind you, but every single day when you put that on, you're wearing your old life."

Nyah shot her a startled look. Her thumbs traced the sleek material, as though reviewing a life via cotton and thread. "It wasn't all bad," she said, eyes fixed on the insignia. "Not all the time."

"I know."

"I didn't hate everything. I didn't even hate everyone either." She gave Lena a hesitant look. "Not entirely."

"I figured."

"Just at the end. I have a limit. We all do. And Tal never saw that. Or he knew and it was inconvenient to admit."

"He's too busy power-tripping over being the boss."

"He's not my boss," Nyah said vehemently. "He was not then, and never will be. My. Boss. That ego-stuffed, orange *frakstit* NEVER deserved to be anyone's boss. He's not a leader. He doesn't grasp what it takes. I tried to talk to him decades ago about what we needed from him. He told me he had it all under control and virtually patted me on the head." Her eyes flashed darkly. "He's a conman out of his depth. He's *nothing* to me. His Facility is nothing to me."

Her raised voice echoed around the room. Abruptly Nyah tore at the top in sharp, furious jerks. Then she yanked off her leggings, shredding them with brute force. When she was done, she stood and held the tattered garments up to the light, staring at them, her breathing harsh and ragged. She bundled them into a tight ball, which she hurled with furious strength to the opposite end of the cave. "I'M NOT YOURS TO OWN!" she raged. Her fists bulged, and her chest rose and fell rapidly.

"You're free of him now. You're free of all of it," Lena said.

Nyah turned sharply, as though she'd forgotten Lena was there. She said nothing for a few moments, and then her shoulders sagged. Her head dropped. "That was a bit pointless," she muttered, as her fury seemed to ebb out of her. She returned to sit beside Lena and gave her a wry glance. "I *will* have to put a uniform back on to get new clothes at some point."

"True," Lena agreed. "But not today. And I bet that felt good." She gave her a nudge and a grin.

Nyah's lips curled at the edges. "Possibly."

Rising, Lena hauled her backpack onto her lap, rummaging through it. She pulled one of her checked shirts out and draped it over Nyah's shoulders. It was far too short and a bit western-tragic for the elegant woman, but Nyah didn't comment. She pulled it closer as Lena sat back down next to her.

Lena pointed at her bandage. "Does it hurt? With your super-metabolism that'll be healed soon, right?"

"I don't...feel any pain. Not much at all now, anyway."

There was a lightness in her eyes that Lena had never seen before. She stared, entranced.

"Really?" Lena realized they weren't talking about physical wounds anymore.

"Really," Nyah confirmed. And then she smiled, a blistering, disarming smile that had never graced any newsreel. Her smile gradually faded but the intensity remained. It was unsettling.

"What?" Lena asked, suddenly aware of their closeness.

Nyah's hand flashed out, forestalling Lena's plan to move, grabbing her forearm. "I just realized something."

"Huh?" Lena said cleverly.

"You're just as intriguing sober as you are drunk. I appreciate that."

"What?" Lena tensed.

"No one ever dares to kiss me." The smile widened, but it had a knowingness to it. "Of course, I have a somewhat intimidating reputation. It is well deserved."

"Yeah, well, I should probably never drink again. That's top of my to-do list." She felt her cheeks flaming.

"How can you to-do a negative?" Nyah teased. "And I didn't say I didn't like it. I know it took courage."

Lena stopped breathing. She'd liked it? As in...*liked* it? Her heart began thumping rapidly and suddenly she didn't know where to look. "Courage, yep," she said, awkwardly. "Or stupidity given it could have ended *really* badly." Bottom of the Baltic Sea badly.

"Oh that too." Nyah's eyes sparkled.

"Are you making fun of me?" Lena asked uncertainly.

"For once, no. But I do want to know one thing—why did you kiss me?"

"I told you. It was the wine. I get like that when I drink." Lena eyed her warily. Couldn't she just drop it?

"So you would kiss anyone in that condition?"

"No, of course not. Well, obviously I don't think you're ugly either." God, this was painful. She hunched down, beyond embarrassed.

"But if I recall, last night you thought I was beautiful." The corners of Nyah's lips were curling.

Of all the maddening…Lena's scowl turned darker. "*Definitely* just the wine."

"So now you don't think I'm beautiful? How fickle women are."

Lena shot her a faux glare. "What do you want me to say?" she asked in exasperation.

Nyah leaned back against the cave wall and watched her with a half-lidded gaze. "The truth. You see, I've reconsidered your offer from last night. So, tell me that you still think it's a good idea, two people seeking comfort. Say that you meant what you said and that's all it would be for you, nothing more, nothing less."

All lightness was gone and Nyah's face became still. Lena understood instantly. This had to be something guardians feared. Fans with their happily-ever-after picket-fence fantasies. Not everything had to be about love.

"I don't want anything else," Lena said with conviction.

Nyah offered a smile that was pure sin.

Lena's mouth went dry.

Slowly, so slowly, Nyah reached over and ran a finger down Lena's cheek then slid it across to her lips. She tapped Lena's lower lip with her thumb. "So soft," she murmured. "Do you want me, Lena?"

Her eyes were gently teasing, and Lena knew the source of her amusement. Didn't everyone want her?

"After all, you did like Shattergirl, didn't you?" Nyah suggested.

Lena paused. Such a loaded question. "Teenagers like a lot of things," she hedged. "But I know the truth about guardians. I've seen what's behind the curtain."

"Yes, you have. It's part of your appeal," Nyah said, her lips lowering to Lena's cheek and brushing against it.

The tiny hairs bent, and a shiver ran through her at the warmth of Nyah's mouth, arousal hitting her straight between the legs. Lena wished she had a modicum of her usual control. How did this woman keep reducing her protective walls to rubble?

"You know *all* our flaws, don't you?" Nyah continued softly, murmuring against her skin. "All our little secrets. You know we bruise and we break. You know all the ways we're self-destructive and imperfect and wrong."

"I also know all the ways you're right too," Lena whispered. "All the ways you keep going when it hurts. The pain you hide. Yes, I liked Shattergirl—who wouldn't? She's larger than life. She's like a goddess in that perfectly sculpted uniform."

Lena's fingers dropped to Nyah's bare ribs, no longer enhanced by her suit's impressive ribbing, and ran them along the bumps to make her point. Goosebumps rose against dark skin. "But the truth is, I prefer Nyah. You're more breathtaking than Shattergirl ever could be. You're *real*."

Lena knew she'd said exactly the right thing when Nyah's lips pressed into her cheek and a murmured "thank you" spilled out.

The drumming rain and wind picked up outside, and it merged with the sound of the blood in Lena's ears.

"But before you get too cocky," Lena said with a teasing smile, pulling back to look her in the eye, "there's something you don't know."

"Oh?" Nyah's eyes lit with curiosity.

"I've tracked down almost seventy of your people over the years," Lena said. "Many of them—men and women—have wanted to fuck over the great Silver for beating them...or just fuck her."

Nyah's breath hitched.

Lena lifted her fingers to her own shirt and began to slowly unbutton it. "I see it in their eyes," she added, sliding the cotton from her shoulders. "They want to possess me, to reclaim their power."

Nyah's deep brown eyes followed her every movement. Lena dropped the shirt on the ground. She pulled her tank top roughly over her chest and head, tossing it to one side. Waiting a few seconds, allowing Nyah's heated gaze to take her in, Lena reached for her white bra and teasingly dusted the cups.

Nyah's eyes darkened.

"They might have wanted me, but they can't have me. Not one single guardian gets to touch Silver." She unhooked her bra and flung it to the ground, her breasts bouncing free. Her nipples hardened when Nyah's gaze instantly slid across her skin like restless fingers. "No one gets to have me—except you."

Lena rose to her feet and unbuttoned her jeans. She pushed them to the ground and stepped out of the denim. Slipping her fingers into the waistband of her boy shorts, she eased them just over her hips and paused a beat. Nyah never blinked or so much as twitched as the material slipped lower and lower down Lena's muscular thighs.

"I see that this pleases you," Lena suggested, "you being the one to have me." She finally stepped out of her underwear.

Nyah didn't offer an agreement or a confession, but her nostrils flared. Her intense gaze flicked to Lena's hard stomach and thighs, and came to rest on the dark curls between. Nyah's eyes darted back up to Lena's. She shifted restlessly. "So what is it I don't know?" she asked hoarsely.

Lena gave her a cocky smile. "That I'm as desirable a prize to your kind as you are to mine."

Nyah hissed in a shaky breath. In less than a second she was off the bed and stepping inside Lena's space. Hands sliding up the back of Lena's head, she crushed their lips together.

Lena couldn't contain her moan. *Soft, so, so soft*, ran through her mind. Her hands roamed, ripping off the borrowed shirt that had been draped across Nyah's shoulders, then her black bra, which she flung across the cave. Finally, her hand was at Nyah's hip, before sliding over to her center, massaging her through the sleek material.

She never expected the heat she could feel nor Nyah's tortured groan. The guardian stilled Lena's hand, cupping it with her own, and took a step back. She pinned her with a heated gaze, and slid her own underwear down.

Magnificent was the only word that lay itself across Lena's mind at the first look at all of her. From clavicles to sculpted, six-pack stomach, and the dip down to glistening black curls, Nyah was stunning. Her toned skin was without blemish beyond the bandage that covered a wound that no longer seemed to trouble her.

Nyah's body was contoured in a way that made Lena desperate to run her hands over every inch of it, stroking the sweep of her ass and those powerful, long, lean legs.

Before she could, Nyah stopped her with a single, knowing look. She placed her hands on her hips, her chin and breasts proudly jutting out. Hips centered and tilted *just so*. Her eyes were dangerous, a sizzling, molten glare that threatened to immolate Lena.

It was Action Shattergirl. The exact pose on Lena's once treasured trading card. Nyah damned well knew it too, if her expression was anything to go by.

"Fuck," Lena hissed. "You just had to go and do *that*."

"I thought maybe there was still a little bit of teenage Lena left who might appreciate it, since adult Lena believes she's above all that." Nyah's eyes glittered.

"Nngh." Lena's muscle cohesion was in serious doubt as she drank in Nyah's pose, her desire rising, scorching along her nerve endings.

Nyah's amused gaze became silky, heated, and most definitely interested. This look was all Nyah, not Shattergirl; something just for Lena. The intimacy of it stole her breath.

Lena pounced, throwing her thighs around Nyah's narrow hips, arms driving past her shoulders and then slinging them around her neck, crushing their lips together. Their tongues brushed, sending arousal rocketing through her. Lena's naked, wet heat pressed against Nyah's stomach, and she groaned at the sensation.

The momentum had thrown Nyah off balance, but it took a moment for Lena's brain to realize they were floating not falling. They were hovering between ceiling and rock, heaven and earth, as they explored each other's mouths and bodies.

Lena kissed, bit, and stroked her way across Nyah's skin, mapping her small breasts and fat, delicious nipples, eliciting a growl when her teeth raked the sensitive flesh. She returned again and again to Nyah's elegant neck, strong jaw, and lips, fighting her own gasps and groans, aware of how much her desperation was on display. It was so revealing. She should be squirming with embarrassment at the way she was undulating against Nyah, her throat uttering sounds so raw and out of control.

But she couldn't stop.

Nyah looked at her with a gaze Lena had never seen before. Naked desire. Need. Nyah was hungry. Starving. For *her*. The look made Lena clench and tremble, and she no longer cared how she must look, desperately grinding into Nyah's body.

Nyah flipped Lena, draping herself weightlessly across her back, cocooning her mid-air, stroking her breasts from behind. Her mouth nuzzled her ear, whispering things into it that Lena couldn't quite make out. They might not even be in an Earth language. But spoken in that voice, all sultry and husky, Lena was fairly sure they were dirty.

It's been so long. The words appeared between them and, in the chaotic rubble of Lena's mind, she wondered whether it was Nyah's thoughts or her own. Or was it both?

Nyah's fingers started biting into her, telegraphing her growing need, and suddenly they were being propelled toward the ground. Lena's knees, and then stomach and breasts, gently impacted her sleeping bag, her back finally pressed down by the weight of six feet of guardian.

Lena gasped at the sensation, pushing up onto all fours. She had never allowed anyone to dominate her in bed. Never would she allow anyone to top her. She'd never before contemplated such a surrender, such a loss of control.

She allowed it now.

The searing heat registered first. Nyah's resting temperature was already much warmer than Lena's, but now the other woman's skin felt like a furnace against Lena's spine and shoulder blades. Goosebumps broke out on Lena's pale skin as Nyah danced her fingertips around Lena's ribs, from her sensitive breasts to her belly button. The taunting hand disappeared lower, slipping into Lena's soaked curls, and nested, tracing idle, light circles.

Her other hand kneaded her ass muscles, powerfully scraping up and down the outside of Lena's thigh. It was as intoxicating as the teasing. Nyah's lips latched onto where Lena's neck joined her shoulder and bit gently. Roaming fingers between Lena's legs grazed her aching clit then retreated.

"More," Lena said, before groaning in frustration. "Stop holding back. I won't break. I'm Silver, damn it. I beat your kind. Start treating me like it!"

Nyah's breathing became harsh and unsteady. Her muscled thighs slammed against the back of Lena's, her breasts and hips pushing hard into her back, flattening her onto the sleeping bag. A thrill skittered through Lena as she felt a taste of the power of the woman, and sensed that her restraint was starting to slip.

"You didn't beat me, though," a taunting voice next to her ear said.

Lena gasped at how sultry she sounded. Her words were dripping in sex.

"I don't even know who Silver is beyond some myth. But Lena Martin's someone worth knowing. Worth sharing my bed. She's so much more than a tracker."

Lena felt the impact of the words like a delicious kiss. Nyah slid her arm out from under Lena's stomach and moved it so it was between their pressed bodies. Her fingers slipped down Lena's back, over her ass, then lower, skidding through her drenched folds. Her fingertips curled up and nudged Lena's clit.

Flares of arousal burned. Nyah's clever fingers wiggled and teased all around the edge of Lena's need, offering themselves. She seized the invitation and ground her hips hard against them, gasping.

Nyah's thumb slid easily just inside her entrance. The amount of wetness made Lena's cheeks flame, but the hissed, gritty words laid against her ear, *"That's it, yes, Lena, use them, use me, come on, do it,"* pushed everything from her mind but arousal.

As Lena rocked and groaned, Nyah pressed her body harder and harder against her. A stream of alien words flowed across her back. Lena turned her head, gasping.

"Beautiful, Lena," she heard. "You're so beautiful." Nyah's words were thick with desire, murmuring all the things she would do to her. All the ways she would have her. All the ways she wanted to make her call out her name. Her fingers impaled Lena, two sliding in and out rapidly.

Lena forced her own hand under herself and frantically rubbed. Nyah ground into her again and again. Teasing, whispering encouragement. Lena was so damn close. So close. She gasped and rocked, over and over.

She came with a sharp, startled cry, and the white-hot blast of arousal was so encompassing that, in the space between heartbeats, she thought maybe she'd discovered a belief in a higher power. Nyah's fingers slipped out but continued to taunt her sensitive center, making Lena twitch with aftershocks. She'd never felt so taken. Sex without an emotional investment could be good, but this? Hell, this was on another level.

Suddenly she was flipped, flattened on her back, and Nyah's mouth was between her legs, lashing her, tasting her, feasting, her tongue flicking her faster than humanly possible.

"Oh," Lena cried out in surprise. "Fuck," she added when her body instantly arched, went taut, and she unexpectedly came again.

Nyah looked up at her from between Lena's legs, eyes alight with pleasure, and a smirk straying across her wet lips.

Oh. Lena exhaled. *Oh my god.* She dropped her head back to the ground with a soft thud, closing her eyes briefly, and then blinked up at the ceiling. What was there left to say after that?

The warmth of the fire threw a glow across her left side. Nyah's furnace of skin, muscle, and sinew shifted, and was pressed full-length beside her. Her finger trailed across Lena's bare hip and it sent fiery trails across her jangled nerve endings.

Lena blew a breath out to get hair out her eyes and caught sight of the naked need on the face of the woman who had thoroughly taken her.

Shattergirl…no, Nyah…wanted her. She studied her face again, seeing the familiar and unfamiliar in the desire. *Oh. Oh fuck.*

Both of them wanted her.

Lena's heart began to pound even faster.

Nyah didn't want to feel this involved.

Lena's proposition had been a simple one. Two lonely people taking what they needed. But the thesis of an enjoyable, uncomplicated, end-of-the-universe coupling had proved flawed. When they'd kissed, it had felt like a star exploding. Lena's touch, her gaze—dark, intrigued, and desperately wanting—had been unexpected. And all Nyah could think as she'd taken Lena and clung to her as she'd come apart so beautifully, so powerfully, was what it would feel like to be on the receiving end of all that focused, intense energy. To be possessed by her. No, she hadn't wanted to feel this involved, but then she hadn't understood anything until Lena Martin was writhing naked against her, issuing soft, desperate cries, and making Nyah feel alive again.

Arousal grew between her thighs as she watched Lena come down from her high. Her pale, glistening hip received Nyah's sweaty finger scribbles, while she watched her recover from her vulnerable moment. She did not have to wait long. Lena rolled her over and kissed her hard, slipping a thigh between hers. Nyah knew the moment Lena had found her wetness by the way her smile brightened. Feeling the proof of Nyah's arousal made her bold.

Lena kissed down her chest, muttering a string of sinful promises that included how Nyah would be lucky if she remembered either of her names by the time Lena was done with her.

With a wicked grin, she took Nyah's dark, plump, erect nipple in her mouth and sucked, sending flares of excitement through her. Nyah's arms fell weakly beside her, clenching and unclenching the slick fabric of the bedding as Lena's busy tongue worked.

She released her nipple with a slippery pop, and slithered down Nyah's body, pushing her thighs apart. Her blue eyes roamed as she closely examined her find. Nyah wondered what she thought, seeing her like this, flaws and all, bared, aroused, wanting. She was anything but the superhero posed on an action card now. Lena ran her fingers through Nyah's soaked dark curls, rubbing her crease with her thumb. Their eyes met and Nyah saw the answer in them.

Admiration. Desire. Pure delight.

She exhaled. Lena bent over her and whispered against her intimate flesh, "You look fucking delicious. Can't wait to taste you."

And then she feasted. Nyah's hands dropped to the top of her head, guiding and tugging as that relentless tongue went to work. Nyah could not stop the bucking of her thighs as Lena's mouth unerringly found where it needed to be.

Finally Lena focused on Nyah's most sensitive spot, an exotic band of three tiny ridges along her clit that emerged when aroused. It pulsed when rubbed against another Arilian female's genitals. Lena took her clit into her mouth and sucked powerfully hard, laving her ridges with her tongue.

"*Frakstit!*" Nyah gasped in shock, as the blast of electricity shooting through her nearly crippled her. "*Oh stars.*"

Not to be outdone, Lena used her teeth next, nudging one ridge at a time, bumping and scraping the slippery pink muscle until Nyah was almost sobbing. She arched and stiffened, bucked and whimpered. Actually *whimpered*.

Things became blurry after that.

"Wow," she dimly heard Lena say. "I could love your body for days."

"Oh," Nyah gasped. "I'm not sure I'd survive."

Lena continued to swirl her tongue around her clit, then nudged a finger inside her entrance, curling it up, stroking.

Nyah spasmed instantly, threw a hand across her clenched eyes, and came in waves. "Enough," she finally croaked and pushed weakly at Lena's forehead. "My god." She gasped for air. "You'd be popular with guardian women if they knew how good you were at that. Even Arilians don't perform *olma* that well."

"Any time," Lena purred, looking altogether too smug.

"A rather tempting offer."

Lena didn't reply, but grinned widely, before rolling onto her side and studying her in the light of the flames. Lena's hand fell between her own thighs, skidding across the gleam of wetness and dipping inside herself. As she did so, she devoured Nyah's naked form with appreciative eyes.

Nyah cocked an eyebrow. "It arouses you, seeing me in disarray?" she asked.

Lena smiled. "Of course. And it arouses you having the one tracker no guardian ever has."

"You think I care about such things?" Nyah asked in a sultry drawl. "Having what no one else can?" Her focus did not shift for a second from Lena's quickening fingers. She bent her own leg back, tilted her hips forward, exposing her folds better to Lena's heated gaze.

Lena's pupils darkened.

"Is that what you think?" Nyah repeated, her breath catching. "That I like having what they can't?"

"You do," Lena said knowingly. Her breath was tight and short. "It's in your eyes. You like that you're special. That I've chosen you."

Nyah smiled, although she'd never admit the truth of Lena's words. She leaned forward and pulled the other woman's hand from between her legs. "That's a poor substitute for what I can offer," she said.

"Oh?" Lena swallowed.

Nyah felt something clench deep inside herself. Something primal, alert, and ravenous. "I'll show you what disarray really means." Her voice was almost a growl.

Hours later, Lena awoke. A gloriously naked woman was sprawled beside her, breathing evenly. Lena peered at her, twisting, trying to gauge the condition of her wound in the low light.

"It's all healed," Nyah said, barely opening her eyes. "It healed hours ago, even before we finished. Don't worry about it." A flash of white teeth lit her face. "Thank you, by the way."

"For what?"

Nyah opened her eyes fully, and rolled to one side, resting her head on her hand. The very edges of her mouth twitched faintly.

"Oh, that? Well, this is the Island of Bliss, right?"

"Not just that. It's been a long time since I've even wanted to feel anything, Lena. For so long, 'feeling' only meant rage or pain. The idea of being with you—of feeling other things for once, no matter how fleeting—appealed to me."

"Ah," Lena said, unsure of how to respond. Saying "you're welcome" seemed a little stupid. "Can I ask something?" she said instead. "Did you read my mind earlier? I thought something about wanting to love your body for days. You replied to me, but I never said my original thought out loud."

Nyah was quiet for a moment. "Sometimes, when you're in moments of high emotion, I hear you. I don't mean to listen. Your talented tongue had me so distracted that I couldn't tell what was spoken and what was thought."

Lena frowned. "My mother said something similar once, that I never could entirely block her out when I was too emotional. So I worked hard to learn to control it. To control myself."

Nyah focus became sharp. She sat up, all signs of languidness gone. "These controls you use...can you tell me about them?"

"It's...hard. And personal."

"I know. You've seen my worst secret, Lena. It helped, you know. Having someone with me there for once." Her hand reached for Lena's and their fingers tangled. "Saying it out loud might help you, too."

Lena *had* seen Nyah's worst pain. Worse, maybe, than what Lena had been through. She glanced at their joined fingers. This was such uncharted territory for her. The look of hope in Nyah's gaze was her undoing.

"I was sixteen," she finally said, shutting her eyes. "I was reacting badly to my situation with my mother. I hated everything about my life. I hated how Mom's migraines made her too ill to function. And I hated her knowing my every thought. I mean, I couldn't have a single private thought. Not even one—if you know what I mean."

"Ah." There was a pause. "That would be awkward."

"It was. She knew before I did when I liked this girl in our church group. It was...not good. I would shout at Mom and demand my privacy, demand she stop reading me, as though it was that easy. She felt guilty all the time. It wasn't her fault, of course. But I made her feel like shit when I got so angry. So we worked on it. We found that if we practiced some meditation techniques, I could sometimes block the occasional stray thought. At first it was just one or two thoughts. Then I was able to do it for five minutes. Then ten. It needed us both working in tandem to be successful, though."

Lena stopped, hating herself for the memory that followed. For what she was about to admit. Opening her eyes, she saw only sympathy and encouragement in Nyah's gaze.

"Go on."

"Mom couldn't focus a lot of the time. She was in agony so it's not like she was in any fit state to concentrate." She remembered that depressing, drowning feeling that this would never end. That she would never be free. Her jaw worked.

"So what happened?" Nyah asked softly.

"I was a teenage girl going through her bratty, pissed phase, where I was all hormones and angst, and I didn't take her 'not todays' well. I demanded she do more. I told her…I-I told her she wasn't trying hard enough. She had to push through. No matter how much it hurt. I told her to do it for me."

Lena squeezed her eyes shut. "She loved me. So she did. She did this for me. She tried so hard. We practiced for hours, even when she was in agony. She'd get these nosebleeds from the exertion—it was a sign she was exhausted beyond all her reserves. And still—even then, even with her crying, I still begged her. I asked if she *really* wanted to stop when we were so close."

Lena's felt the shame wash through her. "God. She was in such an awful state. And I was a selfish little shit and I just wanted her out of my thoughts, so I guilted her into doing more than she ever should have. It became this fucked-up Catch 22. The more she suffered, the guiltier I felt, which made me more angry. And then Mom would feel my anger and feel bad she'd caused it, and work even harder. I was convinced she'd give up if I didn't push her. I thought we were so near the end. *Then* we could rest. She could rest."

Lena couldn't bear to look at Nyah's face. She had no doubt it would contain disgust at what she'd done to her own mother. She gave a cynical bark of laughter. "But then one day we did it. Complete blockage for a day. I was so happy. I didn't...I didn't notice what it cost her. I begged her to do it again the very next day, so I could make sure it wasn't a fluke. Then again and again. Finally, after a few weeks I could block her effortlessly. I was able to practice on my own, strengthening it. I do it now without even thinking, but back then it needed a lot of work. Still, I was so excited. I thought we were both free."

"So you solved it," Nyah said cautiously.

"Yes. We did. You know what my first thought was? 'I don't need my mother any more. I'm finally free of her.'" She forced back a sob trying to escape. Something inside Lena tore as she remembered the rest. "I didn't mean it. Not like that. For years I wondered if she heard that awful stray thought."

"I'm sure she knew what you meant."

"Maybe."

"But your mother also found the peace she sought? A cure to her curse?"

"Yes."

"How?"

The tension and wonder in Nyah's voice, her desperate need to know, made Lena drop her gaze. "A bullet to her brain. No one's thoughts ever bothered her again. She got her greatest wish. She looked so happy when they found her."

Nyah's pained gasp made Lena clench her eyes shut again. "So you see? I killed her," she mumbled. "She'd be alive today if I hadn't forced her to help me. I was so fucking selfish. I'm...not someone you'd want to know. But that's what happened. All of it. So...now you know."

Silence filled the air for a few minutes before Lena dared open her eyes. Nyah was looking at her with an unreadable look.

"Yes. Now I know." She dipped her head. "I'm sorry for your loss, Lena." Nyah's fingers gripped hers, and Lena trembled.

"I'm sorry the answer is not something you're looking for," Lena said shakily. "I'm sorry it can't help you. I can probably teach others how to block a scan, but not how to prevent a receiver like you from hearing people's thoughts."

Nyah regarded her, eyes gentle. "I suppose it's just as well I'm at the ends of the earth then. It doesn't matter that there's no cure for my curse. Few people get close enough to bother me these days. And if they do, Iblis does the trick."

Lena could detect the disappointment in her voice that she was trying to hide. "I'm sorry," she repeated. "I wish something good could come out of this."

"It's okay." Nyah slid a hesitant arm around Lena's shoulders. It was a gesture so intimate that Lena had to fight not to pull away. "I'm fine. And you seem to have done well."

"Oh, yep, I'm great," Lena said sarcastically. "A woman good at only one thing. Manipulating overdues to make them want to return."

"Lena, no one's worth is so limited."

"Mine is. I literally have no other skill. Hell, I even guilted my mother into doing exactly what I wanted. I was a prodigy in manipulation. Scary how brilliant I was at it. Look how well that turned out." She gave a hollow laugh.

"You were a teenager, Lena, who had no outside help, and you were terrified. You had no one to talk to, and even your own mind didn't feel a safe place to hide. So you found a solution and you clung to it desperately. But you were not the adult in this situation. Your mother was. You didn't control her. She chose to do what she did, every step of the way. That is *not* your fault. And if she were here, she would tell you that too."

Nyah tightened her arm around Lena, her fingers pressing into her biceps, seemingly willing her to believe her.

"Have you ever considered that you didn't drive her to suicide," Nyah continued, "but that she waited until you were strong enough to cope on your own before she did what she'd always planned? It's no coincidence that you found a solution, found your own power and independence, and only then she ended her life."

Lena stared at her, frozen in shock.

"And you're far more than a tracker. More than the angry, terrified teenager who had no hope back then. I see a clever, analytical thinker in a world full of drones. Unique. You have such strength, and you don't even know it. I upended your entire world view on guardians. I showed you things that would break a lesser person. I told you things that *did* break me. I expected you to run as far as you could after the first few stops of my hell tour. And then I was certain you'd walk away in disgust after hearing about how I failed Lucy. Instead…instead, you stayed by my side. You bore witness with me. It made a difference. It helped."

A small smile touched Nyah's lips. "And then you tried to make me feel better about everything I've gone through. The 'Vengeance Manifesto'—it wasn't entirely some silly joke to me. It was like being allowed to breathe again after years suffocating." Her smile widened. "You also kissed me, Lena."

Lena gave a low moan, still embarrassed that she'd made such a fool of herself, despite what had happened later.

"No," Nyah said, seeing her expression. "Stop that. It took such courage. Even if I could get intoxicated, I doubt I'd have worked up the bravery to kiss you first. Anyway, my point is you came from nothing, had every obstacle, had your privacy torn from you every day. And despite this, you set your mind on the task of improving things. Yes, you made mistakes. So did your mother. But you set yourself goal after goal. And, for good measure, you rose to the top—*worldwide*—of your chosen profession. Tell me again how that isn't impressive?"

Lena felt her cheeks flame and was lost for words. No one had ever understood. No one had ever acknowledged her fight. Her hands trembled so hard that she clenched them tight.

"I see you, Lena," Nyah said, and trailed a finger down her cheek to her jaw. "For who you are. When you go back home, and long after you forget all about the woman you shared something profound with during a storm at the end of the world, take this with you—I now know why I find you so intriguing."

Lena lifted her head to meet her gaze.

"White crows, Lena, are not as rare as you think."

CHAPTER 13

IN THE SPACE BETWEEN BREATHS, in the space between hurts, in the sliver of frozen nothingness Lena encountered whenever she gazed into the night sky, she felt lost and small. It's why she usually never spent much time looking up. Nyah, on the other hand, seemed languid and content as she stared up, mesmerized by the heavens. They were on the ledge outside the cave, leaning into each other, sharing body heat.

Lena wasn't sure why she hadn't left Socotra earlier in the day as she'd planned. But without discussing it, she'd stayed, and Nyah hadn't said a word.

Pulling her knees under her chin, Lena gazed at the inky blanket with its white flickers of light. Vast and pointless. Why were they here again? Why did Nyah say she had something important to show her? They sat in silence for a long time, Lena pulling Nyah's borrowed blanket closer around both their shoulders.

"What do you see up there?" Nyah asked.

Lena squinted. "Nothing."

Nyah's head tilted. "You must see something."

Emptiness. Doubt. Reminders of how small I am. "No. Nothing. What do you see?"

"Your stars are so different to mine, but in my mind's eye I see parts of the route plotted to PHGTX-459 from Aril. That's where I hope my people live now."

"Catchy name."

Nyah chuckled. "I have no doubt it's been renamed New Aril or something equally unimaginative by now."

"Your people were unimaginative?" Lena picked up on the admission in surprise.

"Let's just say as poets, artists, and writers my people made excellent scientists. It's one area where Earth's people evolved far beyond ours. Do you not stargaze at all?"

"No," Lena said. "It's hard in the city anyway. Too much ambient light and smog."

"There are some clearer nights," Nyah suggested. "Not even then?"

Lena shook her head. "I don't like the reminder of how hopeless it all is."

"Hopeless?"

"Life. Come on, you of all people must get what I mean. We're insignificant specks, and how we feel, how we live, it doesn't mean a thing. Whether I'm lonely or sad or can't even stand the thought of making friends because it's hard opening up to people...it's all pointless when you look up. The stars mock us and our worthless dreams."

Nyah's laugh was rich and beautiful, and did all sorts of interesting things to Lena's insides.

"Is that so? Well, see that star right there, hanging a bit below those two side by side? That's my own personal pointer to Aril. I see it and remember my old world before the end. Knowing what lies beyond these stars reminds me that my people live on. The stars don't mock us, Lena. Far from it. They give us what we need. Stars give us hope."

"You really believe that?"

"Some days it's harder than others. But here, on Socotra, with millions of stars all laid out like a map? It's easier to be reminded."

Lena tried her luck again, and peered up. "I still don't see anything."

"Then you're not looking hard enough."

"I don't understand," Lena said in frustration after a few minutes. "This. Or you."

"No one does. Well, maybe you understand me a little. More than most, actually."

Lena digested that, pride swelling at the admission. "It's pretty funny when you think about," she said. "Me, a semi-literate tracker, and you, a brilliant scientist from another world. We probably have less in common than any two people in the history of ever."

"That's true," Nyah agreed lazily.

"Yet look at us. How do we even share the same plane of existence? Let alone sit together staring at the same stars?"

"At any other time, maybe we wouldn't," Nyah said thoughtfully. "But I believe that sometimes in life someone's path intersects with the person they need most at any given moment. They walk together for a little while, sharing the road for as long or as short a time as they need each other."

Lena stared into the abyss. "I really like that idea."

"Mm. So do I."

Lena hesitated for a moment. "I'm really bad at living in the middle of nowhere," she said quietly. "I did it as a kid once for a few years. The stillness drove me nuts. I need to be in a city with full-on energy. I need the loudness to drown out my thoughts. Or at least to drown out the reminder that sometimes thoughts can be heard. I feel safer there, in the chaos."

"And Socotra has a lot of quiet," Nyah said.

"Yeah. It really does. More than anywhere I've ever been."

"I loathe the city," Nyah replied. "All those voices shouting in my brain."

"I'd hate it too if I were you."

They sat in silence for a few moments, digesting their unspoken understanding. Lena elbowed Nyah gently in the ribs and smiled. "Besides, we'd kill each other in a month if we ever tried to make a go of this."

"A month is probably generous," Nyah deadpanned. Then she turned and met Lena's gaze earnestly. "No matter what, I want you to know that it means something that you're here, right now. You matter. This wasn't nothing to me."

"I... Yeah?" Delight flooded her.

"We may be incongruous together, and this whole thing probably makes no sense at all. But, even so, it made a difference. At least to me."

The power of the statement was humbling. Lena closed her eyes so she could say what she had to without seeing those intense brown irises on her.

"Before I met you, I never let down my guard with anyone," she admitted. "When I was with someone, I never let them touch me. I just touched them. It always felt like they wanted something I couldn't give, like they were taking it from me whether I wanted them to or not. It's too close to what happened with...with how I grew up. With you, I never felt like that. I felt safe. I know us being together makes zero sense, I know there's no 'us', but I'm really glad we met. Even if I don't understand why any of this happened."

Nyah's fingers tangled with Lena's and squeezed them.

Lena sighed, opening her eyes. "I've also been thinking. When I get home, maybe I should try more with people. I haven't been making any effort. It's too complicated. Relationships, friendships, they're just…so freaking hard for me."

"And you're not ready to trust."

"No. Well, I haven't been. But I think maybe it's time I crawled out of my comfort zone. Took a chance or two."

"I know the feeling."

Lena looked at Nyah in surprise.

"I find myself feeling…well, guilty is too strong a word," Nyah said, "but you reminded me I am capable of much more than just hiding out, feeling bitter about what drove me here. I'm not sure if I have a duty to use my abilities and be some force for greatness or not. The idea is still intolerable to me, yet now I face the uncomfortable thought that stewing in a cave might not be the right decision either."

"Nyah," Lena said quietly, "there is a middle ground."

"Oh?"

"It's not important to live a great life, but it *is* important to live."

There was a long pause, and Nyah seemed to stop breathing. Finally she exhaled shakily.

"Now you see?" Nyah said softly. "*That's* why you're here, right now. Saying just the right thing." She gave Lena a fond look. "But I know you don't yet believe that anything you do in this world is important."

Lena blinked, startled.

"So don't overthink any of this," Nyah added with a smile. "In fact, don't think about it at all. Come on, let's make the most of these stars. There's enough hope in them for everyone. Even for Lena Martin."

Lena stared into the inkiness, in the space between nothingness where time sat still, and this time she searched.

CHAPTER 14

N<small>YAH'S GAZE SWEPT THE SMALL</small> clearing at Homhil. A road led off to one side, and a cluster of rangy trees with scaly bark and bright red flowers were all she could see on the other. She settled herself onto a large boulder and waited. Why Lena thought to ask her to meet here was a mystery. But the curious tracker had made an art form out of surprising her.

It had been the most unexpected few days of her life. From the moment the woman had rolled up over the edge of her cliff and come to a panting stop at her feet, Nyah had been intrigued.

She'd clocked her as a tracker almost immediately, of course. She'd also noticed the cocky human didn't have any thoughts about having been almost pulverized under Nyah's rock shower. Or any thoughts about anything at all. A common who could block her? That definitely required a second look.

Although Nyah would never tell her, Lena's mental block was far from perfect. She leaked emotions more often than she knew, usually the intense ones anyone would struggle to keep inside. She had heard her pain outside the cave in the middle of the storm when she'd broken down the first time. And she had felt her unmasked joy when she came undone in Nyah's arms.

She smiled and let the warmth of that memory fill her. She'd never expected to have another woman in her bed again after Isabella had left her. But something about Lena had been irresistible. She knew the exact moment something had shifted inside her. Nyah had clutched her bleeding side, striding into the cave, and one look at the concern and fear on Lena's face told her she truly cared what happened to her. There was no faking that reaction.

Nyah ran her hand over the textured surface of the granite, and admitted a truth. She always, always, did the safe thing. The logical thing.

The scientist thing. She always had. When it came to her personal life, she never did anything crazy or spontaneous or what felt good in the moment. Her hand warmed under the heat of the early morning sun on the rock.

Lena was so different. She was terrified of trust, but still she took huge risks. She had kissed her. Nyah had gone to bed that night and had spent hours listening to the gentle snores from the sleeping bag near the fire, thinking of all the ways she wasn't brave. All the times when logic won. Why did she always hold back? Even as a child she'd chosen the cleanest path through life, without ties or attachments that would get in the way of her work or duty.

Isabella had been the rare exception, not the rule.

Nyah's drought in the bedroom had stretched to more than a decade before Lena's arrival. And when Lena had kissed her sloppily and hopefully that first time, desire shining in her eyes, her plea so simple—a shared night without strings attached—her heart had begun hammering at the thought of what it might feel like to just say yes.

The next day Lena had blamed alcohol for their first kiss, but Nyah had seen the truth in her eyes. She probably would have done it anyway.

So brave.

Later, Nyah had taken her own leap of faith. She'd been right. Lena was irresistible. Not just for her brazenness and spark, but for her flaws too. So many of Lena's vulnerabilities she'd recognized in herself. A pair of cracked mirrors, side by side. Not quite showing the same reflection, but if you tilted your head just so, their broken souls had a similar shimmer. Nyah doubted anyone else could have done what Lena had, and so easily slid past her careful defenses. How had she done this? How had she made her question everything?

White crow, indeed.

She'd miss her. Nyah wasn't even shocked to admit that. She ran her hands down her thighs and looked around impatiently.

Lena had been a balm when Nyah needed it. She'd been wallowing too long. Lucy's death had shattered her into pieces. Maybe she never would entirely get over the little girl's tragic end. Some days were harder than others. But today was not one of those days. Today she could see the pieces clearly in her mind, catalogue them, and she felt confident in her ability to face the world again. All it had taken was a curious, definitely-not-Earth-standard tracker, with probing blue eyes and a cocky grin that hid so much pain.

Nyah wondered if Lena would ever come to see herself as she did. Maybe she'd even let her walls down a crack to trust others, as she had with Nyah. They'd already said their goodbyes at dawn, with Lena refusing an offer to be flown to the outskirts of the airport.

"Not going to the airport," Lena had said, voice teasing. "But meet me here at noon." She'd pointed to a spot on her FacTrack's map. Then she'd almost shyly kissed Nyah goodbye and given her a strained half hug. It was awkward enough for Nyah to lift her eyebrow.

"I've never done a goodbye before," was all Lena would say. "Well, not with someone I give a *tagshart* about."

"I'm honored," Nyah had replied, amused.

"You should be."

And that had been that. Lena had headed off, sliding over the edge of the cliff, and disappearing from sight.

A rumble in the distance made Nyah turn. A white SUV was making its way along the road toward her position. She could make out two figures inside, and rose, shielding her eyes to see who was coming.

The vehicle came to a dusty stop a few feet away, and Lena jumped out from the passenger seat, a ready grin on her face. She pushed her sunglasses to the top of her head, and Nyah could see excitement in her eyes. Her gaze drifted to the driver. A tall woman in jeans and a long, cotton shirt with rolled-up sleeves slid elegantly from the vehicle. She wore a scarf, and her complexion was so pale that her eyebrows were almost translucent.

Nyah was immediately wary, taking an involuntary step backwards. What on earth was Lena thinking? She knew Nyah didn't like meeting others. And she certainly didn't want to be near anyone who might recognize her and end her splendid isolation.

"Nyah!" Lena waved. "I'd like you to meet Dr. Anna Larsen. She's the head botanist of the scientific research team on Homhil Plateau. When I explained your situation, she was dying to meet you."

Nyah slowly faced Lena, her brows knitting together. "My *situation*?" she asked tightly.

"Yes," Lena said, hesitating at her expression. "I explained you're a retired botanist who misses hanging out with other botanists and talking shop."

"Trading war stories," Dr. Larsen inserted. "This is how I believe she put it. Although we have no wars, us botanists, beyond those fought out in science journals." She offered her hand. "Always an honor to meet another colleague in our field."

Nyah studied the hand in surprise. Commons never shook a guardian's hand, so she was caught off guard by the gesture. She realized her hesitation was rude. Belatedly, Nyah reached out, connected, feeling the roughness of skin clearly used to being buried in soil and taking samples.

Her gaze slid back over to Lena, arching an eyebrow. The woman was practically vibrating on the spot with excitement. A second later came a blast of Lena's emotional leakage. It was so powerful it rocked Nyah back on her heels. Okay, she was *really* excited to have done this for Nyah. Lena's walls went back up a split second later, and Nyah found herself missing her uncensored exuberance.

Dr. Larsen was still waiting for a reaction. *Oh.* "Good to meet you," Nyah said cautiously.

If the good doctor was offended by the less-than-effusive greeting, it didn't show, and nor did Nyah sense it. Instead, she felt a steady thread of curiosity, refinement, and intelligence. Larsen's mind was filled almost entirely with scientific questions.

"Tell me, Nyah, are you interested in endemism? For instance, that tree behind you—"

"*Boswellia ameero*," Nyah said. "Yes, it's native and unique to Socotra, and makes, or so I read, medium-quality chewing gum."

"On the contrary, Nyah, it makes *excellent* chewing gum if you have the right scientist in your team. I must introduce you to Dr. Muller next."

Next? When had a "next" been decided? She hadn't even agreed to a "first."

Dr. Larsen glanced to Lena and back. "Lena tells me you are in need of some work? I have a vacancy since one of my researchers had to rush home. It's most inconvenient. But I do need some spare hands to gather samples. Right now I need some more *Aloe squarrosa*, but it is so rare, so hard to reach in the mountains. Is that something you might be willing to help us with? Are you good with heights?"

Lena abruptly turned away, but not before Nyah caught the laugh she was trying to suppress as Dr. Larsen waited for her answer.

"It depends how high," Nyah said evenly. "But I'm not sure…"

"Good! Excellent! With my best researcher gone, I'm left with Dr. Lawrence, and he turns pale if he has to climb three feet. It's not his fault. We all have our gifts, don't you agree? Never mind, you'll meet him soon enough, along with the rest."

Nyah paused. Had she actually agreed to any of this?

Dr. Larsen finished her pitch. "I can't pay much, but I promise mediocre food, except for the excellent chewing gum, of course, and a convivial atmosphere of intelligent minds. That is all we need, yes?"

Nyah exhaled. Her gaze slid back to Lena, feeling nothing but gratitude, even as she nodded to Larsen. This might be exactly what she needed.

Lena smiled broadly and shouldered her backpack, tightening the straps, preparing to leave.

"Excellent," Dr. Larsen continued. "I can take you back to camp now, if that is acceptable? No time like the present, don't they say?"

"Yes. All right. But could you excuse me a moment, Doctor?"

The scientist turned and wandered off to study the *Boswellia ameero* with a fascination that was probably not merited. Although with botanists, who could say?

"Leaving so soon?" Nyah whispered in Lena's ear.

"It's time. This way it's easier for both of us. You may have noticed, I do a lousy farewell."

"I did notice. But this is unexpected." She glanced pointedly at Larsen.

"Yeah, well, I thought you two would hit it off."

"Lena," Nyah said sincerely, "thank you."

"Sure thing. Okay, since Dr. Larsen's going the other way back to her camp, I'm gonna head to town on foot where I can hitch a ride to the airport. You should go with her, get to know her first without the whole team being there."

Nyah didn't speak, overwhelmed by the opportunity and by Lena, who had done this for her. Lena, who was leaving. Right now.

Lena studied her anxiously. "You *are* happy, right? You're not mad with me? Cos I was really hoping you wouldn't toss me into the Baltic Sea for presuming."

"You need not unpack your life preserver," Nyah said dryly. "I can see Dr. Larsen is certainly enthusiastic about her work. I believe I'd enjoy working with her."

"So this is your excited-puppy face? You *are* glad, right? I mean, if you could have seen how you looked when you talked about missing science and not having colleagues to talk to."

Nyah gave Lena her best po-faced look and shot another glance at Dr. Larsen. She'd wandered off even further. Then she smiled at Lena, hiding nothing, and pulled her into a tight hug. "You won't believe me, of course, but for the record, you're impressive."

"Glad you think so," Lena said and blushed as Nyah's fingers stroked her cheek.

She studied Lena's reddening skin with amusement before stepping back. It was time. She felt a flash of regret and loss.

"Hey," Lena said brightly, "don't worry about Talon Man. I'll just say I couldn't find you. He'll have to suck it up without you for the ceremony."

"About that," Nyah said thoughtfully, "I think I may have a solution. There's someone you should look up."

"Oh?"

"Give me your FacTrack. I'll enter the details. Time's tight so call from the first place you can on the way home. Trust me."

"I do." Lena stared at her intently.

Nyah paused, then blinked. She wondered when the last time was Lena had said that to anyone—if ever. Nyah couldn't think how to respond to that.

Lena didn't seem to want a reply, and held out her FacTrack. "I think you had some info to enter?"

Nyah quickly tapped in the information and stepped back. "It's been fun, Lena Martin."

"That's one word for it. A better word is life changing. Or mind blowing."

"That's two words. Four, if you want to get technical."

"Hilarious." Lena rolled her eyes.

They shared a smile. Lena stepped back a few feet, lifted her hand, turned, and strode off, calling out a farewell to Dr. Larsen as she passed her. Nyah watched her go until the botanist pivoted and headed back towards her.

"You know," Dr. Larsen said conversationally, "if I'd known the Iblis demon was so interesting, I might have sought her out long ago."

"Iblis? I don't—"

"Please do not insult my considerable intelligence with a lie. It's fine. I also won't tell anyone you're Shattergirl. But if you want to join my team, it might be best if you updated your wardrobe, yes? I have a change of clothes in my car that might fit you before we get to camp. We are about the same build and height."

Nyah's eyes flitted uncertainly to Lena's silhouette, wondering just how much she had shared.

"She was the model of discretion," Dr. Larsen said, catching the look. "But I do pay attention to the news feeds every once in a while, unlike the rest of my team who probably wouldn't even be able to pick Talon Man out of a line-up. Besides, you are far too arresting to forget. Now come, I still need some *Aloe suarrosa* from *that* peak before dusk. And you are the best qualified for the job. This I know to be true." She winked.

Nyah gave her an amused glance and didn't disagree.

"I also suspect you have a few theories that might rock our world," Dr. Larsen continued, walking back to her car. "I would love to hear your thoughts."

The smile on Nyah's face couldn't have been dimmed by a nuclear winter.

CHAPTER 15

LENA WAS MET OFF THE plane from Socotra by the Facility's impassive man-mountain security guard who offered her a lift into the city. Not that she had any say in it. She eyed the back of his rock-like head.

"Do I want to know?" she asked. "Why I'm here?" she clarified.

He didn't reply, but when they stopped at lights, he turned and pointed to her FacTrack.

Lena got the hint and lifted her wrist, scrolling through her data uploads. Her eyes widened at the newest one. She turned to stare out the window as they pulled into the Grand Palace Complex, which was lined with thousands of queuing people.

Lena sat there, dazed, as security met her and held open her door. Receiving a backstage VIP pass to the most keenly awaited event in human history was shock enough. Seeing Talon Man's personal signature authorizing it was an even bigger one. Why he had bothered with her, one tracker among a hundred of them, was beyond her, but she wasn't going to protest. The Guardian Landfall Centenary Celebration was a once-in-a-lifetime event, regardless of how cynical she felt about the circus surrounding it.

She looked around the wings, as production managers and tech people rushed past, talking rapidly into earpieces, holding clipboards and body mics, wondering if any other trackers had been invited. Surely her boss? But Bruce Dutton was nowhere to be seen. She recognized no one.

The buzz was palpable, and not surprising given the event was broadcasting live on every news and web feed on the planet. She stepped back into the shadows as, one by one, the founders passed her and walked out on stage, waved, and took their seats in front of an enormous crowd. Large screens behind them played highlights of their heroic deeds. The ceremony was broadcast backstage on a sea of monitors.

When Shattergirl, in her sleek, trademark black uniform, sauntered past, Lena smirked, greatly pleased, then watched her join the rest of the guardians on stage.

After all fifty were on stage, a video package of their time on Earth began playing on the screens backed by a live orchestra. A 1,000-voice international children's choir was unveiled on the far side of the stage. It was over-produced to hell—as befitting the Hollywood mega-producer behind it—but it ticked every emotional box. And judging by the wild roars of delight and claps, the crowd was lapping it up.

Lena watched the monitors showing the highlights. Fires put out. Crashed trains righted. Landslides thwarted. She spotted Shattergirl in that footage, and her heart almost seized as the guardian barely escaped being buried alive herself.

Then came the speeches, which included stars and world leaders offering congratulations, and archival footage of the founders' first moments on Earth. Finally, the halftime entertainment started up and the guardians filed off stage for a break.

"Tracker Martin?"

She spun around at hearing a voice she'd recognize anywhere. She'd grown up with it, like pretty much everyone else. His voice was rich and authoritative—befitting the used-car salesman he'd once been. Now the guardians' leader stood before her like he was posing for a statue in his honor.

"Talon Man."

"We meet finally. The tracker who brought Shattergirl back into the fold. Quite an achievement. Her reputation for being difficult is well known."

Lena bristled at the implication.

He laughed. "You misunderstand. It was not an insult. She's independent, free-spirited, and smarter than all the other founders put together," he said genially. "Even I'd never argue otherwise. Of course, she'd have her own way of doing things. Like turning up at the last minute for the biggest ceremony in a century."

He smiled broadly but Lena could smell the *tagshart*.

Talon Man leaned closer, his voice dropping to a low whisper. "But can you just tell me one thing?"

"What?"

"Is she happy, wherever she is? Because I know Eloise Pittman by now. We all do, given we've seen so much of her over the years ever since Nyah first hired her as an impersonator. She gave you Eloise's details then? Told you she's her best Shattergirl double?"

Shocked by his accuracy, Lena didn't reply. To hell she'd admit that.

Talon Man continued, "If you've hired Eloise, that means you were successful in finding Nyah. So, well done, my dear, on that much at least. A shame you couldn't drag her here in person, of course."

Lena gritted her teeth.

"We're not stupid, Tracker Martin. We *do* know our own people. Don't make me ask Eloise for a flying demonstration to prove what you and I both know. So tell me, *is* Nyah happy now?"

Crap. He had her there. Lena gave a curt nod. "Yes. And she'd like to be left in peace."

Talon Man pursed his lips and nodded. "I see. Well, I suppose we'll have to make do without her. Perhaps we'll keep Eloise on the books for any future events. These days Nyah's more trouble to us than she's worth anyway."

Lena shot him a venomous look.

Talon Man's bushy eyebrow hiked in response. "Interesting. Very interesting," he said, assessing her, looking her up and down in a way that was borderline insulting. "Nyah doesn't usually play well with others. Not with the founders and especially not *tagshart* trackers. Those would be her words, not mine, of course. Here, we highly value the work our hard-working trackers do for us."

Lena said nothing. She wasn't entirely sure what he was looking for, but she wasn't about to provide it.

"All right," he finally said. "I'll leave her be and send no one else after her. However that's not the reason I wanted to talk to you."

Lena blinked. She couldn't actually imagine anything she did being of interest to Talon Man.

"You recall when we hired you? You'd been jobless. Homeless. You had a bit of an attitude. We didn't have to give you a job. No one else wanted you. And with high school scores like yours, frankly you were a joke. Not to mention you were a mess."

Steadily eyeing him, Lena folded her arms. She pushed her anger down and waited for him to get to a point.

"We felt sorry for you—but we don't hire on the basis of pity. It was only Mind Merge's glowing recommendation that got you through to the second stage."

"Mind Merge? I've never even met him."

"Well, he knows you. He's been aware of your progress your whole life. How do you think you got an offer to interview with us in the first place?"

"Why would he do that for a stranger?"

"Except he's not a stranger, at least not to one of your relatives. Your late grandmother, on your mother's side, I believe? He never could keep his tights on."

Lena had to force herself not to reel at the implication.

"If you recall, a DNA sample was taken at your medical on the day of your interview," Talon Man continued. "It confirmed what Mind Merge told us—you are a third-generation guardian. That's why you got hired. You're one of us. Where do you think you got that impressive silver tongue from? Certainly not from the common side of your uninspiring gene pool." He laughed.

Shock coursed through Lena, and her ears began to buzz. Dropping her hands to her thighs, she leaned forward, breathing deeply. She'd spent her whole life pitted against guardians. Tracking them. Hating them as pathetic whiners. And now *she* was part guardian? *A third-gen!* God, she used to mock the third-gens as entitled, arrogant wastes of space. Her stomach churned. And that wasn't even the worst of it. Her only skill that made her valuable, the only thing that was special about her, might be just some inherited power? She sucked in a ragged breath, desperate for oxygen to clear her head, as another thought hit her.

Had Nyah known?

The guardian's cryptic statement came back to her from when she'd told her about her mother's mental ability: *Who was it?*

Fuck. She'd known. Of course she had. She was a goddamn scientist, and had put it together in seconds. It was Lena who was the stupid *shreekopf* who'd never figured out how such an alien thing as mind-reading had suddenly entered her family's genetic makeup. It was so obvious now she thought of it.

Talon Man was watching her reaction, distaste warring with amusement on his rugged features. "A bit of a shock then? Well, you can't choose family. But I'll cut to the chase for you. You owe us for the opportunity that no one else would give you."

Shooting bolt upright, squaring her back, Lena eyed him coldly. "You could have damn well told me. And in case you're blind, I haven't let you down," she said, words shaking as she spat them out. "I'm your top tracker in the world right now."

"Oh I know, I know. You've done very well for yourself despite your... shortcomings earlier in life. But you need to know that while we protect our own, it cuts both ways. We also expect you to protect us."

"From what?"

"From whatever tall tales Nyah has likely told you about what it's like being a guardian. I'd hate for you to suddenly decide to share her theories and grievances. Spread lies. Because it's just one person's perspective, and it's a twisted one at that. She's bitter for reasons that have nothing to do with being a guardian. Let's just say she's had a difficult transition on Earth."

Lena gaped at him stupidly. Of all the asshole things to say about her.

He gave her an oily smile as he studied her stupefied expression. "Oh that's right, your limited schooling again. I'm sorry if I'm not making myself clear enough for you. I'll break it down for you very simply. Clause 47.2b of your Non-Disclosure Agreement that you signed when you joined us prevents you from writing or speaking to the media or the public about anything that could cause damage to guardians or impugn the Facility in any way. That means, in layman's terms, you keep your big trap shut. Got it?"

Lena peered at him. "No. Actually you've lost me. What tales can I tell? What are you even talking about? You guys are guardians, right? Heroes! There *is* nothing damaging to say about you. So why would I ever say otherwise? I really don't get it."

Talon Man tilted his head as he examined her closely. It was a gesture so achingly familiar. Nyah would do that too when she wanted to make sense of something.

Finally, the guardian leader smiled again, and it was a smile so patronizing that she had to swallow a nasty insult.

"Well, well, how convenient for us." His shoulders relaxed and he took a step back. "You really aren't at much of a risk for spraining any brain cells are you? Must be your grandmother's side. Your school marks truly didn't lie. Did they, my dear?"

"What the hell?" Lena said indignantly. "Did you just insult my nan?"

"If you have to ask," he murmured, his eyes amused. His insincere expression shifted to placating. "Sorry, I had to ask, you understand. I needed to know that you're loyal. That we can rely on you," he said, patting her arm. Lena fought the urge to wrench it out of his reach. She'd give it an extra wash later.

"Rely on me? I still don't get it." She gave him a perplexed look.

"Which is profoundly gratifying." The music began, signaling that the second half of the ceremony was about to begin. "Ah, my cue." He studied her for a moment longer, snorted, and shook his head, suppressing laughter as he headed for the stage.

Lena watched him go. The moment his back was turned, she allowed an unamused smile. The arrogant were always the easiest to manipulate. You simply fed them the narrative that most closely matched what they already thought of you. He assumed she was a simpleton. Now he was convinced she was with every fiber of his being. You had to love the universe's sense of humor. Her manipulation of the guardian who'd hired and trained her to manipulate guardians. Allowing Talon Man to believe he'd won his little game was the safest place to leave him. Of course, punching that smug smile off his plastic face would have been another good place.

She turned to leave when a shadow fell over her. The Facility's enormous security guard—and occasional driver, apparently—stared down at her.

"What?" she asked waspishly.

"You are like her."

It was the first time she'd ever heard him speak, and his voice was so low and deep it felt as though the ground beneath her feet was rumbling. "Who?"

"Nyah."

"A good thing," she snapped.

"A very good thing," he agreed. "Despite what Tal said, the other founders appreciate Nyah and want her to be content. Were you honest when you told him that she's happy now?"

"Yeah. She's with her people again. A team of botanists."

His face split into a wide smile. "Well, I am most glad to hear this. She deserved much more than she received in her life here, especially being who she was."

Lena peered at him uncertainly. "What do you mean?"

The giant guardian studied her in confusion. "Do you truly not know who she is to us? Did she not tell you?"

"A scientist," Lena said, suddenly filled with doubt. "Botanist?"

"Nyah was a botanist, yes. She was also Aril's chief scientist."

"Oh. That's pretty high up, right?"

"Tracker Martin, Nyah was our *chief scientist*—on a *science planet*. She was our world's leader. This was why she was on the last ship that escaped our world. She wouldn't abandon her duty or her home until every other citizen was safe. All the other scientists had long left. The guardians on Earth all admire her a great deal, but we are not like her. We are not her peers, and we did not truly understand her. But we did understand the sacrifices she made for our safety."

"You let your world's *president* be replaced by a used-car salesman?" Outrage coursed through Lena. It was one thing believing Nyah was the smartest guardian among the founders who'd been somehow overlooked. But it was appalling hearing she was already their leader and had been tossed aside like some shameful secret.

"It was her decision to hide her true identity. She knew she would not be accepted by your people back then. We all felt the hostility and suspicion our arrival caused. She needed to overcome it rapidly, so she allowed Tal to assume her position. She had hoped he would be better at it than he has been."

Lena's voice rose an octave. "She could have changed Earth's history if she'd announced she was your leader. Can you imagine? A woman, not white or straight, in the 1900s showing the world what was possible?"

"Or it would have signed our death warrants. The times were stifling and hostile to one such as her. She did what she had to. She protected us all that day. She was a true leader."

"That must have been fun for her." Lena scowled.

"It is a sadness to us that she was the only one among our kind who immediately despised the job the humans gave us. She did it for a century, even so. Could anyone else have done this? I don't think so." He shook his massive head. "So I hope you will do us a favor?"

"What is it?"

"When you see her again, tell her she is the best of us. We're sorry she felt she had to leave us. But we understand. All of us just want her to be happy, wherever she is."

"I'm not sure I will see her again."

He tilted his head. "Then you are fortunate to have shared even a little time with her. She is remarkable."

The music on the stage changed and the guardian pivoted to face the entrance to it. "My turn."

"Wait! You're a founder?" She looked at him in confusion. She knew all fifty and he was not...

His body fluttered and shimmered, and suddenly the tall, broad-shouldered Volcano Man appeared.

"I like my anonymity," he explained, before pausing, as though remembering something. "By the way, can you remind Eloise to stop smiling or people will become suspicious. Shattergirl doesn't smile. She has never smiled even once since I've known her."

He gave her a sad look at that thought, and then nodded, heading for the stage. A roar of applause greeted him. Lena turned over his words. It was not true. Not anymore. Shattergirl *does* smile, Lena wanted to tell him.

She just needs a reason to.

CHAPTER 16

Lena knocked on her neighbor's door, leaning heavily against the frame, still jet-lagged and feeling less than sociable after too much interaction with her fellow man at the Guardian Ceremony the previous night.

Mrs. Finkel opened it. She smiled warmly as she took Lena's measure, peering at her over her spectacles, her gaze dropping to her arm, which now bore a distinctive Beast Lord scar, and then back to Lena's face. Her greying eyebrows lifted.

"Hey," Lena said tiredly.

"Lena, dear, welcome back. I have your mail for you. All bills, unfortunately. I'll grab it in a minute. Do you want a coffee first?"

"No thanks. I'm here to… I have to ask you something."

"Yes? What is it?"

"Can you, um, come with me for a sec?"

Mrs. Finkel looked intrigued as she nodded and followed Lena back to her apartment across the hall. Lena closed the door firmly, and gestured to her coffee table. It was littered with worn notebooks and printouts from her FacTrack data files.

"It's like this," Lena said, shoving her hands in her pockets and looking at her sideways. "I need someone who can spell to, you know, organize all my work notes. Type them up for me."

Mrs. Finkel lowered herself to the sofa, shock registering on her features.

Lena knew exactly how it sounded. In all her years of living here she'd never once volunteered a single scrap of information about her working life. Nor had she ever invited Mrs. Finkel into her home, much less allowed her to see the contents of her notebooks, filled with her embarrassing child-like scrawl. A child-like scrawl that could blow the world apart.

Mrs. Finkel picked up a notebook and began to read. She paused after a sentence. "Beast Lord?" she enquired. "Why are you looking for a Beast Lord? Is that…is he a guardian? Now wait, why would anyone have cause to chase down a guardian?"

"I can't discuss my work matters with someone outside of the Facility. I signed a binding non-disclosure agreement." Lena looked at her pointedly.

Mrs. Finkel stared at her hard, curiosity flitting past on its way to excitement. "An NDA?" she replied lightly. "Well, that sounds terribly constrictive." She met her eye. "Is that a problem?"

"I suspect my employers don't even properly read what they had us sign. I read all forty-nine pages in detail on the plane ride home. The contract prohibits *commons* from writing about guardian secrets. It doesn't say a thing about what third-gens can share."

Mrs. Finkel's expression told her that she didn't understand what she was saying, but knew she wasn't meant to. She nodded for Lena to continue.

"But we're not here to discuss my contract," Lena said casually. "We're here because, well…look at this mess. It's chaos. How can I concentrate?"

She tossed a carefully selected pile of papers Mrs. Finkel's way, and one spun into view. A particularly interesting one.

"The Facility," Mrs. Finkel read aloud, and flipped to the next page. She glanced up. "Well, that's where they train all the guardians, isn't it?"

"Among other things," Lena said tightly. "Anyway, can you do it? I can't pay much but…I think, um, organization is good? Right?"

"*Organization…*" Mrs. Finkel repeated.

She stopped again, and Lena knew she had just seen the subheadings: "Splats" and "Breaks."

The wrinkles around her pale eyes tightened as she read on.

Lena knew exactly what was on that page. A list of numbers which were coded names of guardians to preserve their privacy, and how each incident was dealt with.

"Yes, dear, organization is very good for the soul," Mrs. Finkel said distractedly. "I'm very glad you brought these to me to, er, type up. Don't worry about payment, I have nothing else to do."

"Being a former news reporter, I'm sure you understand this is very sensitive information," Lena said casually. "I couldn't, for example, go to a media outlet and mention any of this stuff. That would end badly."

"Yes, I completely understand how explosive this could be. If...that's what you want?" Mrs. Finkel asked carefully. "If you're sure?" She peered at her over her glasses.

"I think it'd be great if there was a frank discussion about certain things, speaking hypothetically, of course. I mean, I'm no reporter. So can *you* do it?" She waited exactly a beat, then added, "Type up my notes, I mean?"

"Yes," Mrs. Finkel agreed, delight lighting her eyes. "I believe I can manage that."

"Great," Lena said. "Please be thorough. I'd hate for anything to be left out. That would be a shame." She nudged another notebook Mrs. Finkel's way. One page was marked—"Slave-like Working Conditions." Another said, "Sub-Levels of The Facility: Drugging Broken Guardians."

"Yes, I see that," Mrs. Finkel said as she scanned the page, her eyes widening. Her head lifted as she added quietly, "You must care very much for the guardians to do this, knowing what will happen."

Lena grabbed a garish pink cushion and squeezed it. She was not comfortable sharing her views on any of the guardians. Especially one in particular. "I just want my notes typed up," she said coolly. "That's all."

"Of course, dear. Well, I can do that and much more. I have many contacts."

Lena gave her a direct look. "I like the sound of that." She gave her scarred arm a distracted rub as Mrs. Finkel began to gather up the mound of notes. Her neighbor picked through the pile until she found the first notebook she'd flipped through. It contained Lena's field notes that she'd written while tracking Beast Lord. It included a simple sketch of him, his three sharp claws of his right arm raised above his head.

Mrs. Finkel paused on that page and held up the illustration right beside Lena's injured arm. The claws and the wound matched perfectly. Lena cocked her eyebrow and said nothing.

Mrs. Finkel shook her head. "I see you've been quite busy. In fact, I think I see a lot of things now."

"Perhaps you do."

They shared a look.

"Don't worry. I never gave up an anonymous source in fifty years of journalism."

"I'm not a source," Lena corrected her. "I'm just the woman who needs her notes typed up. What happens beyond that is out of my hands."

"My mistake," Mrs. Finkel said, sounding amused. She seemed to have a sudden thought. "Did you have a deadline in mind?"

"Two days' time would be good."

Mrs. Finkel nodded slowly. "Two days? Ah. When that commemorative guardian collector's book is out that the whole world is waiting for? That's…"

Lena gave her a look.

"Quite a coincidence," her neighbor finished smoothly.

"Yes, it really is." Lena sank back into her chair in relief that everything was sorted exactly as she'd planned on her plane trip home, and smiled.

"You know, that look suits you," Mrs. Finkel said, shuffling the notes into a neat stack.

"What look?"

"I don't recall ever seeing you so relaxed."

"I don't relax," Lena scoffed.

A withered hand leaned over to pat hers. "The world won't end if you let go a little. It's not natural being so controlled all the time. Let your hair down, have some fun, and make some friends. I'm not judging you, dear. It's just, I've been worried. You've obviously lived a hard life. I'm saying, it's time for some changes. Especially with what's about to happen. Don't waste the rest of it."

All the defensiveness Lena usually felt when given unsolicited life advice didn't constrict her throat as it usually did. Instead, she offered another smile.

"Goodness, you really are different," Mrs. Finkel said in surprise. "Something changed you on your last assignment. And for the better."

Lena met her kind gaze and admitted nothing.

"Well, I can see that's as much as I'll get out of you today," her neighbor said with a chuckle. "Let me make you a coffee while we plan a revolution."

"Plan a 'typing assignment' you mean."

"Same thing." Mrs. Finkel's eyes sparkled.

"Another day, thanks," Lena said and climbed to her feet. "I'm washed out right now."

She waited for the elderly woman to get the hint, gather up the papers, and leave. Lena then headed to her bathroom, finding her mirror. She studied her reflection, trying to see what had changed that Mrs. Finkel had noticed. Plain blue eyes stared back. The same blonde sweep of hair. The same snub nose and ears that stuck out just a tiny bit. The same wide mouth and pale lips.

She inhaled at a memory. Lips that Nyah had worshipped. The guardian had explored her for hours, before holding Lena like she meant something to the world. Like she mattered. Even knowing who she was and what she'd done to guardians and her own mother, she'd held her. And she'd told her, that in her shattered, messed-up soul hid a white crow.

Lena smiled softly. She straightened, decision made. "Okay then," she sternly told her jagged reflection in the broken mirror. She nodded more firmly, gathering her courage. "Okay."

She went to her fridge door and took down the business card stuck to it by a magnet. Diane Finkel. The granddaughter looking for someone interesting to hang out with. Lena supposed she constituted that at least.

She hesitated for only a moment. And then she picked up her phone.

CHAPTER 17

THE TRUTH ABOUT GUARDIANS

THE SUPERHEROES WE DRUG, CONTROL, HIDE, DESTROY, AND SECRETLY BURY

WORLD EXCLUSIVE

BY JOSEPHINE FINKEL

Guardians are having mental breakdowns at a devastating rate, before being hidden and drugged in secret wards in the lower levels of the Facility buildings worldwide.

Deaths are being covered up as well, with manipulated footage and images released to the public to give the impression Earth's protectors are all alive and well.

Shocking figures and testimony from an inside source leaked exclusively to this paper reveal the scale of the global outrage:

- Eighty-seven guardians have died in the past century, nearly all while saving humans. (List of the dead on page 3)

- Two hundred and eighty-five guardians have had mental breakdowns. All incidents have been covered up, the guardians' absences hidden from the world.

- Teams of secret enforcers, called trackers, have been finding and bringing back any guardians who go on the run to escape their restrictive lives.

- Guardians are forced to work in slave-like conditions, never able to take a vacation as they are always on standby. This has led to a dramatic spike in breakdowns in the past few years.

- Despite requests by guardians over the years for their leader, Talon Man, to improve working conditions, he has refused, citing the Pact's clauses as binding.

Our source alleges that the cover-ups, lies, and ill-treatment of guardians have all been done to protect the myth of guardian perfection established by Talon Man.

World-renowned psychiatrist, Dr. Francis Butler, from the Institute of Mental Health Research in Boston, said the guardians' inability to have any say in their own lives or career choices would put them under "an enormous and heartbreaking amount of stress."

"The only shock for me is it's taken this long for us to hear about their breakdowns," Dr. Butler said.

He believed that locking up emotionally injured guardians without proper care and counseling from experts in post-traumatic stress disorder was "the worst possible treatment and a form of abuse that should be addressed urgently."

A spokeswoman for Amnesty International, Melissa Goodwin, said the allegations should "shock all decent humans to their core" and must be investigated immediately.

"Make no mistake," Ms. Goodwin said, "the disgrace is ours. How was it that the human race never stopped to ask whether our protectors took breaks and were well cared for when seeing things that would shake a hardened soldier? Amnesty International calls on the United Nations to tear up the Pact and rewrite it, allowing our superheroes the same freedoms that we all enjoy."

Talon Man, when asked to comment, denied all claims vehemently.

"You're being lied to," he said. "By a bitter former employee, no doubt, with an agenda of hate and jealousy. Why would I abuse and neglect my own people? Why would I not want what's best for my own kind? This is absurd.

"After a lifetime of selflessly helping your planet, you accuse me of this? The Facility has nothing to hide. This is a fiction. I'm disappointed you would stoop to this level in printing such baseless lies. If there was any truth to these claims, don't you think it would have come out years ago?"

Talon Man hung up when we asked for a tour of the sub-levels of the Facility buildings. An hour later he posted on his social media account, @talonmanhero, warning people to ignore any forthcoming "smear campaigns" put out by our "terrible rag of a paper."

Three independent experts in video and digital manipulation were asked to look at recent Facility-issued footage of guardians saving lives—guardians who our source tells us are actually dead. All experts confirmed that the footage is a series of brilliantly crafted fakes.

One of the experts, Roger Copeland of Special FX Imagineers, said: "There are certainly lies here—Talon Man's right about that—but they are being told by the Facility and its leader."

Turn to **Pages 2–4** for our list of the dead guardians, obituaries, and statistics of guardians who have had breakdowns.

Page 5: Full analysis of the fake footage that has fooled the world.

Page 6: The NDAs Facility employees are forced to sign—hear from the former mental health nurse ruined for trying to reveal the truth decades ago.

Pages 7–23: More stories and an in-depth analysis of how the Pact and Talon Man's quest for perfection has been killing our heroes.

The Facility buildings were burning. Everywhere Lena looked, news footage showed outraged protestors gathering in front of the towers worldwide. In Paris, students were burning cars and mobbing the entrances. In Istanbul and Athens, they were throwing fire bombs at the buildings. Sydney's protestors had dumped a truckload of manure in front of the Facility. And in cities across the US, chanting protestors in their thousands burnt effigies of Talon Man, his orange outfit blistering in the flames. A thick cordon of riot police forced them back in every city, but it was only a matter of time before the Facility buildings fell, one by one.

There were rumblings now. Every day she heard more. A civilian taskforce might be set up and everyone would be fired. Bruce Dutton was rubbing his thinning hair, looking anxious and fearful. Most of her colleagues were looking for new jobs. Well, those who hadn't already resigned.

Lena supposed she should feel guilty about all of it.

She didn't.

Talon Man had disappeared from the feeds now. It was incredible. After a lifetime of seeing him wall-to-wall on the news monitors each day when Lena arrived to work, suddenly they were all black.

She'd seen the guardian leader twice in the office, stalking through it, jaw tight with fury. His empire was falling. He wasn't taking it well. And he still didn't seem to really believe it. He'd actually stopped once as he passed, looking at Lena speculatively, wondering at her loyalties no doubt. The timing of everything imploding looked incriminating for her, of course. But it was also entirely circumstantial.

She'd done her best to return his look with a projection of idiocy and confusion so perfect that he'd shaken his head and kept on walking. A man like that, always sure his outlook was right, always convinced he could read people with accuracy, was child's play to manipulate.

Lena went back to work. She had a gardener on the fourth floor to see and a deal to make.

Another week had passed. Lena slipped around the back of the building—late for work again. No one commented on it these days. It was lucky if any employees got through the dense circle of protestors, even with the riot police forcing paths through the baying mob for employees.

Moscow Facility had shocked everyone by falling overnight. Rioters had torn the place apart looking for the sub-levels and the hidden, injured guardians. The security on those levels—complete with biometric scans in elevators—prevented their access, of course. That wouldn't last. Not when the UN finally agreed to rip up the Pact, throw out Talon Man's self-governance clauses, and intervene. A vote was due any day now on that. Everyone already knew what the result would be. Soldiers were on standby in every nation that housed a Facility, just waiting for the order to go in. The world was holding its breath.

Lena picked up her pace, the wind carrying the latest chants from the front of the Facility her way.

"Ho-ho, hey-hey, how many guardians did you drug today?"

Catchy.

She couldn't blame them their rage, and didn't complain that she now had to go almost a block out of her way to use one of the hidden rear entrances, connected via a storage facility. Another tidbit she'd learned about, thanks to her (now fracturing) network of insiders.

A high-pitched noise cut through the air. Skidding to a halt, Lena turned her head to listen. A series of heavy squeals of air brakes punctured the silence. Five squeals, one after the other. Lena waited a few minutes. Then, there it was. Marching. Toward the Facility. The cadence was heavy and in step. So, military then, not protestors.

The vote had to have happened at the UN. That meant it was on. *Right now.* Lena yanked out her phone and scrolled to a number she knew by heart.

"It's me," she said urgently. "They're going in now. Soldiers. Five trucks' worth. They'll have to be popping the cork on the sub-levels now so you'll need to be here with a video crew for when they bring them all out. This is the footage that'll break him. It'll break *everything.*"

There was a soft inhalation. Then she heard, "Of course, dear. Thanks for letting me know. Stay safe."

Lena ended the call to Mrs. Finkel. *Stay safe?* Funny thing was she'd never once feared for her life in all this. Sure, there'd been injuries overseas when Facility staff and protestors clashed, but no deaths. The anger was all spitting and curling Talon Man's way. The only real danger, she thought, was his lies *not* being exposed. Of his protests of innocence being believed.

It was the reason why she stayed on at work, feeding Mrs. Finkel updates as the world came apart around her ears.

Sirens shrieked, announcing the arrival of ambulances. She'd been right. They were going in to rescue the breaks. There would be chaos when they surfaced. Lena considered her options. Work was a write-off now. It would all be over soon. The Facility buildings everywhere would be cleared, and that would be that. So what should she do now? Her mind blanked. It really was over.

She stared vacantly at the alley in front of her, when a movement caught her eye. The door from the Facility's storage building had opened. She crept over for a better angle and watched as a figure emerged.

Rats and sinking ships came to mind.

Grimly, Lena dropped her hand to her hip, unlatching the clip holding her Dazr. The figure hadn't seen her yet. Pressing herself against the brick wall behind her, into the shadows, she aimed her weapon, and thumbed up the power setting.

Once set, she coughed.

Talon Man jumped in shock. His stance was wide, an arm lifting, ready to launch into the skies.

Lena waggled her Dazr. "I wouldn't. You'll drop like a bowling ball if I paralyze you midair. Might even kill you."

She stepped out of the shadows, and he looked at her, then at the gun, and back to her.

"You," he muttered in recognition. "Wait...*you?*" he asked again, incredulously. "After everything we've done for you? After our little chat about loyalty, you want to *arrest* me?"

Lena made a show of tapping the safety off and waited for him to finally join the dots. It took almost a minute.

"You disgusting gutter *shreekopf!* YOU were the leak?"

And there it was.

His chest puffed out in fury, and he jabbed a small, stubby finger in her direction. "My staff suggested it might be you, but I told them it was absurd. You lack the intelligence to mastermind any of this. So who was behind it? Really?"

Lena said nothing, but her mocking expression required no words.

His mouth fell open when he understood. "I'll sue you for breach of contract," he snarled. "That NDA is iron-clad."

"Is it? You had a third-gen guardian sign a clause written for commons. And you think *I'm* stupid?"

"*You* really did this?" Shock covered his features. "Don't you see what you've done? Do you even care? It's in ruins. Everything I've built."

"It deserves to be. Look at what this place did to your people. All by trying to make them live a lie. No one's perfect, and it's cruel forcing that standard on anyone."

"You don't understand anything! Humans would have slaughtered us all the day we arrived if we hadn't shown we were better than them. They had to see. Be impressed by us. They had to know that we were worthy of saving." His voice broke. "Perfect."

Lena stared at him, aghast. "Oh my God, that was a century ago. Are you kidding me? Are you really still that frightened alien sitting on the grass in England, terrified by the guns trained at your heads? Is this what this whole fucked-up thing has all been about? Building an empire so big and so powerful that no one will ever try to hurt you again? All this time you've just been *scared*?"

Hate filled his eyes. "You'll never understand what we went through. We'd lost our whole world, and your planet wanted us dead. They shot at us before they even spoke to us. They made us perform for them like animals to prove our worth. They could have killed us at any moment, and do you know the only thing that saved us? They didn't know they could." He gave an incredulous laugh. "So that lie of perfection that you mock so much saved us many times. It's why you're alive today. Not that you'd ever grasp that. You're just a *shreekopf* traitor."

Lena glared at him. "Are you done? Because what I see is a frightened little man who had no clue how to lead, and who built his house on sand. You tortured and drugged your own people to shore up your empire, yet you call me the traitor? You're as screwed up as those you sent to the sub-levels. But you don't care about them—only your own hide. You disgust me."

He gave her a toneless laugh. "What are you going to do?"

For all his cockiness, Lena heard a ripple of fear in his voice.

"Hey, listen," Lena said, angling her head in the direction of the Facility. "They're chanting your name. They sound angry, don't they? They have a right to be. So I think I'll give them what they're demanding. You'd hate that wouldn't you? Being humiliated? Me dragging you out there? Not only less than perfect, but exposed for the slippery speed agent and fraud you are."

"What do you want? Money?" Talon Man hurled at her angrily. "Name it. I have resources."

"Can't you hear them? *'Talon Man, Talon Man',*" she said copying the sing-song chants. "Is it just me or does it sound like more of them than before?"

"I can give you Mind Merge!" Talon Man said suddenly, looking paler. "Family! I can make it so he's in your life. You'll have a grandfather. You want that? Family. Since your mother…" He faded out.

Lena stared at him. "You're unbelievable. You think I give a *tagshart* about some stranger who was nowhere around back when it might have mattered? Is that how pathetic I seem to you? Or is it all humans? Christ, to think our world worships you. Sorry," Lena corrected helpfully, "make that *worshipped*. Past tense."

Wails and furious shouts began to fill the air from a block away.

"I'd say by the crowd reaction, your time's up," Lena continued. "Sounds like the first of your broken guardians are surfacing. What *will* they do to you when I haul your ass out there?"

"Please!" His whole body shivered with the word. "Please," he said again, even more desperately. His mouth moved wordlessly. The bravado had completely evaporated.

Lena gaped at him, never expecting this. It was worse than a meltdown. It was a complete capitulation. Or was she being manipulated? She narrowed her eyes, seeking the lies. She couldn't find them, though. Was the man really this cowardly?

"We share the same blood lines," he whispered, his voice shaking. "Doesn't that mean something? Don't do this." Panic covered his face. "Just tell me what your price is. Tell me!"

"My price?" Lena mocked him. "You don't have it in you."

His head snapped up, sensing a crack, a sliver of hope. His eyes filled with the possibilities. He looked exactly like the scheming used-car salesman he was deep down. Still trying to do a deal from the bottom of a manure heap.

"You're not fit to be a leader," Lena ground out in distaste. "You had a real leader and you treated her like dirt."

"I know. I'm sorry." He stopped abruptly. "Is that what you want to hear from me?" he asked, almost eagerly. He straightened and affected a sincere voice. "I'm profoundly sorry for what we did to Nyah. She deserved better. We should have told the world who she really was years ago."

"Try decades ago." Lena rolled her eyes. "And what's all this 'we' crap. You ran a fucking dictatorship."

"Yes." His hands trembled as the crowd's chants grew angrier. "I did. I…a lapse of judgment. Sorry."

Christ, could he even hear himself? A lapse of freaking judgment? *Sorry?*

"Sorry for your freefalling reputation, you mean," Lena said sharply, "but never a thought for your own people. You haven't even mentioned them once, have you? Not the broken ones. The drugged ones. The dead ones. Not the ones run into the ground with your expectations of perfection. *That* was the price you had to pay to prevent your public humiliation, in case you're wondering. They're who you forgot to be sorry about." She shook her head in disgust. "What's wrong with you? You had one job! You were supposed to protect your people, not make their lives worse. You are a failure." She waved her Dazr indicating the alley leading to the front of the Facility. "Let's go. It's time you greeted your adoring fans."

There was a civilian committee overseeing the guardians now. Lena had seen it on the news the day it had sent her an automated message ordering her to turn in all her office-issued gear at a specified address. It had contained a charming postscript explaining that she was also fired.

Lena thought she'd care more. She really didn't.

Her old boss, Bruce Dutton, had become a "temporary transitional advisor" to the civilian committee. Lena only knew that because he'd called her to a meeting at some plush hotel that the committee was operating out of until it could get its own headquarters.

She sat opposite him on an overstuffed sofa that was covered in swirls of lime and white, while his fingers flew across the keyboard of the laptop on the coffee table between them.

"Thanks for coming in, Silver, especially seeing you don't work for me anymore." He adjusted his glasses but didn't look up. "The committee's first order of business is to set up a meeting with Shattergirl. They want her to be the new guardian leader. She'd be a vast improvement on her predecessor. And, apparently, she has some experience."

Clearly someone, somewhere, had done their research on the origins of Nyah. Lena nodded, just as Dutton glanced up.

"You don't seem surprised," he noted carefully.

Lena immediately realized her mistake.

Before she could answer, he continued. "We both know that wasn't her at the ceremony. I've never seen so many teeth on Shattergirl in my life."

"She's always been a smiler, that impersonator," Lena agreed. "Or so Volcano Man tells me."

"Mm," Dutton said. He tapped on his computer and then paused, eyeing her, his fingers poised over the keyboard. "I always said that if anyone could get Shattergirl, it'd be you. Clearly, you know more than you're letting on. So, what did you find? All of it."

Lena stared at him, right *into* him, injecting every ounce of sincerity into her expression. When she spoke, her words dripped with conviction. "Nothing." She sighed. "Just some ancient myth about an Iblis demon that the locals thought was real. Turned out to be some grumpy hermit who throws rocks at trespassers. So if anyone hears any other reports of Shattergirl from out Socotra way, it'll just be that old story getting recycled. Waste of my time the whole trip. Put that in your report."

Dutton's eyebrows lifted, challenging her, seeking out the lie. But Lena hadn't been called Silver for nothing. She drew on everything, every skill in this twisted art she'd ever possessed, and stared him down with utter confidence. She held his gaze evenly until she saw his brown eyes soften and turn to belief. He nodded then, and his fingers shifted to the keys.

"There was nothing of Shattergirl," she repeated slowly as he began to type. "No trace at all."

EPILOGUE

Six Months Later

LENA ADJUSTED THE BLANKETS AND cushions on the rooftop of her apartment building and lay back. The area made for a meager and ugly sun deck by day, but that was okay, since Lena preferred to be here at night. Old air-conditioning units were hidden by a collection of lush, exotic plants.

Yellow eyes regarded her from between the fronds of one particularly lumpy looking plant.

"What do you want?" she asked Bernstein, the smug, pigeon-shredding cat. "I'm not feeding you. This is strictly a beer night."

The cat watched her sullenly, narrowing its eyes to slits, and swished its tail before disappearing back into the foliage.

Lena turned her attention skywards. Clouds disrupted the view, but she could see a few stars peeking out. Nothing like what she'd seen on Socotra, but enough. She searched unsuccessfully for two stars, side by side, to find the one beneath it that Nyah had shown her was the pointer to Aril. She peered in vain. Maybe the stars around here were different to those she'd seen on Socotra.

"Hey," said a familiar voice behind her. "Got your note."

Lena turned and smiled up at Diane who was waving the scrap of paper Lena had stuck to her own apartment door. Mrs. Finkel's granddaughter, intrepid war correspondent and, of late, somewhat amusing drinking buddy.

Now, thanks to a certain world exclusive that destroyed any secrecy about trackers, Lena was free to swap war stories with Diane. Their accounts became increasingly absurd and all the more entertaining whenever they were nine sheets to the wind.

The woman was long limbed and filled out her soft jeans nicely. Her brown hair was pulled into a careless ponytail. She zipped up her leather jacket tighter against the night air and glanced around the rooftop with interest. Her eyes widened.

"Crap on a crust, Martin, these plants! Where'd you get them from? I've never seen anything like them." She twisted her head towards a potted tree in the corner with a doily-like spread of leaves. "And that thing looks like it should be in some sort of sci-fi exhibit."

Lena shrugged. "You can get the darnedest things via mail order these days."

Diane bent over, sniffing the foliage in rapture.

"What are you doing?" Lena laughed. "They just smell of green and dirt. Come on, pull up a cushion. Wanna beer?"

"Sure."

Diane lowered herself onto the sea of cushions, crossing her booted feet at the ankles. She caught the bottle Lena tossed her way.

"So, where were we last time?" Lena asked. "You were negotiating with rebels?"

"Oh yeah. Right of free passage for my photographer and me. The bastard in charge stole my iPhone and said I was okay to go. I saw red. That thing is my baby. So I told him if he kept it he'd be creating an international incident because Americans don't negotiate with kidnappers," Diane said, deadpan.

"Wait, you're claiming your iPhone was a hostage? You are so full of shit," Lena said, rolling her eyes, but she still laughed at the stupid story.

"You should talk. Still not convinced that the Lava Eyes guardian is real. How come I never heard about him anywhere else?"

"Talon Man's censorship was complete."

"Oh that's convenient. At least *my* stories are verifiable. Well, the true ones are." Diane grinned.

"I knew it! All lies! So tell me something true then."

"Something true?" Diane sipped her beer thoughtfully, and then slid her eyes over to Lena. "I think it's true you're Nan's source on her exclusive... Hell, I know you are, not that she'd ever admit it. But come on. I'm amazed Talon Man never worked it out."

"Funny thing is that for some reason Talon Man thought I was a knuckle-dragging imbecile."

"Well, that's weird." Diane looked at her in confusion. "Guess it doesn't matter now, does it? It's all over for him."

That was the understatement. In the months since Mrs. Finkel's story, all the Facility buildings not ripped down by protestors were in the process of being dismantled. What had ruined Talon Man was the condition of the drugged guardians the day they'd been brought up, blinking and stumbling into the light. The news feeds played the footage on a loop for weeks.

Beast Lord's gaunt figure had been the final straw for many. He'd stopped, lifted his face to the sun, and just stood there, soaking it in, on the steps of the Facility, like he'd never seen sunlight before. Lena had appeared in the background, pressing Talon Man toward the front of the chanting crowd, with a Dazr in the small of his back, to where soldiers were milling. The guardian leader's head had stayed bowed as she forced him into the open.

Those brazen claims that this was all just a bitter campaign against him dissolved the moment he locked eyes with the sunken-faced guardian who'd once terrified the people of Oymyakon, Siberia. Guilt radiated from Talon Man's face. Then shock as he took in his wasted, thin condition.

Beast Lord's once-proud eyes filled with angry tears and he said only three words to Talon Man, his voice choked and rough from lack of use, "I hate you."

It had been the front-page headline in enormous, 120-point letters on dozens of newspapers worldwide the next day.

The shamed leader had been under indefinite house arrest since. The civilian committee had offered all the other guardians their existing jobs, with paid vacations and every other benefit they could imagine, if they still wanted them. Some stayed and could still be seen on the daily news feeds saving lives. The rest of the guardians had scattered to the winds.

Or so it had seemed.

Lena had set herself up as a survivalist instructor, and many of her clients turned out to be guardians, curious to learn how to live off the grid from none other than Silver herself. It was surprisingly fulfilling work. Turned out there *was* something else she was good at.

"So," Diane said, eyeing her curiously. "*Are* you Nan's source?"

Lena smiled and took another swallow of her beer.

"You have a dreadful poker face, especially when you're drunk."

"I'm not drunk!" Lena protested.

"Allegedly." Diane regarded her for a moment. "You have lived one batshit crazy life, Lena Martin. You're damned impressive."

"Not really. It's just life," Lena said. "Now *you*—you've been living the crazy. That tinpot dictator interview? Gold."

Diane sighed. "Wish I'd had your gift of the gab then. I got stuck in a jail for three weeks while they decided whether my questions had been impertinent or not."

"You? Impertinent?" Lena asked. "Shocking."

"I know, right?" Diane said, feigning surprise. "I was totally mystified."

They both laughed. It felt good. *This* felt good. Friendship? Laughter? Since when did Lena do this? Not before Socotra, she knew that much.

"I'm glad we met," Lena suddenly said. She stared accusingly at her beer, astonished she'd said that out loud.

Diane glanced at her, not milking the admission for once, and tilted her beer bottle at her. "Back at ya."

Lena could see the sincerity in her eyes, laced with something else. Something more. A hopefulness. She focused hard on her beer, drawing her thumb down the side, creating condensation trails. *Oh! No way.*

Why not, though? a little voice asked in the back of her head. The idea of having something more with Diane shouldn't be that crazy. It's just they were so relaxed together, Lena hadn't thought about it. Before Socotra, she'd never had a thing with someone she called a friend. She frowned at her beer bottle. Then again, she'd never really had friends before either. Hmm. She'd kick this around later, when she was sober.

Lena broke the silence after a few moments. "Thanks for stargazing with me, stupid as it is with these skies."

Diane glanced up. "Nah, it's a relaxing diversion. So spill, why do you stargaze?"

"A friend put me onto it. Thinks I need more hope in my life."

Diane's eyebrows shot up and she smiled broadly. "Is she, like, seventy-one and makes crap coffee?"

"No. Not your nan."

"Ah. A *special friend* then. Got it."

Lena ignored the innuendo, her gaze tracking a shifting cloud.

Diane considered her for a moment. "You miss her. Your friend."

"I do. She's like no one else on Earth." *Or off it.* "We were there for each other when we both needed it. We had to get our butts kicked out of our ruts. But it's worked out the way it's meant to. For both of us." Lena lifted her beer to her lips. "She's happy now." She swallowed, feeling the tasty brew spill across her tongue.

Diane nodded and her eyes became unfocused. "The special ones stay with us, don't they? Like chapters in the book of our life. We look back from time to time and remember how things were. It's important. Our sense of who we were comes back. For good and for bad."

"That's true."

They lay in a relaxed silence until Bernstein knocked over one of the potted plants and yowled balefully, scaring Lena into the middle of next week.

"Damn it, cat!" Diane said, wincing as she scooped up the caterwauling interloper. "I'll take him. Sorry. I'll raid Nan's pantry while I'm dropping him home. We definitely need snacks. Be right back."

"Sure."

Lena settled back and contemplated the skies when a dark shadow rose up from behind the rooftop.

"You're late," Lena said, climbing to her feet.

"I had a storm to go around. And you looked busy." Nyah floated over the lip of the roof and then landed. She wore jeans, boots, and a thick, padded, long-sleeved shirt. "I circled the block until you weren't."

Lena smiled as she saw what she was holding. "What have you brought this month?"

Nyah held out a knotty, leafy green plant with a bulging trunk, and set it down next to the others. She stood back, regarding it, then leaned forward, rotating the pot a few degrees. "*Dorstenia gigas.* It's a rare caudex-forming species."

At Lena's glazed look, Nyah added with a fond eye roll, "It has a fat trunk. Needs mild weather. Try not to kill it. The care details are on the tag."

"Thanks," Lena said. "Your *klava*'s in the usual spot. Don't drink it all at once."

Nyah picked up the brick-sized wrapped box that had been tucked safely under the lip of the roof edge. "Excellent. I'm all out."

Their eyes met knowingly. They were well aware that Nyah could just ask Lena to source her a *klava* plant from the Facility's former gardener so she could grow her own beans on Socotra. But that would mean Nyah would have no need for regular visits. The fact she had never asked for the plant warmed Lena's heart immensely.

"You look well," Nyah said, after a pause. "Life—and living—suits you."

"Could say the same for you. How's Dr. Larsen? Still into her endemic thingies?"

"Of course. What's not to love?"

"Love, huh?" Lena asked suggestively. "Well it's to be expected. Larson's like nerd catnip to you science types. Nice legs too."

Nyah rolled her eyes, but a smile twitched the corners of her mouth. "We're not actually..." She trailed off. "Not...yet."

There was longing in her words and Lena's breath caught, surprised. "Yet?" she prodded.

Nyah's brows drew together. "She made an offer that was extremely flattering. I-I...actually find myself seriously considering it."

Lena picked apart what she wasn't saying and suddenly understood her hesitation. "You're considering something serious, you mean. That's...wow. That's great. This is...it's not before time, right?"

Nyah's eyes warmed in agreement. Instead of answering, she said, "Anna says hello. How's your war correspondent? Still telling ridiculous tall tales?"

"Yeah. Still making me laugh."

"I'm glad." Nyah looked it. "You need that. It's important."

A thought struck Lena, and she shook her head in amazement.

"What?"

"Who'd have thought it?" Lena said. "Us, realizing that maybe, just maybe, we need people."

"Hm. This outlandish theory doesn't sound like us at all."

Lena grinned. "I notice you didn't disagree with me, though. I'd never admit it to another living soul, but I think we're going soft."

"Speak for yourself," Nyah said, eyes crinkling. "By the way, your amusing beer companion is clomping her way back up your stairs as we speak." She straightened and shifted the brown-wrapped parcel firmly under one arm. "I should go."

Lena hesitated for a moment, then pulled her into a brusque hug. It was brief, but she hoped it conveyed all the gratitude and care that she felt for someone who had changed everything. She was still terrible at hugs.

"Stay longer next time," she told Nyah firmly. "We'll catch up properly. Shoot the breeze. Mock the *shreekopf*s, the usual."

Nyah offered her a slow, genuine smile. "I'd like that. It may be a while, though. We've possibly found a new species of succulent. Anna's thrilled."

"Ooh, exciting."

"Yes. It is." Nyah ignored the sarcasm, joy filling her eyes.

Lena's breath caught at the breathtaking change.

Nyah tilted her head towards the door. "Your reporter's about to open the door."

"Okay." Lena stepped back with a grin and patted her arm. She left her fingers there and squeezed, appreciating the solid connection, wanting to convey her earnestness. "I'm really happy for you. Stay safe. Be happy."

Their eyes locked. "You too," Nyah said softly.

Lena stepped back. Nyah smiled at her, lifted her chin, and in an instant, her friend was gone.

Friend. Lena shook her head at the mere idea of it. This friendship business was getting habit forming. She followed Nyah's dark streak along the horizon until she was gone.

"Hey," said a warm voice behind her.

Lena spun around and laughed at the sight that greeted her. Diane's arms were stuffed with all manner of fatty, salt-laden almost-food.

"Wait, what on earth is *that*?" Diane frowned, dropping her junk pile on the cushions, and pointed at the *Dorstenia gigas*. "That wasn't there before."

"Wasn't it?" Lena arched an eyebrow. "It must have just arrived."

Diane stared at it balefully. "I know I haven't been gone *that* long. It's just...I'm sure I'd have remembered that."

"Thanks for the snacks," Lena said. "Bernstein safely inside?"

"Howling like a two-year-old." Diane gave the plant one last, suspicious glare and flopped on her back.

Lena joined her, settling in closer, enjoying the cozy warmth and her faint smell of cologne. She could get used to this. Whatever this was.

Diane turned to Lena. "Now, what were we discussing? You were telling me what's up there. What you see when you look."

Lena didn't reply immediately. Contentment washed over her as she turned the question around in her mind and realized she felt relaxed in a way that she hadn't in years. So much had changed since that night at the end of the world, side by side with Nyah. A night when Lena had seen nothing in the heavens but had also realized for the first time just how empty her life really was. She'd gazed at millions of brilliant white stars and finally understood what Nyah had been telling her. That her life didn't have to stay that way.

"What do I see?"

Lena Martin closed her eyes and smiled.

ABOUT LEE WINTER

Lee Winter is an award-winning veteran newspaper journalist who has lived in almost every Australian state, covering courts, crime, news, features and humour writing. Now a full-time author and part-time editor, Lee is also a 2015 Lambda Literary Award finalist and Golden Crown Literary Award winner. She lives in Western Australia with her long-time girlfriend, where she spends much time ruminating on her garden, US politics, and shiny, new gadgets.

CONNECT WITH LEE
Website: www.leewinterauthor.com

OTHER BOOKS FROM YLVA PUBLISHING

www.ylva-publishing.com

REQUIEM FOR IMMORTALS

Lee Winter

ISBN: 978-3-95533-710-0
Length: 263 pages (86,000 words)

Requiem is a brilliant cellist with a secret. The dispassionate assassin has made an art form out of killing Australia's underworld figures without a thought. One day she's hired to kill a sweet and unassuming innocent. Requiem can't work out why anyone would want her dead—and why she should even care.

EX-WIVES OF DRACULA

Georgette Kaplan

ISBN: 978-3-95533-410-9
Length: 338 pages (122,000 words)

Mindy's best friend, Lucia, is a vampire. Every second Mindy spends with her she's in danger of becoming dinner. But Lucia needs help. To keep her alive they need fresh blood, and to cure her they have to kill her sire. So why is it that Nosferatu, the cops, and the chance of becoming an unwilling blood donor don't scare Mindy half as much as the way she feels when Lucia looks at her?

THE TEA MACHINE

Gill McKnight

ISBN: 978-3-95533-432-1
Length: 321 pages (97,000 words)

Spinster by choice, Millicent Aberly has managed to catapult herself from her lovely Victorian mews house into a strange future full of giant space squid, Roman empires, and a most annoying centurion to whom she owes her life. Decanus Sangfroid was just doing her job rescuing the weird little scientist chick from a squid attack. Now she finds herself in London, 1862, and it's not a good fit.

DEFENSIVE MINDSET

Wendy Temple

ISBN: 978-3-95533-837-4
Length: 276 pages (100,000 words)

Star footballer and successful businesswoman Jessie Grainger has her life set, and doesn't need anything getting in the way. That includes rebellious rival player Fran Docherty, a burnt-out barmaid with a past as messed up as her attitude. So when the clashing pair find themselves on the same Edinburgh women's football team, how will they survive each other, let alone play to win?

COMING FROM YLVA PUBLISHING

www.ylva-publishing.com

THE POWER OF MERCY

Fiona Zedde

To her family, Mai Redstone is weak. Her shape-shifting power is nowhere near as impressive as their abilities to literally alter the world around them. But when she puts on the costume to become Mercy, a rooftop-climbing chameleon with a thousand disguises and at least nine lives, she feels almost invincible. When a local politician is murdered and the police call Mercy in to help, the stability Mai has built out of past pain threatens to crumble. The dead politician turns out to be her uncle, a man who made her childhood a living hell. Caught between giving a medal to the killer and being forced to find the murderer for her family, Mai must make the difficult choice between family loyalty and self-preservation. Mercy is a blade that can cut both ways.

Shattered
© 2017 by Lee Winter

ISBN: 978-3-95533-563-2

Also available as e-book.

Published by Ylva Publishing, legal entity of Ylva Verlag, e.Kfr.
Ylva Verlag, e.Kfr.
Owner: Astrid Ohletz
Am Kirschgarten 2
65830 Kriftel
Germany

www.ylva-publishing.com

First edition: 2017

Credits
Edited by Astrid Ohletz
Proofread by Joanie Bassler
Cover Design and Print Layout by Streetlight Graphics

Printed by
booksfactory
PRINT GROUP Sp. z o.o.
ul. Ks. Witolda 7-9
71-063 Szczecin
Poland
tel./fax 91 812-43-49
NIP/USt-IdNr.: PL8522520116